Seeker

THE SHILOH SERIES
BOOK TWO

SEEKER

HELENA SORENSEN

Seeker © 2014, 2015 by Helena Sorensen

All rights reserved. No part of this publication may be reproduced, distributed, or transmitted in any form or by any means, including photocopying, recording, or other electronic or mechanical methods, without the prior written permission of the publisher, except in the case of brief quotations embodied in critical reviews and certain other noncommercial uses permitted by copyright law. For permission requests, write to the publisher, addressed "Attention: Permissions Coordinator," at info@brightenerbooks.com.

A Brightener Book
www.brightenerbooks.com

Trade Paperback edition ISBN: 978-0-9964368-8-5
Also available in eBook

Cover design by Pear Creative, www.pearcreative.ca
Map created by Robert Altbauer, www.fantasy-map.net
Previously published by MyInkBooks.com in 2014, ISBN: 978-1-928021-08-7

Printed in the United States of America
15 16 17 18 19 20   01 02 03 04 05

www.brightenerbooks.com

Contents

Prologue 7
Chapter One 9
Chapter Two 15
Chapter Three 23
Chapter Four 33
Chapter Five 41
Chapter Six 49
Chapter Seven 57
Chapter Eight 65
Chapter Nine 73
Chapter Ten 83
Chapter Eleven 91
Chapter Twelve 105
Chapter Thirteen 111
Chapter Fourteen 123
Chapter Fifteen 129
Chapter Sixteen 139
Chapter Seventeen 149
Chapter Eighteen 157
Chapter Nineteen 163
Chapter Twenty 175
Chapter Twenty-One 183
Chapter Twenty-Two 191

Helena Sorensen

Chapter Twenty-Three 197
Chapter Twenty-Four 203
Chapter Twenty-Five 213
Chapter Twenty-Six 221
Chapter Twenty-Seven 233
Chapter Twenty-Eight 241
Chapter Twenty-Nine 249
Chapter Thirty 261
Chapter Thirty-One 267
Chapter Thirty-Two 273
Chapter Thirty-Three 279
Epilogue 287
Pronunciation 293
About the Author 295

Prologue

Their voices echo still, in the winds that whip down from the mountains, in the rush of the stream that winds its way around the forgotten village and plunges into the pool where lazy currents of black water drift below ice-crusted banks. But all else is silent. Charred stones and decaying boards, like discarded bones, peek through a blanket of snow. The lanes that wind between the shells of collapsed cottages are empty apart from the snow that collects in ever-rising drifts. The furnace in the hillside, once bright with fires and the varied colors of cooling glass panes, is cold and black.

To the east is a strange, broken forest. The blackened stumps of ancient trees squat on the ground, shouldering their heavy snow burdens. Hundreds of years of fallen leaves and flowers rot beneath the snow, in layer upon layer of death. No man who sees this desolation could envision the gentle rain of pink petals in the heart of the Fayrewood in spring, or the clear green of the fan-shaped leaves in summer, or their transformation to vivid gold in autumn. All of that is lost.

When the snows thaw, little clusters of bleeding flowers will spring up again on the hillside. Nectar will gather on the tip of each folded, velvet petal and fall to the ground, sinking like blood into the soil. The flowers could tell the tale. They remember the colored wood and the bright lanterns, the loveliness that blossomed, for a time, beneath the Shadow. The remnant that retreated to the village of Fleete could tell it, too, though their version could hardly be trusted. The others are gone, lost. Women of great beauty and courage and children who hardly knew how much they had to fear vanished in the tangled gloom of the Whispering Wood. Fierce warriors, men of skill and daring and cunning, faded into the darkness of the Black Mountains, never to return.

This is the story of the Sun Clan, the *Lost* Clan, and all that was lost with them.

One

The girl on the doorstep was all eyes, it seemed. They were huge and bright and hungry, and the only thing that drew Evander's attention away from them was the streak of gray hair that burst out from the girl's right temple and wound its way into her unruly black waves.

"They called me Grey," she said.

Evander hesitated, at a loss to comprehend how this child could have reached the northernmost village of Shiloh, a village resting in the very shadow of the Pallid Peaks, in the dead of winter. He leaned over her head, peering into the lane. The lantern that hung by the door on the cottage nearest his was all but obscured by the storm, no more than a breath of gold in a tempest of snow and dark. The snow on the ground was knee-deep, and deepening, and the wind came careening down from the mountains in gusts that would knock a sturdy man on his back.

"How'd ya cross the Cutting?" he asked.

Grey stared back, her chin quivering with cold. The faint movement snapped Evander out of his confusion, and he took her arm and pulled her inside.

"Fergive me," he said. "Ya took me by surprise." He grabbed a thick blanket from the end of his cot and knelt to wrap it around the girl's shoulders. He looked into her eyes. She stared back, unblinking.

"What's the Cutting?" she asked. She was very pale, and she trembled as she clutched the blanket.

"It's the stream that wraps around the village. Runs down from the Peaks." It moved too swiftly to freeze over, but the water was brutally cold, and the people of Holt called it "Cutting" with good reason.

"There was a log," she said.

Ah, Evander thought. *Must've washed downstream.*

"And what of yer ma?" he asked.

Grey looked at the floor and said nothing.

"Yer da?"

Grey didn't answer, just reached to her neck and pulled away a stiff, filthy bit of cloth. Her eyes closed and her lips tightened against the pain of the wound. Four gashes marked her neck, and the surrounding skin was a bright, angry red. Evander knew at once that this was the work of a Shadow Wolf. He could only wonder how the girl had escaped.

"Ya lost both o' them, then?" he asked, his voice unsteady.

"Aye," Grey said. Her eyes filled with tears, and she rested her head on Evander's shoulder. He put his arms around the child and held her while she cried.

When she quieted, Evander washed her neck and covered the wound with salve and a clean bandage. He gave her a bowl of warm broth, pulled wool socks onto her dirty feet, and tucked her into his cot. She turned on her side to face him and watched as he sat by the fire, the lids of her eyes growing heavier and heavier. When they shut at last, and her breathing was steady, he rose and crossed to the cot.

He was surprised and a little frightened by the ferocity of the feelings that uncurled within him as he watched her sleep. He wondered again and again how she'd survived. She was so small, just skinny arms and legs, a mass of black hair, and those enormous eyes. Evander knew the wolves. His many scars bore evidence of a long and intimate knowledge. He'd seen more than one seasoned hunter fall to that tireless enemy. His father had fallen. How could a child survive when both her parents were lost? Unless they died protecting her. Evander had no sister, no daughter, but it's what he would have done. He fought the tears that rose as pity and rage and tenderness and resolve bloomed together. He brushed the hair from Grey's brow and kissed her forehead.

In the back room, unaware of Grey's arrival, Maeve was dreaming.

Her first dream had come when she carried Evander in her belly. It had thrilled and terrified her, for there were no Dreamers in those days. She had not spoken of it. As the years passed, the frequency and intensity of the dreams had increased, and what Maeve saw on the night of Grey's arrival was nothing short of wondrous.

She was walking through the Fayrewood, and the dazzling gold of the leaves overhead told her that it was autumn. She walked along a cool carpet of leaves, and the wash of gold above and below gradually came together, blending into one enormous body of light. She walked on, the trunks of the trees and the scattered stones of the Fayrewood falling away as she stepped out on nothing. The world was blue and immense, not heavy and pressing, but wide and open and far-flung. And that golden light, so huge, so bright, was almost within reach. *The sun.* She knew its name. Her eyes ached from the beautiful glare of it, but she refused to close them.

Behind her, there was a vicious growl. She felt sharp teeth snag her shift, and she was dragged away from the brilliant light, back into the darkness.

She woke bathed in sweat. Her fair hair was plastered against her face and neck. She glanced to the windowsill and saw the failing light of the fire reflected in the drops of nectar that hung from the black petals of the bleeding flowers.

All was well. Maeve breathed a heavy sigh. She rested back on her cot and fell asleep.

Evander was weary next morning, and stiff with cold. His sleep had been troubled. He eased out of his chair and built up the fire on the hearth before going to the front window. There was a little depression in the stones to the left of the glass, just at the height of his shoulder. It was the perfect spot for leaning, and, as Evander couldn't pace the room for fear of waking Grey, he sank against the wall and watched the swirling snow.

The winters in Holt were so long. They always stretched to the very limits of his endurance. As the days passed, the cottage grew smaller, the food more stale. Evander grew thin and nearly wild with restlessness. He longed to take Rogue out into the hills with his men. *Soon*, he told himself. Soon the bridges would go up and his band of hunters would set out.

He sensed someone watching him and turned to see Grey, sitting up, her legs dangling over the edge of the cot, her eyes bright and curious.

"Did ya sleep at all?" she asked.

"Aye," Evander replied. "A little." He crossed to the table in the center of the room. "Hungry?"

Grey nodded, and Evander took a couple of small, brownish cakes and tossed one to her. "This time o' year, everything's dried . . . the fruit, the meat. What's left o' the meat, that is. Even the vegetables in the soups were dried before the first frost." He shook his head in annoyance and took a bite. Grey devoured her cake without complaint.

He leaned against the front wall again, staring out the window and absently rubbing his knuckles against his chin. "If the snow doesn't get ya, the food will. It's enough ta make a man mad, waiting fer spring , waiting fer some sign o' life."

Grey licked the crumbs from her fingers. "Is there any more?" she asked.

Evander tossed her the rest of his cake and watched her eat. He wanted very much to ask about her parents, about how she had come to this place. But he couldn't bring himself to do it, not this morning. He went to check her bandage instead. He lifted the dressing and swore, looking hard into Grey's eyes before studying the wound more closely. The night phlox salve was useful for many things, cuts and scrapes and burns among them. Evander had hoped that it might stave off infection, but it appeared to have worked a wonder. Swollen red skin and deep gashes had been replaced by healthy skin with faint pink scars.

"I'll leave it on another day, just ta be safe."

"Who's this?" Maeve asked. She stood in the doorway that led to the back room.

"Grey," the girl said, turning to face the fair-haired, blue-eyed woman.

"She came last night," Evander said, "during the storm."

"When will she be going?" Maeve asked.

Evander crossed to his mother in a few long strides and lowered his voice. "She's got nowhere ta go, Ma. She's only just escaped the wolves."

Maeve looked past Evander, looked into Grey's fathomless eyes and held her gaze. She was silent so long that Evander touched her shoulder, trying to draw her back from wherever she'd gone.

"She can't stay here."

"She won't disturb ya, Ma. I'll make certain of it. But I won't send 'er away. Any longer in that cold and she'll die."

Maeve looked her over again, studying the bandage on her neck, the hollow, hungry look in her eyes, the thin, bony limbs that swam inside her ragged shift.

"No good will come of it," Maeve said.

"If it were a wounded dog, we'd shelter it until the weather cleared, at the very least. I'll do no less fer a child."

"What if she touches the flowers?" Maeve asked.

"She won't," Evander replied.

And it was settled.

Two

That was the winter Valour came to the village. Mina was among the first to see her, gliding through the center of Holt with a calm, curious look, as if she weren't the most extraordinary woman anyone had ever seen. She walked with her mother while her father handled the horse-drawn carts piled high with furniture and crates. She wore a heavy, fleece-lined coat with the hood thrown back, and the lantern she carried scattered beams of light over flame-red hair and flashing blue eyes.

Mina watched the villagers as they stepped into the bitter cold to peer at the newcomers. She saw many eyes fill with wonder and some with hunger as Valour and her parents made their way toward the western side of the village, near the furnace. Mina loaded squares of turf into her apron and wondered what it must be like to be beautiful.

Mina was strong and lean, and rather too square. Her smile was lovely, so lovely that it might easily have captured a man who took the time to notice her. But Mina had no interest in being noticed, and she rarely smiled. More often, her face was set and stern, a faint line between her brows betraying the toilsome nature of her days.

"Mina, where's the turf? It's freezing!" Reed, her younger brother, was poking his head out of the cottage when he saw the disturbance. "By the gods, who's that?"

Mina shushed him and shoved him back inside, where she unloaded the thick chunks of dried peat and set about refueling the fire.

"Did ya see 'er, Mina?" Reed asked.

Mina threw a chunk of turf at him. He dodged it and turned his attention to his mother. "Ma, her hair was *red*, red as flame, near as red as blood, Ma. Red!"

"Calm yerself, boy," his father said. Jameson was sitting in the chair where Mina did her mending and sewing, the chair by the southfacing window. It offered an unobstructed view of the hillside. He'd seen the family come into town.

"What do ya think brought 'em here, ta Holt?" Reed asked. "And why now? Why not wait 'til spring?"

Jameson sat back in the chair and squinted at the window. There was nothing left to see but snow and Shadow. "He's a craftsman, no doubt, come ta get 'is share out o' the Cutting."

"Who's a craftsman?" Reed asked.

"The man who's just arrived. Girl's father, I'd wager," he said. "They'll be takin' Barclay's cottage. Wonder how they heard it was empty." He chewed the inside of his cheek for a moment, considering. "Well, it's like I always said, there's a good livin' ta be made out o' the Cutting, so long as a man knows what ta look for, so long as there's someone ta teach 'im." Jameson grunted, shifted in his chair, and turned to Mina's mother. Tilly was sorting through a basket of sickly, shriveled vegetables. "Tilly, what do we have to offer the newcomers?"

"Just a bit o' soup, love," Tilly said.

"Make it up, then, and we'll take it over."

Her mother made no protest, but Mina cringed inwardly at the thought of bringing a thin broth with the pitiful remains of last summer's vegetables to the new family. She did not want to stand in the same cottage as that radiant beauty, nor hear her father make his awkward introductions, nor even consider how Reed might behave. She envied her older brother, Chase. He was hunting in the hills around Holt, thinking his own thoughts, no doubt, and enjoying the quiet company of the Fell horses.

The dread of the evening's visit grew larger in her mind as Mina poked at the fire, pushing the half-burned logs back to the center and surrounding them with peat. Her father would probably urge her to wear her coming-of-age shift, the one with the little brown tree embroidered at the neckline. It was pretty enough, the nicest thing she owned, in fact. But Mina hated how even that small spot of embroidery could draw unwanted attention.

When the fire was roaring on the hearth, its warmth spreading to the farthest corners of the cottage, Mina went to her mother. With just a glance, she asked. With just a nod, Tilly answered. *I've got it. There's time. Go.* Mina grabbed her coat and gloves and went.

She took no torch or lantern. It was near midday, so she could see a little way ahead through the thin, gray light and the silent snowfall. In truth, she could've managed the journey in the pressing dark of night, so well did she know the way. She cut through the cottages, heading east, and waded down the hillside through the snow until she reached an opening in a cluster of trunks that formed the entrance to the Fayrewood. She stepped in, breathing deeply. The air was sharp and cold, familiar and beloved. Mina wandered along a favorite path, and shimmied up a tree. *Her* tree. She brushed the snow from off a wide branch, *her* branch, and lay back to listen to the moaning and cracking of ice-laden trees. Her dark hair spilled over the branch, and one booted foot swung back and forth. She forgot the cold.

There was no one in Shiloh who knew the Fayrewood like Mina. She had climbed every tree that could be climbed on this side of the Turn, and she knew every shrub and flower, every root and berry, every stone and leaf by touch and smell. She knew the Fayrewood in seasons, and the coming of each was like the arrival of an old and dear friend. Even the winter was lovely here, with ice and snow bouncing silver-white light in a thousand directions. Mina knew the Fayrewood in layers. There were layers of color, layers of motion and sound, and each was ever changing, endlessly transformed by the shifting of seasons and the passing of time. Mina knew them all.

In the Fayrewood, Mina was as free as she could imagine being. She was free to see and free from the fear of being seen. The beauty of the wood surrounded her, enveloped her. She was radiant and still; she was part of the Fayrewood. Mina breathed, one delicious breath after another. She thought of nothing. The faint line between her brows softened and disappeared. She smiled.

After a time, there was a tugging sensation, as if her bones were roped to the village and the slack had gone out. She sighed, hopped down two branches and leapt from the tree, hurrying back to the main path in the center of the wood.

Evander patted Rogue's back as they crossed the bridge. Six hunters followed, mounted on powerful Fell horses. It was early yet for a hunt, but Evander's restlessness had driven him to risk riding out in the snow, to risk reassembling the main bridge over the Cutting before the spring floods. His men hadn't argued. They had all grown thin and hungry, their families with them, and they were eager to improve their fare. But the hunt had proved fruitless, and the hunters' faces were grim as they led their horses toward the island of lights at the top of the hill. *At least we've all*

returned, Evander thought, *all seven whole*. That was something.

"We should race ta the falls, Evander," Knox was saying. "The falls and back. Always said Frost could outrun Rogue if she had a bit of open space ta stretch 'er legs." He stroked Frost's neck. It was white as new-fallen snow, and her wavy mane hung loose. Gray spots appeared across her belly and back, collecting and multiplying until they darkened her hindquarters to a deep, uniform gray. She was strong, broad chested with thick legs, and her hooves were curtained in thick feather. Like all the Fell horses, she was suited to the bitter winters that descended on the lands south of the Pallid Peaks, and Knox was more affectionate with her than he was with his three younger brothers.

"In spring, perhaps," Evander answered.

"Ah, you're always putting me off," Knox said. "Ya know well enough what the outcome would be. Why not let it be settled?" He laughed and prodded Frost, picking up the pace as the band of hunters neared the stable.

Evander kept Rogue at a steady trot and let Knox race ahead. His eyes were on a figure slipping into the village from the direction of the Fayrewood. Torchlight and lantern light fell over it as it moved in among the cottages. Then the figure slipped around a corner and vanished. A woman, by the look of it. *Strange*, Evander thought. *No one goes to the Fayrewood in winter*. Most of the villagers never went at all. But his thoughts were lost in the flurry of their homecoming. Women rushed out of their cottages, searching for the faces of sons and husbands. Children surrounded the band of hunters, hoping for food, their faces alight. It tore at Evander's heart to send them home again with nothing.

Evander dismounted and took the reins from some of his men. He often stabled, groomed, and fed the horses, especially for those men with pressing duties at home. He didn't mind.

"Ya can't wait forever, Evander," Knox called as he approached, leading Frost and two other horses. He lowered his voice. "Wouldn't want the men ta think you're afraid, would ya?" He smiled and slapped Evander across the back.

"In the spring, Knox. Ya have my word." He extended his arm, and Knox grasped it, hand to elbow. They entered the stable.

"First Market?"

"Done."

Knox cheered. "This is the day, Evander! Come with me!"

"No."

"The whole company home unharmed and a race set fer spring. Can't think of a better time ta start. I'll make a man of you yet!"

Evander shook his head and laughed. "No, Knox. I've no taste fer it."

"I'll pull out the huckleberry ale. Been saving it." He raised his eyebrows as he led the horses into their stalls. "Last chance."

"Come by later if you've a mind. Grey'll want ta hear about the hunt."

Knox swatted him away in disgust. "Suit yerself." He closed the gates on three of the stalls and left.

Evander watched him fade into the shifting shadows of the shops and cottages, his boots crunching in the snow. He knew Knox wouldn't come to see Grey. Knox would spend the evening with his ale and forget that Evander had ever given the invitation. He sighed, removing Rogue's saddle and bridle and tossing him a pile of hay before moving on to the other animals.

There was a delicious peace in this ritual. Evander loved the smell of the hay, loved the gentle nickering and blowing of the horses, loved the lulling repetition of each brushstroke on their thick coats. The work wasn't hard. It gave him time to think, and his mind was just drifting back to the figure returning from the Fayrewood when Chase came in.

"Evander."

"Aye?"

"There's news," Chase said. "New family in the village. Just arrived today, it seems. Taking Barclay's old cottage."

"Couldn't wait 'til the snows passed?" Evander asked.

"My da seems ta think the man's a craftsman, come ta draw 'is fortune out o' the stream."

"Ah," Evander said. He continued his work, wondering why Chase should have sought him out to deliver such unremarkable news.

"The girl's something ta see. Whole village is talking. Reed won't shut up about 'er. Says she's got blue eyes —"

"Mmmm," Evander mumbled. His mother had blue eyes. They'd been the talk of the village once.

"— and *red* hair." Chase's eyes twinkled.

Evander looked up at last. "Red?"

"So it seems," Chase replied. "Going ta welcome them tonight. Ma's bringing a pot o' soup or some such. Like ta join us?" He grinned.

Evander thought a moment. He wondered if this girl was anything like his mother, if she was plagued by dreams or visions of her own. Her unusual appearance was some sign from the gods, surely. He sighed.

"No. I should see about Ma and Grey," he said.

Chase's grin faded and he turned to leave.

"Chase," Evander called. "Thanks."

Chase nodded and closed the stable door behind him.

Evander stayed until Rogue, Frost, and five other horses had been watered, fed, and brushed. When he stepped outside, he stood a while against the stable wall, ignoring his weariness and his hollow, aching belly. The Shadow hung low, wrapping the flickering fires of the village in mist and darkness. In his mind's eye, Evander saw the wide plain that stretched northward from the hill where Holt was perched. He saw the Pallid Peaks, rising from the plain in a solid wall of stone. In this corner of Shiloh, the Shadow was sometimes frayed and fitful. Once or twice, Evander had seen the air clear a little, as though the mountains held up the weight of the Shadow with their pointed, snow-capped peaks. On this evening, as his eyes searched the darkness, he imagined the Shadow parting and the hills blossoming with color. The slopes of the mountains would be gilded in red-gold light, as though someone had dipped them in molten edanna. The snow would sparkle, and the dull stone of lanes and cottages would awaken. He imagined his home clothed in a light he had never seen — the light of the sun.

Three

Valour tucked a strand of hair back into her braid and glanced at Chase, who was trying not to stare. Valour was familiar with such behavior, and she much preferred boyish grins and stolen glances to the burning stares some men gave her. She smiled at Chase, and he blushed. He stood in the front room of their cottage with his parents, a sister who seemed to melt into the wall, and a younger brother who gawked at everything in the room. An unappealing pot of thin soup sat on the front table.

Valour dreaded the many introductions that lay ahead. She wondered how long it would take before the questions ran out, before people regarded her as a young woman and not an oddity or an emissary of the gods. Already she missed the rocky, windswept village of Fleete, missed the cottage where she'd been born and the friends she'd loved. She missed her father's workshop and the cherry trees in the valley. And more than anything, she missed the solitude of her retreat on the summit of the hill.

Her father was confident that he could increase their fortunes if they came to Holt. When he'd heard of the death of one of the town's metalworkers at a market where he sold some of his pieces, he'd come home and announced the move to his wife and daughter. They had balked. Holt was the northernmost village in Shiloh, lying right under the shadow of the Pallid Peaks, right on the doorstep of the dragons. To the east was a terrible forest that rose up to the Black Mountains. South of the forest was a pool where little currents of black water could be traced all the way down to the dark and forbidding Lake Morrison.

But some of the Clan of the White Tree had settled there, in that perilous place, to draw the ores from the Cutting Stream. The frigid water, pouring over the falls from the heights of the Peaks, cut a path around the village. Swirling in its currents were flecks of edanna and other, lesser-known metals whose scarcity made them even more valuable than the red-gold ore. A man who knew what to look for could pull wealth untold from the Cutting, and Cole assured Ada and Valour that he was such a man.

At the moment, her father was indulging Jameson, showing him some of the pieces he'd unpacked from the crates. Reed circled the men, exclaiming over the beauty and value of delicately wrought lanterns, chains, charms, and daggers. Her mother made polite conversation with Tilly, thanking her for the soup and inquiring about the best time for planting a garden.

Valour followed their lead, striking up a conversation with Chase and his sister.

"I know little of Holt," she said.

"Ya know of the Fayrewood, surely," said Chase, still grinning.

"Aye," Valour replied. "I've heard o' the colored wood."

"It's not much ta see now," Chase said. Valour thought his sister bristled at the words. "But soon, it'll be full o' pink blossoms." He turned and gestured to Mina. "Mina knows it well, better than anyone, I expect."

Valour smiled at Mina. "That's pretty embroidery," she said, admiring the small tree sewn into the neckline of Mina's shift.

Mina blushed, shrank even more thoroughly against the wall of the cottage, and said, "Thank you." Then, as though she felt obligated to offer a compliment in return, she said, "Yer chain is beautiful."

Valour reached to touch the red-gold chain around her neck. The sign of their clan, a tree with spreading roots and spreading branches, hung from the chain. "Da made it fer my coming of age." Her smile fell when she realized that Mina's simple shift was probably her best, and that she wore no jewelry of any kind. Even the girl's braid was tied with a scrap of string, and her shoes looked thin and worn. She changed the subject.

"Do ya have much music in Holt? Any dancing?"

"We've the Midsummer dance," Chase said. "The Dance o' the Lantern Light."

"Midsummer?!" Valour said. "That's months away." She sat down, the weariness of the day's journey coming over her suddenly. "This winter's gone on fer ages."

"They always do," Chase said. "Ya might persuade Lachlan ta play a tune fer ya."

"Thank you," Valour said, and gave him such a genuine smile that Chase looked away, embarrassed.

"Never had anyone ta teach me the craft," Jameson was saying, as her father steered him toward the door. Mina smiled a hasty farewell and slipped outside with her mother. They linked arms and struck out through the snow. Jameson left only after Cole promised to talk with him on the first market day. Reed followed, leaving Chase on the threshold, hesitating.

"Pleasure ta meet ya," Valour said, and Chase seemed satisfied. He turned his boyish grin away, and her father closed the door behind him before putting a hand on her arm.

"I grow weary of saying it, Valour. It's cruel to encourage them so."

"I didn't encourage anything, Da. They brought soup, and I was friendly, and that's all."

"If ya were an ordinary girl, like that dull creature who came tonight, it would make no difference. But a friendly smile and a kind word from *you* is enough ta raise a man's hopes. And if ya ever decide ta raise a man's hopes, I beg ya, daughter, don't let it be some starving hunter."

"Hunting's respectable, Da," Valour said, rehearsing a familiar argument. "Someone's got ta do it, else we all starve."

"Respectable, aye. All those standing around 'is funeral pyre will doubtless respect the boy."

"Da!"

"Tell 'er, Ada," he said, moving to the back of the room and fishing through the unpacked carts for his tools. "I thought she'd seen enough ta know, but perhaps not. Tell 'er!"

Valour's mother gave her a pleading glance. "Hunters leave too many widows and starving babes behind. They could never give ya what yer da's given me . . . given us."

Cole grunted approval. "Marry a craftsman, Valour, a man ya won't have ta watch the road for."

Valour gazed out the front window at the torches and lanterns adorning the walls of the surrounding cottages. She wondered what it would be like to watch her husband ride out into the Shadow, to know with absolute certainty that one day he would not ride home. The wolves would devour him, or the dragons. What remained of his body would be burned quickly, without ceremony. His steady warmth would be replaced by cold and want. Her necklace, her shift, all the lovely things with which she surrounded herself would be sold to feed her children. And what then? "Alright, Da," she said, as her fingertips brushed the delicate chain around her neck.

Evander was surprised to find Maeve sitting in the front room, in his own chair by the fire. She rarely moved so far from her flowers. He went to the back of the chair and leaned down to kiss the top of her head. Her hair hung loose over her shoulders in wisps of pale gold. Evander had always envisioned the sun in that same shade of gold. The idea may have been birthed in his infancy, when Maeve cradled him and sang to him of her strange dreams. Perhaps he would forever see that splendid light as he had seen her golden hair spilling down around him.

Maeve's fingers worked at an intricate pattern along the hem of a shift. She embroidered little circles that connected to one another through an unusual arrangement of long and short, straight and curved lines. Evander had seen the pattern many times. It was his mother's favorite. She could embroider anything, creating scenes so vibrant Evander could have sworn they lived and breathed. Flowers looked as though their sweet nectar might spill out and stain the fabric. Tongues of flame seemed almost to flicker. Roots of trees stretched, imperceptibly, toward hemlines. But Maeve preferred the sun pattern above all else.

She hummed a tune as she worked. The sound of her voice as she sang it was Evander's first memory, and he heard the words in his head as she hummed.

> Tiny drop
> Clear as glass
> Hold the light
> When lanterns pass
>
> Watch fer dawn
> Wait fer sun
> On the petal's
> Velvet tongue
>
> Fade ta red
> Turn ta blood

Weep fer all
That once was good

Loose yer hold
Stain the ground
All is lost
That once was found

It was the Song of the Bleeding Flower, and the tune was haunting. It always filled Evander with an aching sense of loss and longing.

It came to him suddenly that something was wrong. A chair had been pulled from a corner and placed next to Maeve's. It was empty, but for a scrap of fabric and some needles. Grey was missing.

"Ma," he said. "Where's Grey?" She had not left the cottage for more than a few moments at a time all winter.

Maeve looked up from her work. "She's in the back room."

Evander gave her a questioning look and walked to the back room of the cottage. The room was chill, the embers on the hearth sooty and silent.

"Grey?" he said, his eyes searching the small room for some sign of her. He was just about to overturn his mother's cot when he saw her, crouched in the corner between the cot and the wall. She was looking up at Maeve's flowers with enormous red-rimmed eyes, and she was shivering and sniffling.

"Grey, you'll freeze back here!" Evander scooped her up into his arms and sat down, wrapping a blanket around her shoulders and pulling her close. She rested her head against his cheek. He could feel the fluttering of her eyelashes and the dampness under her eyes. "What's wrong?"

"It was the song," she said, and her voice caught on a little sob. "It was terrible." She looked up at Evander. "What does it mean?"

Evander shook his head. "It's nothing, little one, nothing ta fret about."

"But what does it mean about waiting fer the sun?"

"I don't know. It's something Ma sees when she sleeps, a great light overhead. She's sung of it, spoken of it fer as long as I can remember. I don't know if it's real."

"What would ya do if there was such a light?"

Evander looked at the ashes in the fireplace as he answered. "If I knew such a thing could be found, I'd go and find it." He sighed heavily. "But it may be only a vision."

Grey put a small hand on Evander's face. "Alright then. If it's no more than a vision, I won't be afraid."

Evander searched her face, surprised. "Afraid? Why would ya be afraid, Grey?"

"The wolves," she whispered, her eyes growing wider than ever. "If you went away, ta find the light, there'd be no one ta keep me safe."

"Oh, Grey," Evander said, wrapping her tightly in his arms and tracing the wild streak of gray hair that shone through the mass of black. "The wolves can't have ya. I won't let 'em."

Poor child, he thought. She still lived in fear that the Shadow Wolves would take her. How did she sleep at all if she imagined them so near, if she expected to be taken at any moment? It explained her reluctance to leave the cottage. He would ask his mother to sing something else. There wasn't much chance of his request being remembered or heeded, but for Grey's sake, he would try.

The fire crackled on the hearth. One log crumbled and fell into the embers with a hiss and a sigh. Mina looked up at the wooden beams above her cot and listened to Reed's steady breathing. Her parents snored at the other end of the cottage, and she heard nothing from Chase. He was probably lying awake as well.

It frustrated Mina that sleep should elude her. Tomorrow's

labor would be no less than today's; the days were unrelenting in their demands, and her body cried out for rest. But her mind would not be stilled. Mina closed her eyes. She imagined herself pressing down a squirming knot of thoughts with both hands. She waited. One thought worked its way to the surface, slipping between her fingers. She picked it up and examined it.

She is so beautiful. This thought was difficult to hold. It hurt, and Mina hardly knew why. She had been stunned by Valour's beauty that evening, had felt incapable of doing anything other than stare. The flaming hair, the eyes clear and bright as the flowers of the morning glory vine. She was a little younger than Mina, had probably come of age within the last year or two, but where Mina was strong and square, Valour was soft and feminine...

And surrounded by beautiful things. This thought came hard on the heels of the first. Mina remembered the edanna chain and charm, the fine wool shift, the cottage overflowing with bright lanterns and finery, more wealth than she had ever seen in one place. It was as if Valour had strolled through the tables on market day and loaded baskets, no, whole carts, with everything that struck her fancy. It was unimaginable prosperity.

My chest aches, she thought. It felt large and hollow, as though the icy winds from the Peaks had found a crack in her skin and swept in, whining and whistling through her.

What is wrong with me? Why should this plague me so? These thoughts were bulky, complicated. She picked at them, searching for the source of her unease. She did not hate Valour. No, it wasn't hatred that she felt, or even jealousy. It was just... she couldn't find the words to frame her grief... it was just that she had never thought to hope for the kind of beauty Valour possessed. She had never felt so discontented with her ordinary brown hair and brown eyes. She had never been so conscious of the dull gray of her shift, never felt so keenly the spreading darkness of the Shadow. The sight of such extraordinary beauty made her want to weep for the life she lived, the face she wore, the future that lay ahead. But she found that she didn't have the courage for tears. Instead, she rolled onto her side and thought of the coming spring. She fell asleep awash in a memory of pink petals falling like snow to the floor of the Fayrewood.

Four

In spring, as melting snow from the Pallid Peaks poured roaring and foaming over the falls and overflowed the banks of the Cutting Stream, the village of Holt came alive. Children ventured out into the warmer air and played in the mud. Women planted their gardens, aired their cottages, and beat the winter's dust from rugs and mattresses. Restless hunters mounted their horses and rode out in search of food. And restless craftsmen came with screens and sieves, with shovels and spoons, ready to glean the precious ores that flowed down from the heights of the mountains.

Their torches and lanterns created a shifting avenue of light as Holt's craftsmen crossed the churning waters of the Cutting. From their cottages and workshops, they brought tools and raw materials, resuming their work in little lean-to huts on the western side of the stream. Beyond the huts, two rounded doorways, spread three or four paces apart, were cut into the rocky slope of the next hill. Behind them was a cave, and inside the cave was a furnace. Its fires flared to life each spring, their smoke escaping through a vent in the top of the hill and mingling with mist and

Shadow. For the people of Holt, the light that poured from the furnace in the hillside was a surer sign of spring than the change in the weather.

Errol was always first to the furnace. He'd learned from his father that pride was only to be found in a hard day's labor, and he had lived nearly sixty years by that principle. He was first to clear a path through the lingering snow, first to gather fuel, first to set the fires roaring. The other craftsmen didn't mind. They even allowed him first pick of the ores that were harvested from the Cutting. For Errol knew what none of the others did. Errol knew how to make the fires burn hotter and last longer. He knew the secret of the Holt lanterns, the key to making smooth, clear, uniform panes of glass. None of the other craftsmen could say how Errol managed it, but they thanked their good fortune and asked no questions.

Errol whistled to himself, rubbing his palms together over the tiny blue flame in the heart of the furnace. He reached into a small jar and pinched a bit of ashy powder between his thumb and forefinger. He was quiet as he tossed the powder into the furnace. The flame coughed and sputtered, shrinking to a small ember, then woke in a flash of red-orange light. He resumed his whistling and set to work cleaning and oiling his tools.

The whistling helped him think, and this year there was much to ponder. He had been gifted with many years of good health and prosperity. But each winter felt longer than the one before it. Errol was not sure how many more winters he would see, how many more he could endure. He had never taken an apprentice, had never shared his knowledge of his craft or revealed his secret to anyone. He'd always kept to himself, had always been content with his work and his secrets. But now he wondered at his choices. He was running out of time. Holt's craftsmen generally took their own sons as apprentices. Errol had no sons, no family at all. He had to choose an apprentice, but who could be trusted?

He scanned the huts along the near side of the stream, then the cottages on the far side. Through the dim morning light, he could just see their western walls. Many of them had small workshops attached, with doors that opened toward the stream and the furnace. He eyed Barclay's old place. Barclay had been what he might have called a friend. But he wouldn't be fashioning any lanterns this year. His pyre was cold. Errol missed him. His tune faltered for a moment. He sighed and rubbed his eyes, leaning back on his stool. He scraped a bit of rust from the tip of an iron rod and considered the family who'd settled in Barclay's cottage. If there was any truth in the snatches of gossip he'd overheard, the father was a highly skilled craftsman, especially gifted in working with edanna. He was also quite prosperous.

Shame he has no sons, Errol thought. And then another thought struck him. It was so ridiculous, so unlikely, that he chuckled to himself. He laid the rod aside and picked up a set of shears, testing the hinge to see if it moved smoothly. The joint caught and scraped, so he oiled it. He was struggling to believe it, but he thought he might have found the apprentice he'd been waiting for all these years.

Mina leaned through the doorway of Moss's shop and inhaled the lingering scents of mandrake and tobacco. The front room of the apothecary's shop was nearly bare, but that was always so in early spring. Winter complaints had depleted Moss's stores, and her shelves and tables looked almost embarrassed by their assortment of empty bottles. The ceiling beams, too, were naked and longing for clusters of dried herbs to clothe them.

"Need the usual today, Moss?" Mina asked.

Moss shuffled into the front room. She was not old, but her knees were arthritic. She eased into a rocking chair by the fire with a groan.

"If by 'the usual,' ya mean every root and herb in the Fayrewood," she said.

Moss looked rather like Mina. She was pleasant enough, but unremarkable, with dark hair braided away from her face and a gray wool shift that fell to her ankles. Both women wore belts and leather boots. But where Mina wore a leather belt with pockets and pouches for gathering, Moss wore a woven belt embroidered with the sign of their clan. The embroidery work was exquisite, the many branches and roots of the trees interweaving as they circled the strip of cloth. Mina hadn't seen it before.

"Should be able ta find some mandrake, but ya know it's early fer anything else," Mina said. "Yer belt, Moss. It's a new one, isn't it? Maeve's work?"

"Aye," Moss replied. She looked down at the interlacing trees and ran a hand over the embroidery. "I could swear the branches move in the wind, Mina. Never seen anyone who could match 'er skill. It's a shame."

Mina knew what Moss meant. As a girl, she'd spent many hours watching Maeve, staring at her bright eyes and golden hair as she stood behind her stall on market days. But Maeve's appearances in the village had grown more and more rare, until one day they'd ceased altogether. Mina had never been inside Maeve's cottage. She knew a little of what kept the woman from leaving those four stone walls, and she guessed a great deal more.

"Do ya believe what they say, Moss, about the belladonna or the mandrake?"

Moss shook her head once and looked into the fire. "Not I. Either o' them could cause hallucinations, if used improperly. But Maeve never came ta me fer any such thing, and I've never known 'er ta go searching the foothills or the Fayrewood fer roots and berries." She leaned back in her chair, grimaced at the pain in her knees, and started to rock. "No, Maeve's visions began when she was with child. It's not uncommon fer a woman ta see and feel all manner o' strange things when she's with child. I was sure it would pass when 'er little one came, but it seems the visions have only come stronger and more frequent over the years."

Mina was quiet for a while. She ached to know all that Moss knew, to ask a hundred questions about Evander's mother, to know what Evander faced when he passed through the doors of his cottage. But she allowed herself the luxury of just one more question.

"Ya think it's raving, then? Madness?"

Moss gave a brief, humorless laugh. "A great light in the sky? A lantern so bright it lights all o' Shiloh?" She turned to Mina, and the look in her eyes told of despair and something else, something childlike. "This is the Shadow Realm, Mina."

It was not a revelation. Mina was familiar with the Shadow. She waited a moment for Moss to speak again, to amend her statement, to offer some hope. But Moss rocked in her chair and said nothing, and Mina left at last, seeking mandrake and consolation in the Fayrewood.

Cormac walked the muddy lanes of Holt, taking in the activity of the village and exchanging words with passing villagers. He told himself that he had no particular destination, that he'd come out to talk with his people and share in the labors and the little joys of their day. His father often did the same. When his stroll brought him to Barclay's old cottage, Cormac told himself that it was only right he should greet the newest residents of Holt, that Valour was no different than any other young woman in the village. He took a faltering breath and stepped up to the door. He raised his hand to knock, heard voices, dropped his hand. He heard footsteps approaching, and he ducked around a corner of the cottage and peeked through a side window. She was there. Valour was inside.

Cormac touched the window, running the tip of his finger over the place where Valour's hair was visible through the glass.

He'll have her, a little voice whispered in his head.

Cormac ground his teeth and pushed the thought aside. *The man who claims such a rare beauty for his own will surely be respected in Holt,* he told himself. A smile of anticipation and satisfaction began to play at the edges of his mouth.

But it won't be you who claims her, the little voice persisted. *Evander will have her, as he has everything you desire.*

Cormac turned away from the window and pounded his fist against the wall of the cottage. He'd only ever wanted one thing: the respect of the men of Holt. As the son of Nolan, the magistrate, it should have been easy enough for Cormac to have his heart's desire. When his father died or became too old to execute his duties, Cormac would assume the leadership of a bustling and prosperous village. He would hold council with other magistrates. He would live in more comfort than the craftsmen, and he would likely live far longer than the hunters. His future should have been bright.

But Cormac believed he would never have his heart's desire so long as Evander lived, or lived in Holt, at least. He'd been born without something that Evander possessed in abundance. What it was, he couldn't say, but even as children, if Cormac urged the village boys toward some mischief or adventure, they declined, chasing after Evander instead. When Cormac came of age, the usual celebrations were held. When Evander came of age on Midsummer's Day, the village was riotous, and the girls swarmed around him like flies.

Cormac could have forgiven him, perhaps, if Evander had treated Cormac as an adversary, if he had reveled in his many victories. But Evander never seemed to notice how men many years his senior deferred to his judgment, or how the mood of the village changed when he returned safe from the hunt. He lightly esteemed what Cormac would have given almost anything to possess, and

Cormac despised him for it. He couldn't bear another loss to Evander. He could not. Not again.

Cormac skulked against the wall, seething over the thousand imagined injuries he'd suffered at Evander's hands, until the shouts of a group of boys playing by the stream woke him to his surroundings. He slipped away from Barclay's cottage without a word to Valour and hurried home.

Five

The Shadow Wolves had been cunning. They waited for Evander to make his move. Three bull elk, all pierced by arrows, were scattered on the ground twenty paces ahead of the little band of hunters. But just beyond, in the trees that lined the valley, the wolves were watching. Their eyes flashed in the darkness, hovering, waiting. Evander's men could turn back and leave their first kills of the year. They could continue their search elsewhere. They could return home empty-handed to greet the gaunt faces of those they loved. Or they could fight.

"The Wheel," Evander said.

Lachlan snatched up the cold torch that hung beside his leg. He thrust it into the flaming torch he already carried, gave a command to his horse, and held his position, fiery torches now raised in both hands. Around him, six hunters circled. Their arrows were nocked, and they moved toward him, their horses weaving in and out. As each arrow was set alight, its bearer turned to face the enemy.

"Grosvenor!" Evander shouted, as the wolves' black coats

caught the light of the fires and the pack descended, snarling, on the hunters.

They released their arrows in quick succession, each man returning to Lachlan's torches with a freshly nocked arrow as soon as he had fired. Most of the men could fire two flaming arrows at once, sending a pair of advancing wolves off in a gust of vapor and smoke.

"Here!" Chase cried. On his side of the Wheel, the wolves were advancing too quickly.

Knox left his position and rode out, drawing off three wolves that had nearly overtaken Chase. He sent his arrows through the first pair, then spurred Frost away from the Wheel. The last wolf followed. As he passed Evander, Knox took another arrow from his quiver, leaned to touch its tip to the arrow Evander was preparing to fire, turned in his saddle, and dispatched the wolf that pursued him.

"Back!" Evander cried. There were more wolves at the edge of the valley. Some hadn't come in the first onslaught. They were waiting.

Knox only laughed in reply, urging Frost toward the fallen elk.

"Knox!" Evander called.

Knox rushed ahead, dismounting between two of the elk and motioning to the others. Lorne and Alistair wanted very much to follow. They had large families to feed, and they sorely needed the meat. But they would not move without Evander's consent. There was a long, slow moment when Knox stared at the hunters as wicked eyes collected in the trees behind him and the hunters looked on, full of dread.

A wave of fitful darkness broke from the tree line. Evander kicked Rogue, surging forward with a growl of frustration. The others followed, expending all but their last arrows to cover him as he leapt from his horse and helped Knox toss the carcass of one elk over Frost's back. Knox was jumping to retrieve another when Evander took his arm.

"Leave 'em!" he roared. The fire in his eyes was bright and fierce, and Knox finally relented. The others hung back, felling two, then three more wolves, before racing behind Knox and Evander out of the narrow valley.

They camped that night on a hilltop half a day's journey south of Holt. They would risk the exposure and the frigid winds in favor of a good vantage point. Alistair and Chase set to work building a fire. Lorne went to see about the elk. Lachlan pulled a pipe from his belt and fiddled with it, warming his fingers and easing his way into a tune. Evander dragged Knox down the hill, where the winds would carry their voices out of hearing.

"Ya can't keep this up, Knox," Evander said. "I won't have any man in my company who'd risk all our lives so freely. It's reckless!"

"What was I ta do?" Knox shrugged, spreading his hands in a gesture of helplessness.

"Ya know as well as I, Knox. Keep ta the Wheel! The Sons of Grosvenor have done as much fer generations. Are ya really so arrogant? Do ya think you know better how ta hunt, how ta defeat the wolves than thousands of men who've gone before ya?"

Knox spat back at him, meeting his eyes with a barely-restrained fire of his own. "What's become of all those hunters, Evander? Did their skills, their knowledge, their *Wheels* keep 'em out o' the jaws o' the Shadow?" He ran a hand along the back of his neck, shaking his head. "Their bones are black, lost beneath a hundred winters' worth o' snow!"

Evander's anger, which had boiled all the way to camp, cooled. He sighed and ran his knuckles over the scar on his chin. This argument was too familiar, and what lay at the heart of it he was powerless to change. Knox had lost three brothers. All had been hunters; all had fallen to the wolves. And Evander still did not know what comfort to offer him.

"What of my leadership, then?" His voice was softer now, reasoning with Knox.

"Bah," Knox replied. "They'd follow ya through the Turn, Evander, right inta the Black Mountains if you asked it. All o' them. My takin' a few risks won't change that."

Evander sighed. "How many more risks, Knox?"

"How many more hunts, Evander?"

The two headed up the hill. A lively tune met them as they entered the camp. Knox gave Evander a slap across the back and went to help Lorne with the elk. Alistair talked with Chase about the wife and five children who waited for him at home. Lachlan leaned against his pack and played his pipe. Hallam motioned Evander to join him.

"That one will be the death of ya, you know."

Evander sat down and took a small roll from his bag. "Aye," he replied. "I know. If this food doesn't kill me first."

"What've ya got?" Hallam asked, leaning over to see Evander's meal. "Cakes? I've got nothing but potatoes. Hand one over."

Evander tossed a cake to Hallam. "It's these late winter stores I can't stand. Withered vegetables, dried venison, dried berry cakes. Doesn't seem right fer a man ta live off o' dead things."

"It's the same every spring," Hallam replied.

"Aye," Evander said. "Every spring." He looked to the north, catching a burst of blue light out of the corner of his eye. *The dragons are waking up.*

Hallam followed his gaze. "The dragons. Something else that's the same every spring."

Evander said nothing.

"Ya know, it helps ta have a woman at home waiting fer ya. Winters don't seem so long. Thin soup doesn't seem so bad. I'm hungry as the next man, of course, but my Emmeline puts a shine on things. She's having twins. Did ya know that?"

"Aye," Evander answered. He looked at Hallam, who was beaming. "I'm glad of it, Hallam."

"Why not marry? Fergive my saying it, but I've never known a man so dissatisfied with 'is lot. You're the best of us, Evander. Maybe a good wife is all ya lack."

"It's not that, Hallam."

Hallam leaned in. "Have ya seen that red-haired beauty?"

Evander laughed. "I have. But it's not that, truly."

"What is it then, Evander? What is it you seek?"

The words caught on the tune Lachlan was playing and bumped around in Evander's head. *What is it you seek, Evander?* He stared at the campfire, at the tongues of flame reaching, stretching, searching . . . for what? He thought of his mother's song. *Tiny drop clear as glass, hold the light when lanterns pass. Watch for dawn, wait for sun . . .*

It was impossible. There could be no light so great, so bright. Such a thing could not exist in the Shadow Realm. If it were real, wouldn't someone have found it? Someone braver and stronger than he? There could be no sun. It was impossible. But something within him ached to know for sure.

The seven hunters returned to Holt at midday, and Evander stabled the horses as usual. When he was finished, he carried his share of venison back to the cottage. He looked forward to roasting the cut of meat over the fire. There was a dusting of dried herbs stored somewhere near the hearth, and some salt. Grey would be thrilled. The girl ate as much as any grown man, though where she put it, Evander could not imagine.

He smiled to himself as he crossed the threshold. But his face fell when he saw Maeve. She was not watching her flowers, not embroidering, not sitting near the fire. She was standing with her arm resting on the back of the rocking chair as though she'd been collecting all her strength for this moment.

"She's gone," Maeve said.

"Gone?" Evander said. "*Grey's* gone?"

"Aye."

"How? When? When did she go?"

Maeve shook her head. "I don't know. It was yesterday, sometime after —"

"Yesterday?! She's been gone all night? Ma, how could ya let 'er go?"

Maeve shook her head over and over. She backed away, slipping into her room and settling herself by the bleeding flowers.

Evander dropped the meat on the cold stones of the threshold and stood for a moment in shock and indecision. What should he do? Where should he even begin to search for her? She'd been alone, in the dark. What if the wolves —

Evander's stomach tightened as the possibilities rolled over him. He ran toward the stable. Wherever he went, he would need Rogue.

He'd not gone three paces before he saw her, walking calmly toward him. "Grey!" Evander called. He ran to her, crouched on one knee, and scooped her up in his arms. "Where have ya been?" He searched her for some sign of injury. There was no mark on her. The old wound on her neck was all but forgotten, no trace of it remaining in her soft skin. "Grey?" he said again.

"I wanted ta see ya come in from the hunt," she said.

"But you've been gone all night. Ma was . . . Ma was beside 'erself."

"I thought ya'd be back last night. Fell asleep in the stable waiting fer ya."

"But I was there, stabling the horses. How did I not see ya?"

"I curled up under the hay."

Evander sighed and stood. "You must be hungry," he said.

"I am," Grey replied, grinning.

"Well, we made a kill at last." He smiled and lifted Grey to his shoulders, carrying her home. "Tonight we feast!"

It was the first time Evander's belly had been full in months, and he blessed Knox for his recklessness. Maeve joined them and ate a little of the roast venison before returning to her embroidery. Grey ate a heaping portion and fell into a contented sleep. Evander tucked her into the cot he'd made for her and sat in front of the fire, listening to the haunting melody of the Song of the Bleeding Flower as Maeve sang from the back room.

Six

Mina was suspended in a heaven of pink blossoms. As the winds liberated the petals one by one, they drifted down around her in shades of palest white-pink and deep blush pink. The Fayrewood trees were in bloom. Mina was stretched out on her favorite branch, watching the petals fall. They fluttered against her skin. Her face was serene. What hair was not braided hung below her, and one soft leather boot. She loved this tree and the wide, smooth branch that broke from the trunk at just the right height. She was not so high that she lost sight of the floor of the wood, not so low that she could be seen by anyone who approached. Not that anyone did, for the most part.

Mina sat up and gazed through the branches toward the lane that ran through the center of the Fayrewood. Petals were hurrying down, carpeting the muddy path, filling it with color. And there were other colors spreading over the floor of the wood. Flowering tobacco in white and yellow and wine-red clustered near moss-blanketed rocks. Star-shaped moonflowers clung to the branches of low shrubs, sometimes closed and shy, sometimes fanned out in full array. Morning glory vines scaled the trunks of the trees, their indigo blooms peeking from lush green leaves. Layer upon layer of color.

Mina breathed it in and sighed. Her world had come alive when her parents had brought her here for the first time. She'd been six or seven, perhaps, and Jameson and Tilly, like most of the people of Holt, brought their children to the Fayrewood out of a vague sense of obligation. They felt that every child should see the wood. Their village was known for it, after all, and there were the Fayrewood lanterns. Children should know why the lanterns were famous, and so forth.

But Mina still wondered that so few came to the Fayrewood after their first visit. She thought the Turn a poor excuse to stay away. She thought that only a fool would allow his fear to rob him of such a gift. In the minds of the people of Holt, however, the mysterious terrors beyond the Turn had blended with the mysterious beauty of the wood. In the minds of the people of Holt, fear and wonder had become inseparable. The Fayrewood was nearly always deserted.

Mina heard a rustling in the lane below. She pulled her legs in close to the trunk of the tree and waited.

It was him. Evander. He walked down the main path, stopping here and there to touch the bark of the trees, or gaze up at the slow descent of thousands of tiny petals. He looked peaceful. He looked happy.

Mina hardly breathed as she watched. All her years had been spent in watching him, and she would spend them so again, and again. Evander was as much a part of her world as the Pallid Peaks that shadowed the village or the Cutting Stream that wrapped it round. To her, his every movement spoke of grace and strength. The sound of his voice was as familiar, as dear, as the sound of the wind in the topmost branches of the Fayrewood trees. Mina did her sewing and mending by the south-facing window so that she might scan the southern border of the village to see when the hunters returned. She'd endured many years of hunts, listening for the noise of the approaching hunters and searching for the white blaze on the muzzle of Evander's horse.

Mina saw when his tunic was threadbare and his trousers torn. She saw when he favored his left arm because of some hidden injury or wound, or when his long, steady gait was halting and slow. The bright flash in Evander's eyes, that light that remained somehow undimmed in the darkness of Shiloh, was clear to any observer. But Mina saw those fleeting moments when it faltered, when his eyes were dark and still, full of longing, and without hope.

Mina understood him and loved him. She knew him almost as she knew herself. It was a knowledge gained from long years of quiet curiosity, of hasty stolen glances. But it was more. If Mina had come to Holt when Valour did, she would still have known and understood him, in part, from the moment she saw his face. Their hearts danced to the same silent music, and Mina heard the song more clearly whenever Evander was near.

The first time she'd seen him walking beneath her in the Fayrewood, she had frozen, her breath catching in her chest, her fingers digging into the grooves of the bark. She had looked on in an agony of delight and embarrassment. She had not sought him out. She would never have so lightly esteemed his time, his solitude, his choice. Those things were sacred to her, as she knew they were to him. To hover in the branches, watching him, was unthinkable. To climb to the floor of the wood and make her presence known was impossible. She could not bear it. So she had turned her face away, wrapping her arms around the trunk of the tree and pressing her cheek to the bark, until the sound of his footsteps had faded to nothing.

On this day, she let her eyes rest on him for one sweet, lingering moment. She was not even certain why she did so. The longer she watched him, the more the wind whistled inside her, and her heart felt hollow, aching. She turned away, closing her eyes and leaning her forehead against the gray-brown grooves of the trunk.

Evander was glad. He was glad that Grey had recovered enough from the loss of her parents to leave the cottage on her own. He was glad to see the winter snows melting, glad to pack up the thick fleece-lined coat he wore through the freezing months. He was glad to see the awakening of the Fayrewood, though even in winter he felt at ease from the moment he stepped into the wide lane in the center of the wood. Something small and tight within him uncurled. He felt himself stretching out into his skin, inhabiting his body as it was meant to be inhabited, and coming alive to the beauty around him.

He placed a hand on one massive trunk, brushing his fingers over the bark. At his feet, roots spread out from the base of the tree and dawdled before plunging into wet, black soil. Evander wondered how deep those roots went and if they ever longed to come up for air. He looked up at the falling petals. In all his years, he had never ceased marveling at how the Shadow pulled away from the trees of the Fayrewood. There must be some enchantment that held back the darkness. Above him, the trees stretched up and up. His eyes searched the topmost branches for some sign of encroaching Shadow. But as far as he could see, the edges of the pink petals were clear and crisp, undimmed by fog or mist.

This was a sacred place to Evander, and as he walked, he cursed himself for failing to come more often. When he stepped over the threshold of his cottage, his mother's needs and Grey's needs overtook him. When he mounted Rogue and set out with his men, the dark and the wolves and the driving need for a successful hunt overcame him. He forgot how desperately he needed this place, forgot what a balm it was for his restless agitation.

As he had done before, he resolved to come every day. When he was not hunting, he would walk in the quiet of the wood, and he would breathe, and he would be glad. His step quickened. He smiled. So long as he had this place, he could settle down. He could marry and have children and find contentment in Holt. In the Fayrewood, he would find peace. In the Fayrewood, his heart would rest.

He took no notice when the path curved sharply to the right and the lane of trees narrowed. He was lost in his thoughts, distantly aware that the edges of the trees had become less distinct, that his eyes could not hold them in focus. His feet had found their rhythm. They did not stop, not yet. He'd only just begun to notice movement on the edges of his vision, only just felt chilled. He was suddenly aware of a single drop of clammy sweat that trailed down the center of his back.

He'd gone beyond the Turn. He stopped, spun, stumbled. He reached out to regain his balance, resting his hand against the nearest tree. The trunk twitched and crawled at his touch. Evander recoiled. He ran, away from the shivering trunks of the dark trees, back into the lane of pink petals. He ran out of the wood, taking a sharp right before plunging into the Cutting, and climbed the hill back to Holt. Inside the cottage, he sat by the fire and steadied his breathing, all the while trying to imagine a world where lovely things never turned, where there was light enough and to spare, and the Shadow quailed before it.

The last snows melted, and little isolated patches of green grass came joyfully together and spread over the foothills. Bright hot fires from the furnace in the hillside bathed Holt in red-orange light. The huts along the Cutting bustled with activity. Apprentices scooped molten glass with iron bowls affixed to iron rods and transferred the various colors to cooling ovens. Workers in iron and edanna pounded their anvils, hammering lantern frames and decorative pieces along with the necessary, mundane axheads and nails.

Cole leaned over a sheet of edanna, making small cuts and grooves in the surface. He was a patient man, and the tedious nature of his work had never plagued him. Each new piece was a challenge, each a delight. The lantern he was planning at the moment would bring a fabulous price, if only he could resist giving it to his daughter. As if hearing his thought, Valour stepped into his workshop. She eyed the metal sheet, squinting as she guessed at some of her father's techniques.

"Ya made that cut with straight sheers?" she asked.

"Aye," he answered.

"This is an intricate piece," she continued, and picked up another scrap of unfinished filigree work. "Mind if I fool with it fer a while?"

"Valour."

"I won't spoil it, Da. Ya taught me better than that."

"That's not what I mean."

"What, then?"

He shook his head. "We've made a new start here. I know I indulged ya in Fleete, but it was seldom. What need have you of learning metalwork?"

"I've a knack fer it, Da. Ya said so yerself."

Cole leaned away from the table and brushed the sweat from his forehead.

"Aye, you've a knack, my lovely daughter, but you've no need o' skills such as these. You ought ta be out with the young people o' the village. The flowers are blooming! Go and talk; go and dance."

Valour left the workshop without a reply, and Cole sank back in his chair. He'd made a habit of giving her what she wanted, but this desire to take up a man's labor confounded him. His daughter was so extraordinary that he was sometimes caught unawares. The lantern light would wash over her hair and it would glow like embers, or she would turn suddenly and her blue eyes would flash and the air would be charged as though struck by lightning. She could have any life she chose, any man she chose, and Cole wanted her to know all the beauty and ease that could be found beneath the Shadow. He smiled tenderly at the spot where Valour had stood and went back to work.

It was the one thing Valour loathed about her beauty, that assumption that she was merely ornamental. She was more than that. She *could be* more. But who was likely to understand her desire if even her father could not? He should have known how much she enjoyed his lessons, should have appreciated how the work gave her a sense of purpose. But he had dismissed her. And what now? If she were in Fleete, she would have climbed to the craggy peak of the hill and let the winds tear at her braids. Or she'd have gone to visit her friend, Fern, who'd never once been intimidated by Valour's beauty. She'd found no one like that in Holt. The girls regarded her from a distance. The boys smiled and teased and stared, but few actually spoke to her. She'd been in Holt long enough to see winter bow to spring; that was all. And already her loneliness threatened to smother her. If she couldn't find something to fill the empty hours, she would run wild.

She loitered in the village for a while, walking the lanes between cottages and observing the progress of the gardens. She wandered south and west, moving steadily toward the raging fires of the furnace in the hillside and the many torches and lanterns that illuminated the western bank of the Cutting. She crossed the newly assembled bridge, turning to glance at the explosions of blue light that emerged from the measureless darkness of the mountains. The craftsmen were pleased to see her, eager to display their skills as she stopped by their huts, asked questions, and complimented their work. The young apprentices were the boldest of the lot, making no effort to conceal their admiration as she moved among them. The boys fritting the sand nearly burned their batches before their masters elbowed them in the ribs or knocked them upside the backs of their heads.

Valour approached one of the low doors that blocked the entrances to the cave and leaned in. A couple of boys were adding fuel to the furnace. Their faces glistened in the firelit darkness. They grinned and mopped the sweat from their foreheads with their forearms. Another man was pouring molten glass onto sheets of iron. He didn't look up. For him, one stolen glance could prove disastrous.

"This is no place fer a lass such as you," an old man said, stepping up to the door from inside the cave. "Dangerous. Get along with yerself, now."

Valour had no wish to be dismissed by two men in the space of a lifetime, much less that of a single hour. She stood her ground. "Not dangerous if ya know what you're about."

There was a cough behind her, a smothered laugh.

But Errol didn't laugh. He raised his brows till they nearly touched his gray-white hair, then lifted his right hand, fingers spread to showcase a missing finger. "I won't embarrass ya by stripping off my tunic and trousers. The work's dangerous, *even if* ya know what you're about." He eyed her closely, appraising her. "Marvelous, but dangerous."

Valour caught the gleam in his eye. She thought, she almost thought, that his words held some kind of offer for her, some kind of proposition.

"Get along with yerself, now," he said, this time stepping out of the cave and hustling Valour away from the heat of the furnace.

"Market day," he said, speaking into the braided hair at the back of her head.

She turned back, gaping, but the door was already swinging shut, and Errol was gone.

Seven

Four drops of nectar held the firelight, suspended like little suns from the petals of the bleeding flowers on the windowsill. The light captured in the droplets was whole, fixed. It did not stretch and strain, like firelight or candlelight, toward some unreachable design. This light was perfect. It was the nearest thing Maeve had ever found to what she saw in her dreams. She watched the drops intently.

Any day, new bleeding flowers would appear on the hillside. She'd have to go out and dig them up. The ones on the sill had kept her company since last spring, and they were beginning to fade. But they lived, and the nectar still gathered on the velvety black petals. Maeve breathed a contented sigh. All was well.

She edged her cot closer to the window, resting her elbow on the sill and her head on her arm. She watched the little suns until the fire on the hearth died and the tiny lights went out. Maeve didn't rise to replenish the fire. She sat in the darkness, eyes fixed on the now dull droplets. Tears slipped, one after another, down her cheeks. But she did not move until the wall behind her, the wall between the front and back rooms, shuddered. The faint disturbance spread to the outside wall of the cottage, tremors passing from stone to stone and then to the window frame. The flowerpot trembled. Maeve stiffened. The droplets shook, perfect globes stretching oblong, each clutching its dark petal. Three absorbed the shock and resumed their circular forms.

One fell.

It splashed onto the windowsill in a red as bright as blood.

"Grey!" Maeve screamed her anguish and stumbled over the cot in her rush to the front room. The girl's eyes were wide, impossibly wide. She was sprawled on the floor next to an overturned chair. A mug was shattered in a hundred jagged shards, and a shelf hung askew from the wall overhead.

"Out!" Maeve screamed. She thought of nothing but the tiny, perfect light that was lost. Lost forever.

Grey hesitated.

"Out!" Maeve screamed again.

This time Grey jumped. She clambered over the chair and fled.

The Cutting Stream, after looping around Holt and turning east, emptied into a wide pool, just south and east of the entrance to the Fayrewood. Currents that began in the heights of the Pallid Peaks, that roared their way past the Shadow Dragons and braved the plunge over the falls, finally slowed and came to rest. Though the pool was deep, no one knew how deep, the waters of the Cutting filled it to overflowing, and some spilled over the rim of the pool and fed the bog. There were other waters that fed the pool. Here and there, a little rivulet trickled its way up from Lake Morrison and swirled in among the waters of the Cutting. The lake water was black, and it curled like inky fog into the clearer water from the mountains. Except on Midsummer's Night, when it was lit with the dancing light of dozens of floating lanterns, the pool was an eerie place.

Knox took no notice. He didn't hear the croaks and shrieks of the creatures that were secreted in the bog. A torch was thrust into the mud beside him. A nearly empty jug of potato beer rested on his thigh.

He rubbed the back of his neck. His hand fell over his forehead and then his eyes. He wept. The beer never banished the sound of their voices, though he returned to it again and again. The voices gained strength as the jug emptied. He could hear them so clearly. Three brothers, each with his own lilt, his own laugh. Seven boys born, and three already taken by the Shadow. Knox wished that the wolves had stripped the sound of their voices from his memory. It would have been just. The beasts were so bent on taking everything else.

He'd put off training his younger brothers to hunt. He'd found excuses to stall. Bowstrings had snapped; arrows had run low. Sometimes he merely disappeared, fleeing the expectant, adoring eyes of his brothers and settling by the pool with a jug. *I'm naught but a coward*, he thought. *I don't deserve to die like them.* He tossed the jug into the pool, watched as it bobbed and settled on the surface, as it took on water, as it slowly sank out of sight. *Better I drowned in the pool.*

He stood and snatched up the torch before stepping to the edge of the pool. The torch cast its light on the fingers of twisting black that leeched into the clear water. Knox watched their progress, wondering what it was his brothers saw after the wolves spilled their blood and their eyes closed forever. He shivered.

I'm naught but a coward, he thought. He took a shaky step back from the pool and stumbled up the hill toward the village. His intent was to return home, to fall into his cot and forget. But the lantern light shining out from the stable drew his attention. He flung open the stable door and found Evander grooming Rogue.

The great Fell horse was calm, and Evander had been murmuring to it before the noise of Knox's entrance shattered their peace.

"Tomorrow!" Knox said, slipping his torch into an iron ring on the wall.

"Midday," Evander replied.

Knox went to Frost and put his hands on either side of her muzzle. "You'll show Rogue, won't ya girl?" He grinned at Evander. "Fastest horse in Shiloh. Bet my life on it."

"Is there anything ya wouldn't bet yer life on, Knox?"

Knox ignored the question and stumbled over to his friend. He leaned against a dividing wall while Evander brushed Rogue's sleek, black coat. "It'll make quite a show fer market day. Imagine the stories they'll tell." He looked up into the rafters, growing thoughtful. "Remember how we'd go down when we were boys. Every spring we'd sneak up ta the falls, hoping ta catch a glimpse o' Sirius's spawn." He laughed to himself. "How many years did I search fer something ta turn my bow as white as Grosvenor's?"

Evander joined him in his laughter, but said nothing.

"I was sure if I had the White Bow, the dragons would fear me. I would be unconquerable, the greatest hunter in all o' Shiloh." He laughed again, this time bitterly, and shook his head.

"It's a risk, Knox. Ta move across the open plain. Ya know as well as I that it could draw them out."

Knox looked into his friend's face, his eyes flickering with pain. "Afraid, Evander?"

Evander shook his head. "It's not that. Just seems so reckless, ta risk yer life fer sport."

"Fer what, exactly, would ya have me risk my life, then?" The words were not spoken in challenge, but in earnest.

"Not this, Knox. Not this way. Is yer life worth so little? Is there nothing you want?"

Knox held his eyes for a long moment. Then he shrugged his shoulders. He ran a hand over his hair and grinned at Frost as he reclaimed his torch and headed out the door.

"Tomorrow, my beauty! Tomorrow we teach this Rogue a lesson!"

Mina rolled onto her side. Her back ached and her feet were sore. She ought to have been asleep hours ago. But her mind whirred with thoughts of the coming day. She loved market days, but that was not unusual. Everyone in Holt looked forward to the color and vigor, the pleasant chatter and chaos that invaded the village twice each month in spring and summer, and twice a month in autumn, so long as the weather held. The hunters would trade meat, tallow, sinew, and skins for herbs and medicines, candles and lanterns, tools and dishes. The craftsmen would trade all manner of handiwork for whatever they and their families needed. It was because of the craftsmen that market days were such a success, for all the villagers. People came from the far reaches of Shiloh to see the famed Fayrewood lanterns and the other pieces boasting colored glass. Mina once overheard a fisherman from the southern moors talking with one of the men of Holt. She'd wondered why anyone would risk such a perilous journey until the fisherman explained. "I had ta see the lanterns," he'd said. "And I swore ta my daughter I'd bring one home if it cost me a summer's worth o' fish."

Maeve's embroidery was also a great favorite with villagers and visitors alike. It was no secret that Maeve had relied on her embroidery to feed herself and her son after her husband's death. Once knowledge of her skill spread, she began receiving commissions from prosperous men in distant villages. The Father of the Fire Clan had paid her a huge sum to embroider his daughter's coming-of-age gown. But, for all that, Maeve would not venture into Market Circle to accept praise from admirers or answer questions about her unusual patterns. She would stay in her cottage, and

Evander would man the table where her work was displayed. He didn't seem to mind.

Mina loved that about him. She turned onto her back and watched the fading firelight lap against the wooden beams overhead.

She had a scrap of memory from the time just after Evander's father had died. Her mother's shift played a prominent role in the memory, for Mina had hidden behind it when Tilly took a little food to Maeve. She knew the rest of the villagers had been generous as well, but in the winter even the richest among them was not rich in food. It was needlework that kept Maeve and Evander from starving. Mina knew Evander was grateful for his mother's skill, for the time it had bought him to be a boy, to duel with wooden daggers and practice his marksmanship. He was grateful for the Fell horse the payments from her larger commissions had bought him. He was grateful, and unashamed, either of his post at the embroidery table or of the mother who was eternally tucked away in her cottage.

Mina knew all this. She'd been watching from the outskirts of Market Circle for year upon year. Evander looked people in the eye when they stepped up to his table. He remarked on his mother's artistry and smiled. He accepted coins and goods in trade. He thanked those who came to buy and those who came only to look. When Knox arrived to vex him, he brushed the teasing aside. And when market day drew to a close, he packed up the delicate cloth and the table and whistled softly as he walked home. Mina had watched him do so for as long as she could remember.

But tomorrow Mina would have a new vantage point. Tomorrow, she would have a table of her own, right there amidst the hubbub of buyers and sellers in Market Circle. It would be small, but it would be hers alone, and the thought of facing customers and answering questions filled her with dread. She shivered, then curled her legs up close to her chest and rolled onto her other side.

It was a good thing. A good thing. She had reminded herself of this over and over, since the idea first struck her while she gathered herbs and flowers in the Fayrewood. Not everything she gathered had to go to Moss. The thought had surprised her at first. She'd collected mandrake and tobacco and many other little things for her family through the years, but the idea that she could make a profit on her own, apart from the small fee Moss paid her for what she needed in the apothecary's shop, was altogether new. It was also, for Mina, very bold. It would require her to be seen by hundreds of people, many of them strangers, on several occasions throughout the year. There was even the possibility that she might be noticed by some of the villagers manning tables in Market Circle.

Mina took a long, slow breath and held it. She stared out her window into the darkness and tried to sort through her fears.

The darkness. That fear came first. The darkness was everywhere, always. In the dead of night, it was complete, impenetrable.

The wolves. Somewhere south of Holt, where the hills rose in wave upon wave, hungry eyes burned through the dark, and the wolves moved as silently as fog. They waited . . . for her father, for Chase, for Evander.

The dragons. Somewhere north of Holt, blue fire spewed from the mouths of the dragons. They had awakened, and they would surely come.

Mina released her breath and clung to thoughts of the darkness, the wolves, and the dragons. On this night, they seemed lesser fears by far than the terrors of the coming day.

Eight

Black night softened to the dense gray of a Shiloh morning, casting a thin light over the clusters of bleeding flowers that had just made their appearance on the hillside. Cutleaf nightshade brightened the lanes between cottages with its fragile, feathery leaves and tiny white blossoms. Morning glory vines clung to cottage walls, flaunting deep purple-blue flowers that drank in the meager morning light.

But the people of Holt had risen well before the morning glories showed their faces. The first market day had come. Cole wrapped jewelry and lanterns in layers of cloth. Maeve folded her embroidery and stacked it in baskets. Moss, whose arthritic knees kept her close to her shop, spread an assortment of glass phials and woolen sacks and clay pots and herbs wrapped with string over the table in her front room and pulled her chair out the front door so that she might watch the comings and goings and doings of the day. Errol had set the furnace blazing even before Moss had eased her creaky knees over the edge of her cot.

Tilly fretted over Mina's wares, arranging them carefully in baskets. Mina hadn't wanted to place herself in competition with Moss, so she'd woven wreaths of flowering tobacco in red and purple, in yellow and pale pink and white. Some she'd woven small enough that the girls could wear them as crowns. It wasn't much to sell, Mina knew. It was rather ridiculous, really, and she wouldn't make much of a profit. But it pleased her to share some of the beauty of the Fayrewood, a beauty even the poorest among them could enjoy.

Chase had disappeared very early, with Lachlan. Market day was busy for the craftsmen, but it was a day of rest and recreation for the hunters, when they were home to enjoy it. Jameson was gone as well. He liked to visit the craftsmen's tables first thing in the morning, to compliment their skills and ask questions before the crowds arrived.

So it was only Reed who was left to help her. He whined as he lifted his end of the kitchen table and grumbled as he and Mina maneuvered it through the doorway. He moaned about his miserable lot as they shuffled toward the opposite end of Holt. He screeched when the corner of the ponderous wooden table came down on his foot. But when he saw the torches and lanterns collecting on the edge of the plain, he forgot his complaints. "They're getting ready fer the race!" he shouted. He dropped his end of the table and ran down the hillside.

Mina had not allowed herself to think about the race. Not yet. There was much to do before midday, much to endure. She hurried home to gather her wreaths. As she walked back to her table, arms sagging with the weight of her baskets, she stopped. This sight always stopped her. It was like the change of seasons in the Fayrewood. No matter how many times she saw it, no matter how familiar she grew with every stone and branch, the sight of the wood in the full glory of each new season always took her breath away. The same was true for the lighting of the lanterns. When the craftsmen were ready to display their work and scores of little flames shone through panes of blue and gold and green and purple glass, the village was transformed. The world was transformed. No one gave a thought to the Shadow.

Mina set her baskets on the ground. Already, handfuls of travelers from nearer villages were making their way toward Market Circle. But she could not go, not yet. When she stepped into that ephemeral world of color and light, she would be busy with her display, busy with customers. She would lose it. The hollow, aching feeling crept over her again. It seemed very strange that she could sit beside a window for hours, mending and sewing, and be content. She could share a meal with her parents and her brothers, and be at peace. But the Fayrewood and this . . . this wonder . . . they plucked at some chord within her that she could not name.

Mina picked up her baskets and found a path to her table through the ever-increasing noise and bustle of Market Circle. The tables were arranged in two open circles, one inside the other. Mina's table was part of the larger, and situated near the back. It was a small comfort. Ahead, and to her left, she saw Valour's braided hair. In the light of the lanterns, it was more magnificent than ever. She stood beside her father, and their table was spread with chains and charms and lanterns that glittered in the dancing light. Three tables to the left of Valour, Maeve's embroidery was displayed. Evander stood behind the table, surveying the crowd. Mina dropped her eyes.

She was startled to find a child staring up at her. The girl was small, and very thin, and her eyes were huge. Mina had seen her once or twice, had heard Chase tell the story of her arrival on Evander's doorstep. But the girl had only just begun to show her face, and the villagers were still not sure what to make of her.

"Are you Grey?" Mina asked.

"Aye," she said. She studied Mina's wreaths, looking at each in turn before reaching to touch a small one with crimson flowers. She looked at Mina with those impossibly large, hungry eyes, and Mina pitied her.

"Are these flowers from the Fayrewood?" Grey asked.

"Aye," Mina answered. "Have ya been ta the wood? It's very beautiful."

"Oh, no," she said, shaking her head. "I couldn't go there."

"Why not? It's lovely. I could take ya. The pink blossoms will be gone soon, but the summer leaves are wonderful, too." She stopped, because Grey didn't seem to be hearing her. Her eyes were wide, and she shook her head in earnest.

"I wouldn't go anywhere near the Turn," Grey said, glancing to her right, toward the wood.

"That's foolishness, Grey. You'd miss all the beauty o' the Fayrewood fer fear o' the Turn?"

As Mina's voice rose, Grey's softened. "It's real, the Turn. And wicked things live there. The Shadow waits there, fer whoever wanders too far down the path."

"Of course it's real, but the poison o' that place doesn't spill out onto the rest o' the wood. Fear would make it so, but you mustn't let it. Ya can't imagine how much is lost by such thinking."

Mina realized that the conversations around her had died away, that her voice was louder than she intended, that people were staring. Her face burned. What was she doing arguing with a pitiful orphaned child? It was natural that the girl should be afraid.

"I'm sorry, Grey," she said, and pushed the red wreath toward her. "Please, take it."

"I've no money," Grey said.

"Please."

The girl nodded and took it. She put the wreath on her head and pressed it down on top of her black waves. The red flowers stood out in bright contrast to the streak of gray at her right temple. She thanked Mina with an odd little smile and disappeared into the crowd.

Valour made her escape on pretense of taking a basket of berries and a bolt of cloth back to the cottage. She left her father to his customers, set the bartered goods just inside the door, and crept out the back, through the workshop. She crossed the bridge. The craftsmen's huts were empty, the whole western bank of the Cutting uncommonly dark and still. But firelight spilled out of the furnace. Valour stepped up to the first entrance and looked inside. Errol was hard at work. With one hand, he tossed bits of ashy powder into the fire and bathed the sweat from his face. With the other, he stirred the molten glass.

She felt a fool for coming. Errol had made no promises. He'd offered her nothing. But here she was, far from the glittering finery on display in Market Circle, far from the adoring eyes of her admirers. She stood on her toes, peering into the sweltering cave, enthralled by the bubbling orange liquid in the oven.

"Yer da won't take ya as apprentice," Errol said, turning toward her. His face was smeared with soot.

"No."

"You'd be better off working with edanna, my girl."

"Aye, I know. Less danger in the work. I'm fond of it, truly, but Da won't teach me."

Errol nodded, laying aside his tools and removing his gloves. He opened the low door and let her inside. "I'd probably do the same if you were my daughter. Must be plenty o' young men keen ta marry a girl such as you. What need does any husband have of a wife who makes glass?"

Valour fiddled with the charm on her neck. She hadn't thought to prepare an argument. "I may not choose ta marry," she said. It was the best she could do off-hand.

Errol chuckled. "You'd let 'em all kill each other fer naught, eh? Seems awfully cruel."

Valour tried again. "If I did marry, and my husband were killed," she began.

"Ah! You're improving, my girl. You'd be better off than most widows in Shiloh if ya had a means ta feed yer little ones." He stopped and gave her a hard look. "Is that really why you've come?"

Valour was flustered. She didn't know what Errol was looking for, and she was beginning to fear that he would send her away. She pulled herself up to her full height. "I want ta do this, please. I've no particular reason except that I want ta *do* something with myself. Is that so terrible?"

Errol's eyes twinkled. He waited for her to continue.

"Anyway, I'd be very glad of anything ya can teach me, so long as it's done in secret."

"Secret?" he said. "And when do ya propose ta come here in secret."

"Ya start the day early, don't ya?" Valour asked.

"Aye, but not so much earlier than the other craftsmen. They'll be swarming in and out o' the hillside within an hour or two o' my coming."

"I'll come earlier, then." Her face was set. "I'll get the furnace going."

"Ha!" the old man laughed sharply. "And how do ya propose ta do that?"

"I've lit many a fire, Errol. I'm capable o' that much."

"It's not any fire in Shiloh can melt the sand into glass, can burn as hot and stay as hot as it must ta do the job."

"What sort o' fire will do the job?"

Errol smiled and patted her shoulder. "I won't go spilling all my secrets just yet, girly. Off ya go, before someone starts asking after ya." He shooed her out the door. "We'll begin tomorrow. Very early."

She looked back, and he winked. "Won't have any apprentice o' mine sleeping the day away when there's work ta be done."

Then the gate was shut behind her and Valour was stumbling down the hill toward the bridge. She smiled to herself. *Apprentice.*

Errol had called her his apprentice.

When she reached the center of town, she followed the crowd that was making its way north. It was time for the race to begin.

Nine

Evander looked around him. To his right was the Fayrewood. He could just make out the first line of trees, splashing color over the gray landscape. Soon, the pink blossoms would give way to tight buds and then to clear green leaves. Evander wanted to see them when they opened. He could just hear the roar of the wind in the treetops over the din of the villagers and visitors crowded behind him. They called and shouted and speculated, their torches and lanterns a chaos of shifting light. Ahead of him was a dim, broad plain. Beyond, out of sight, stretching impossibly high, until their peaks were lost in Shadow, were the mountains. And somewhere, far ahead and to his left, the falls spilled over a lofty crag in ceaseless thunder.

Rogue stamped beneath him, sensing his anxiety. Frost was nearby, looking as skittish as her competitor. Knox did nothing to calm her. He was not drunk, but neither was he sober. Evander wished he would take this challenge seriously, win it cleanly, and have done with it. It was a vain hope. Knowing Knox, he'd concoct some other reckless plan before the close of market day. It made

Evander wonder, yet again, if he'd lavished his unflinching loyalty on all the wrong people.

"Would ya like ta make a wager, my friend?" Knox asked.

"No," Evander replied.

"You're seated beside a champion, Evander. Why not at least earn some reward fer engaging in this hopeless contest?" Knox raised his brows, spreading his hands magnanimously.

Evander offered him a level gaze. "Alright then, Knox. I forfeit. I surrender. Let us be done with this."

Knox grinned and motioned for the magistrate. Nolan positioned himself in front of Rogue and Frost, facing back toward the crowd.

"Torches ready?" he asked. Knox and Evander nodded. They were accustomed to carrying torches, in turns, when they hunted. It took no small strength to carry a torch aloft for an hour or two at a time. But these men were fierce, and hardened by many years' journeys, and both were expert at riding with one hand.

"Horses ready?" Nolan asked. Frost gave an impatient whinny, and tense laughter rippled through the crowd. The men nodded.

Nolan took a step back, raised a lantern in front of him, and lowered his voice. "Knox?" he said, searching Knox's face. Knox gave him a defiant grin. "Evander?" He held Evander's eyes for just a little longer. Evander nodded.

The crowd was silent, every breath held. The torches flickered, and far off, the falls thundered. Nolan opened the glass door at the back of his lantern and blew a little puff of air. The flame was gone. And the horses were off, their riders spurring them on at a maddening pace.

Evander could hear the shouts and cheers that erupted behind him, but the pounding of the horses' hooves soon drowned all other sound but the roar of the falls. He knew that the crowd was following the progress of the torches. It was the only way to gauge the race in such scant light. Even then, the torchlight would be swallowed by mist and darkness before ever the riders reached the falls.

The falls and back, Evander thought. *The falls and back.* He pushed everything else from his mind and concentrated on his goal. He ignored Knox's wild laughter, ignored the protest of the torch fires as they struggled against the wind, ignored the panting of his beautiful black horse. His face was set, the muscles in his legs gripping his seat, one hand clutching the torch and the other holding the reins.

Frost pulled ahead, but Rogue dogged her heels. The Fell horses were finding their rhythm, eating up the land between the village and the Pallid Peaks.

A gust of icy wind came careening out of the mountains, and Knox's torch was snuffed out. Evander rose in his saddle, eyes trained on the figure that pushed ahead into the thickening dark without the slightest hesitation.

"Come on, Rogue," he said. "We can't lose 'im."

He urged the animal forward, into the roar of the approaching waterfall, into the mist that obscured the ground around it. He came to the edge of the falls. He could hardly think for the din of rushing water. He stopped, turned Rogue back toward the village, and searched the mist for some sign of Knox. Evander lifted one foot from its stirrup, preparing to dismount. Then, a shadowy form shot past him, laughing, the mist swirling in his wake. Evander growled and set off after Knox. There was no torch to follow, and the lights of the village were not visible from this distance. As near as he could judge, he pointed Rogue south and east, and leaned in to the pursuit.

After a moment, he thought he could just see the faint glimmer of Frost's white coat. "Let's go, Rogue!" *The falls and back. The falls and back.*

A gust of wind, not icy but torrid, extinguished Evander's torch. He was riding blind. He could not make out the lights of Holt, could see no sign of his friend. The world around him was gray. And blue.

Great wings beat the air. Screams broke over the roar of the falls, and Evander's blood went cold. Two dragons belched blue fire in waves that lit the open plain. Evander saw Knox, perhaps thirty paces ahead. The village was within sight now, its many-colored lights suddenly bathed in the blue of dragon fire.

Evander spurred Rogue onward, clenching the sides of the horse with his knees, holding tightly to the darkened torch. The air above was hot and foul, and he could think of nothing but his goal. *The falls and back.* One dragon swooped down on the assembled crowd. Its immense wings, as ragged and black as if they'd been torn from the Shadow itself, blotted out the lights of the village. Evander rode harder, racing toward the distant cries of his people.

But the other dragon seemed set on pursuing him alone. The beast swept in on his left, rose, descended on his right. It was toying with him, scorching the grass on either side of his path. Rogue screamed in terror, his mouth foaming, his eyes wild. Evander was consumed with pity for them: for the horse he could not save, the people he could not reach. And a fire was kindled in him. His face shone with it. He leaned against Rogue's neck and shouted in his ear, "Straight on, Rogue!"

The dragon pulled up, hovering. It gathered its legs beneath its great armored belly and prepared for another dive. Evander wrapped the reins around the palm of his left hand. He pressed his right hand, still gripping the torch, against the horn of the saddle. He lifted one foot, then the other, onto Rogue's back. His feet pivoted, turning him around, and he fell into the saddle with his left arm behind him and the reins held at his back.

Overhead, blue eyes marked him.

"No more games, worm!" he roared. "Come and get me!"

A sound like the shattering of a mountain of glass broke from the dragon's throat. Wave upon wave of blue flame billowed down. Evander thrust his torch into the fire until it caught. He dropped the reins, snatched a dagger from his belt, and hurled it into the dragon's mouth. The blue fire sputtered and faltered, and the beast retreated.

Now the cries of the villagers rang in his ears. Women and children, young and old, fled from the fury of the remaining dragon. They rushed to their cottages. They cringed in narrow lanes, cowering beneath the eaves. They ducked into the cave in the hillside. Anything to stay out of sight.

But the men among them came out to fight. Evander breathed his relief as he rode up the hill and found Knox, Hallam, Chase, Lachlan, Lorne, and Alistair moving their horses into formation. Two other bands of hunters did the same, and all eyes were trained on him. He carried with him their only hope, for dragon fire alone could conquer the dragons.

He rode to the center of each band of hunters, lighting the torches in the hands of the men at the hub of each Wheel. He guided Rogue around the rubble and wreckage of the tables as the hunters lit their arrows with blue fire, then took his place in the center of his own band.

From the southern end of Holt came the sounds of stones crunching against one another, of slate tiles shattering, of screaming and bleating.

"Grosvenor!" Evander shouted. And all the hunters echoed his cry.

Cormac had been first to see the dragon fire. While the crowd waited, breathless, at the bottom of the hill, to see the outcome of the race, Cormac skulked near his cottage. His were the only eyes not fixed on the plain, straining to determine which torch would be first to emerge from the gloom. He saw the blue fire before anyone. He knew what was coming, and he froze.

He should cry out. He knew he should. His father was with the crowd, and his mother and sister. Hundreds waited, unknowing. He should warn them. He would lead these people one day; he could lead them now.

Cormac took a step down the hill. The blood beat in his ears, and the words rose to his lips.

Run.

But it was the voice in his head that spoke. No sound came from his mouth. He turned and hurried into the safety of his cottage and closed the door behind him. Then the cries erupted from the crowd and a wave of panic broke over the village and the people ran in terror. He watched them through the window.

The door swung open, banging against the wall. His mother and sister stumbled in, with Nolan behind them. Cormac didn't intend to do it. By accident, he met his father's eyes, and what he saw there shamed him so deeply that he hung his head. Nolan turned and ran back into the village. He left the door open.

Cormac took a deep breath. He found a scrap of courage, buried deep, and seized it. He knew, all at once, exactly how he wanted to use it.

A handful of craftsmen were emptying water troughs over the little fires that broke out in Market Circle when the tables and lanterns fell. Cormac ran past them. He'd last seen her on the far side of the crowd, near the Cutting. While the hunters faced the dragon, Cormac searched for Valour.

He spotted her at last, running into her father's workshop. He followed, rushing through the door behind her. She searched the cottage, frantic, then turned and jumped at the sight of him.

"What are you . . ." she began. She shook her head, agitated. "I didn't see 'em in the crowd. Did you?" She took a dagger in hand. "Did ya see my parents?" she asked again. She reached for the door. "I've got ta find them."

"No!" Cormac took her arm, loosened her grip on the dagger, and slipped it out of her hand. He set it on the table and pulled her to a seat away from the windows. "Ya mustn't be seen."

"I can't just stay here," Valour insisted, rising.

"Ya can, and you must." Cormac took her shoulders and pushed her gently back into her chair. "You're still too bright."

"What are you talking about?"

"The dragons! Did ya never see them in Fleete?"

"Almost never. Why? What does it matter?"

Cormac looked at her, overwhelmed for a moment by her beauty. He swallowed, then went to a window and looked furtively out. "The dragons come fer bright things."

A little girl rushed into the lane, crossing from one shadowy hideout to another. Her light was erratic, one moment flaring and the next almost vanishing. The dragon saw and swooped in. The hunters followed. Their arrows flew, sending blue fire searing through the ragged wings. The dragon crashed into a cottage on the eastern edge of Holt. It thrashed its great tail, black scales clanking and fire billowing from its jaws. The hunters gathered around the desolation, this time aiming for the beast's eyes and the softer skin beneath its legs.

The walls of the cottage, or what remained of them, collapsed. The dragon writhed. Acrid smoke rose from its nostrils. Its head twitched, and then it was still.

Evander looked around him. The faces of the hunters were grim. The villagers, and those in town for Market, were just beginning to emerge. He did not see Nolan.

He turned to his men. "Lorne, Alistair, Lachlan, Hallam, go and make a search o' the village. If any are wounded, take 'em ta Moss. Chase, if you'll see about the wreckage o' the tables and goods. I've no doubt you'll find ample help." He looked at Knox, who was trembling and who could not quite meet his eyes. "You can see about the carcass."

No one questioned Evander's orders. The other bands of hunters joined his men in their tasks. Even Nolan, when he appeared, only nodded to Evander and went to help Knox with his unenviable job.

Evander slumped in his saddle and dismounted. He led Rogue to the stable. He closed the horse in his stall, gave him water and hay, and set out toward the cottage.

No one noticed when Cormac showed up with Valour in tow. The villagers all moved about with purpose, comforting children, assessing the damage, tending to the most pressing needs. Valour spotted her father. She pulled away from Cormac's grip and ran, and Cormac went in search of his own father. But Nolan was not at home. He was not in Market Circle. He was not standing in the center of Holt directing the villagers in their tasks. Cormac's frustration grew. He stopped two craftsmen who helped an injured boy toward the apothecary's shop.

"Where's the magistrate?" he asked.

"He's working on the carcass," one said.

"The carcass?"

"Aye. Evander and his men brought it down." He pointed in the direction of the dragon.

Cormac sighed. "Alright. I won't hold you any longer. Mustn't interfere with the magistrate's orders."

"No orders, Cormac," the craftsman said. "Evander set his men ta work, and we just fell in with 'em." They moved off toward Moss's shop.

Cormac closed his eyes, the hatred inside him expanding until he nearly choked on it. Evander had rallied the hunters and saved the village. In the wake of the attack, Evander hadn't taken charge.

He'd merely set his men to work, and everyone else had followed. Simple as that. And what had he done while Evander won such glory? He'd kept Valour prisoner in hopes of saving her, in hopes of earning her gratitude, her love.

On that day, Cormac was the only defeated man in Holt. He skirted the western edge of the village, keeping well away from the dragon, and went home.

Evander relaxed when he saw the cottage. It hadn't been damaged in the attack. The light was failing, the day drawing to a close. He hoped . . . he hoped that his mother and Grey were safe inside. He stepped through the door, surveyed the front room, and found Grey sitting at the table. She was asleep, her head resting on her left arm, her right hand wrapped around a wreath of red flowers. Evander carried her to bed. He leaned down and kissed her forehead, stroking the tendrils of hair that fell over her thin face.

In the back room, Maeve sat on the edge of her chair, waiting. Her fingers moved as if working her needles, but her hands were empty. She stared into the fire.

"Ma," Evander said.

She stood, turned, reached out to him. "Are ya well, my son?"

"Aye, Ma. Well enough." He took her hands and pulled her close, embracing her.

"My brave son," she said. "Why do they come? Why must they come?"

Evander only shook his head. He was very weary, too weary to ask or answer such questions. But he fell asleep that night with his mind full of the memory of the little girl, wavering between darkness and light, and the dragon descending.

Ten

Valour sifted through shards of broken glass and scraps of twisted, misshapen filigree. They'd cleared away the tables the night before, had salvaged the pieces that could be saved. But this morning's task was more disheartening. So much had been trampled as the people fled from the dragon, so much destroyed.

She filled her basket with all sorts of debris, but jagged pieces of colored glass made up the greatest portion. She lifted a piece of amethyst glass and raised it to the light of the simple lantern she'd brought from home. Only one corner of the panel was chipped, and Valour grieved at such waste. She wondered if any of the craftsmen could design a lantern frame that would make use of some of the broken pieces.

She gasped when she saw an edanna chain that had been overlooked the night before. This, too, she lifted to the light, and smiled. She draped it over the handle of her basket and sat back on her heels.

There were others helping to clear Market Circle, and many had lost more than her family. One pitiful girl at the edge of the circle gathered crushed wreaths, their flowers now bruised and torn.

This time of year, the flowers were easily replaced, but the sight of the girl retrieving them, placing each one tenderly in her basket, was far worse than the sight of the ruined cottage where the dragon fell or the shards of glass in her hands. It broke Valour's heart.

She knew that girl. She'd certainly seen her before. Yes, her brother was the hunter. Chase. Valour fumbled around in her memory for the girl's name, but it would not come. She resumed her work, remembering too late that she'd promised to beat Errol to the furnace that morning. She would go tomorrow. Considering the attack, the old man would surely understand.

Errol did not understand. And when Valour appeared, next morning, long before the impassable darkness showed any sign of yielding, Errol was in a huff.

"Hard ta sneak off on such a morning, I grant ya, but of all mornings!" he said.

Valour jumped out of his way as he shuffled from one corner of the cave to the other, gathering small clay pots, arranging and rearranging them, and muttering under his breath.

"Of all mornings ta miss! I could've shown ya . . . never shown anyone . . . it was a gift . . . a gift from the gods." He stopped, gave Valour a sharp look.

"Any losses?" he asked. "From the attack?"

She shook her head. "None dead. Two injured."

"Aye? Well then." He gave an approving nod to the collection of pots on his worktable and rubbed his hands together. He leaned in toward Valour. "I got it, see. Before they burned the carcass." He motioned her closer with one knobby, calloused finger. "Dragon fire," he whispered, smiling.

Valour blinked, wondering suddenly if the old man was a bit mad.

Errol checked to be sure no one was loitering around the entrances to the cave before pulling something from his pocket. It was black and leathery, rather like a pepper that had spent a few winters in the bottom of a basket. "Dried it yesterday," he said. He handed it to Valour, and she turned it over in her hands carefully. She poked it once and sniffed it.

"Ugh, it's horrid," she said, thrusting it back at Errol.

"Dragon fire," he said again. He slipped a knife into one corner of the shriveled thing and slid the blade along the edge. Opening it slowly, he dumped the contents into an empty pot. It looked like black powder, like ash. Errol took a flint-and-iron from his belt and went to the furnace. He struck the metal against the stone, sending sparks into the kindling. When a tiny fledgling flame caught, he tossed a pinch of the black powder into the fire and the flame turned blue. Errol looked over his shoulder at Valour's astonished expression. His own face was bright and merry in the dancing blue light. He took a bit of another black powder from a satchel on his belt. When that powder hit the fire, it flamed red. It looked like any ordinary fire.

"This little mixture is my own recipe. Hides the blue o' the flame, but it still burns hotter than any fire in Shiloh. Hotter and longer. There's a reason we make such lovely glass in Holt."

"Errol, could this be used against the dragons, when they attack?"

"I've tried many times, my girl. The powder'll only change a fire that's already burning, no more than that."

"You're certain?" Valour asked.

Errol's eyebrows rose slowly, in surprise and challenge. "I can't decide if you're insolent or merely bold. To ask me such a thing on yer first morning as apprentice . . ." He shook his head and moved away from the growing heat of the furnace. "I'll say this, Valour. There are ores running through the Cutting that we've found no use for. I doubt they're useless. Their virtues may be vast. They may hold answers fer questions we've not thought to ask. But I've yet ta master 'em." He leaned against the wall of the cave and crossed his arms. "I've never found a means ta use the black powder against the dragons. My da didn't either, nor his father before 'im. Are ya satisfied?"

Valour nodded, momentarily subdued. "But why not tell the other craftsmen? Is the dragon fire not a danger ta them?"

"Well, the secret has its uses. I do get first pick o' the ores and tools. But the fire's no particular danger. Any fire'd burn the flesh from their bones, not just dragon fire. Besides, they'd be opposed."

"Why?" Valour asked. "If it's the secret o' their trade, their prosperity, why would they object?"

"'Evil,' they'd say. 'Ulff's work'. They'd want no part of it."

Valour shuddered. The Lord of Shadows was rarely spoken of. And Valour much preferred to fear the overhanging darkness and the creatures of Shadow than to imagine that some larger evil directed his malice toward them, that he organized and orchestrated their doom. She turned her thoughts instead to the worktable and its collection of pots and powders.

"I know what you're thinking, my girl," Errol said. "I take too great a risk, perhaps."

"In truth, Errol," she said, "I was wondering how I'll ever learn ta tell one o' these powders from the other. Fully half o' them are gray or black."

Errol laughed, a short back of a laugh, and the glint returned to his eye. He chose one of the pots on the corner of the table. "We'll start with this one."

Mina was weary of the conversation, and it had only just begun. They sat at the table, she and her two brothers on one bench and her parents opposite, eating supper. The fare had improved of late. There was fresh meat in the stew. Fresh herbs as well, and berries were mounded in a bowl at the end of the table. Reed stole them by ones and twos, popping them into his mouth when he thought no one was looking.

"Something should be done," her father was saying.

"Something *was* done," Chase replied.

"We did as we've always done, and it's not enough."

"The dragon is dead and burned and nothing lost."

"Nothing lost? What o' the two boys injured and the trampled goods in Market Circle?" Jameson said. "What of those who came from other villages? Will they come again? How long will they risk the wrath o' the dragons ta buy lanterns?"

"Ya know they always come back, Da. Besides, the dragon is dead. What more would ya have us do?"

Jameson took a bite and chewed as he thought. Mina and her mother exchanged glances.

"There has ta be a better way. If we had some strategy, something surer than the mad risks of one man —"

"Mad risks?" Chase said. "You'd call Evander mad fer what 'e did? There's no knowing what might have become of Holt had 'e not taken such a *mad* risk. I won't hear ya speak ill of 'im, Da."

"Now wait, Chase. I don't speak ill of Evander. I only mean ta say that we can't depend on one man ta defend us from the dragons. There must be more we can do."

If any man can defend us from the dragons, it's Evander, Mina thought. But she ate her stew without comment. When Reed stole another berry from the bowl, she kicked him under the table.

"We'll discuss it at the meeting," Chase said.

"The meeting?" Reed asked, finally focusing on the conversation. "When? Who's going?"

Jameson shook his head, "Only those come of age, Reed. They've invited men from Fleete as well. But I don't want ta come to a decision at the meeting. I'd like ta bring a proposal, have something to offer."

They ate quietly for a while, and the sound of Mina's voice startled them when she spoke.

"We could do what Evander did."

They stared at her, spoons in midair, little bits of potato and venison plopping back into their bowls. Mina sighed and continued. "Have cold torches ready, soaked in tallow, waiting ta catch the fire when the dragons come."

Her father's eyes widened. Chase's narrowed.

"They'd have ta be high up, attached ta the rooftops, maybe." Chase said.

Mina nodded.

"It'd be dangerous," Jameson said, "climbing up ta the torches and lighting the arrows. Dragons wheeling past, spewing flames. Awfully exposed that high up."

"Aye," Chase said. "It would be dangerous, as it always is when they come, but not mad. If the torches caught fire at several points across the village, any number of men could retrieve the fire and mount an assault." Chase looked pointedly at his father. "Less likely you'd have ta rely on the madness of one man, eh, Da?"

Mina beamed at him, and in that moment, Chase knew and understood. Mina could see it in his eyes, realization blended with pity.

"Well," Jameson said. "It's something. We'll see what the others make of it."

Mina cleared the table, loading the used dishes into a basket to carry to the stream. Her mother watched her as she worked. Mina caught her glances once or twice, but that was not unusual. It was Chase's discovery that made her stomach tighten, and she found, when she noticed him watching her, that she could not hold his gaze.

They assembled in the large front room of the magistrate's cottage. Evander sat quietly while Nolan discussed what remained to be done before the next market day. He took some small pleasure in watching a few of the older craftsmen reproach Knox for his recklessness. He noticed Cormac, sitting near the front of the room, watching him. Evander couldn't imagine what he'd done to earn Cormac's hatred, couldn't recall when it had begun. He looked away, focusing on Jameson as he shared his idea about mounting torches on the rooftops of Holt. Nolan praised the suggestion, and some of the village men were assigned to the task. The men visiting from Fleete thought the idea a brilliant one. Fleete was further south, and the dragons rarely ventured so far from the mountains, but having a defensive strategy was a great comfort to them. It was so simple, so obvious, they marveled that they had not thought of it before, and they were eager to return to Fleete and raise torches of their own.

Only Evander left the assembly feeling frustrated. Everyone else, Knox included, seemed hopeful about the new plan. But Evander could not shake the feeling that they had accomplished nothing, that they only put off the inevitable. A man might just as well wrap a fine embroidered cloth around a boil. The problem, the infection, was left to fester. And Maeve's words kept running around and around in his head. *Why do they come? Why must they come?* These were questions no one seemed willing to ask, questions for which he still had no answers.

Eleven

As spring gave way to summer and the weather warmed, Evander's band of hunters traveled farther from Holt. South of the foothills, near Lake Morrison in the east and in the open plains to the west, there were herds of deer and elk that made easy prey if the hunters could avoid the wolves. Even the rabbits they encountered on their journeys were a gift, for they fed the men as they hunted, and they were easy to clean and cook.

In the evenings, weary from the day's pursuit, they camped in a circle around the largest fire they could build. In forested land, their campfires were more akin to bonfires, and the warm light was all the more welcome because it offered an ever-present weapon against the wolves.

Lorne and Alistair sometimes entertained the younger men with the stories of how they wooed their wives (or kidnapped them, in Lorne's case). Lorne was not a cruel man, but when the time had come to marry, there had been no young women recently come of age in Holt, so he'd brought one home from Fleete. Lorne's stories of their first years of marriage always set the men laughing, for, by

Lorne's account, his young wife had tried to poison him on several occasions.

"Thought she filled the soup with enough nightshade ta kill a man." Lorne threw back his head and howled. "Poor girl didn't know it was cutleaf, not deadly nightshade! I've often wondered what it was 'er mother taught 'er if she couldn't tell the difference." He wiped the tears from his eyes and caught his breath. "Gave me quite a bellyache, though."

Hallam laughed and shook his head before launching into a list of Emmeline's virtues and sharing his hopes about becoming a father of twins. Knox and Chase talked of many things, of their families and their exploits and the girls who caught their eye. Lachlan often played on his pipe, for it cheered and relaxed him, and the others were glad of it.

Evander spoke very little. He was the leader of this band of warriors, though he was neither the oldest nor the most experienced. He just had a way about him. Other men deferred to his opinion, respected his choices, followed where he led. It had always been so, and Evander didn't give it much thought. But though he loved his men, would have taken an arrow for any one of them, he still found that he had very little to say to them.

He was different somehow. Separate. And it was not because he was their leader. It was something else he could not quite name, and even in the midst of laughter and tales and music, Evander was lonely. He had wondered countless times why this should be. He'd considered the possibility that it was because of his father's death. Alistair had hunted with his father years ago, had seen him die. But every man in this band had lost someone to the wolves or the dragons. Hallam had lost a younger sister to hunger during a harsh winter a few years back. No, his men knew loss only too well, and that shared grief should have been a bridge connecting him and them.

It could have been Maeve, though it was not her strange behavior or her seclusion that caused a rift between Evander and his men. It was true that none of them spoke of her, but neither did Evander. There was nothing to speak of, and if Maeve caused division, it was only because Evander used her to isolate himself.

There was something else. Evander leaned back against his packs and took in the scene before him. Chase was telling a story about his brother, and the others were listening and laughing. Hallam passed a jug of beer around the circle, and the men drank. All but Evander. He'd never had a taste for beer, or even the cherry ale that men sometimes gave in trade on market days. He seized on that for a moment. Perhaps if he drank with his friends, he would be one of them. He would feel as they did, finding delight and contentment in fireside stories and roasted rabbit and beer.

He motioned for the jug, and Knox abused him heartily before handing it over. He raised the jug to his lips and drank. The others roared with laughter as he winced and forced himself to swallow. He detested the bitter taste of the drink, the sick, sour feel of it in his belly.

"He can turn flips on the back of a galloping horse and thrust 'is torch inta the mouth of a dragon," Knox teased, "but he's no match fer a swig o' beer!"

Evander smiled, shrugged, and passed the jug back to Knox. If drinking was the only way to connect with his men, he supposed he'd have to settle for loneliness. Chase continued his story. Evander was too restless to stay by the fire. He went to see how Rogue fared, then checked on the other horses, taking special time and care with each one.

When the men had settled down and the camp had quieted, Evander went reluctantly back to his place. He sat with the others, watching the movement of the firelight. Out of the silence, suddenly, Lachlan began a new tune. It was strange and haunting and lovely. It filled Evander with a terrible longing for . . . something. When the song was finished, he asked Lachlan where he'd learned the tune.

"Nowhere," Lachlan said. "Just a little tune o' my own."

"How do ya come up with tunes ya never heard before?" Evander asked. His mother sang songs no one else knew, but he'd always imagined she heard them in her dreams.

Lachlan hesitated. "I don't know, exactly. One day there's nothing, and then the next day there's something. It's just there, see? The tune shows up without my asking fer it. And I play it. That's all."

Evander nodded understanding, though he did not understand.

"Know any songs, Evander?" Lachlan asked. "We all of us sing from time ta time, but I've never heard you."

"Aye." The others took up Lachlan's request. "Honor us, Evander," they said. "Give us a song." They would have none of his excuses, so Evander gave in at last. He lowered his head and cleared his throat, then raised his eyes to the firelight and sang.

"Another day has died
The faded light now deeper fading
And still I watch the sky
Watch in sorrow, hoping, waiting

The endless mountains rise
Through seas of snow and cold winds wailing
And I would scale the heights
Ta find a warmth, a light unfailing

The Shadow covers all
This smoth'ring dark my nearest brother
What hope fer bright ones born
Who seek the bosom of another?

Another day has died
Another night descends, unyielding
No strength ta watch the skies

The breathless dark too heavy lies
And I must close my weary eyes
My fragile torch and lantern wielding"

There was quiet around the camp. The flames crackled. The embers hissed. One thick log split open and tumbled to the ground in two red-gold slabs. It was Lorne who spoke first.

"Was it yer ma, Evander? Did she teach ya that song?"

Evander thought. "She sings some of 'er own, but this one, I think, she learned from 'er mother."

Lorne nodded. "I thought as much. I've heard it before."

"She still sees them, then? These night visions?" Alistair asked.

"Dreams," Evander said.

"She sees lights?" Chase asked. The younger men shifted their weight, seeming as uncomfortable as Evander was with the increasing intimacy of the questions.

"Just one light, mainly," Evander said. "The sun, she calls it. A great light that hangs in the sky, a light that burns away the Shadow."

No one spoke at all, until Knox tossed a scrap of food into the fire and spat. "Visions like that would drive any man mad."

Muscles tensed all over the camp. The hunters waited, stealing glances at Evander and glaring at Knox.

It took a moment for Evander to reply, but when he did, his eyes met Knox's with a challenge. "It's the darkness that drives a man mad."

Hallam sighed heavily before speaking. "My da used ta tell stories," he said, "of a time when the world shook, when the land was changed and the Shadow took hold. He stopped telling 'em after my sis died."

Lorne nodded. "My Da did the same, but I've told no tales ta my sons and daughters." He dropped his eyes and picked at the grass. "They fade so quickly as it is."

"Ya think they'd fade faster if they heard the stories?" Evander asked.

"Can't say," Lorne replied. "But it seems cruel ta tell 'em tales o' things they'll never see."

"You've a bit o' fire about ya still, Evander," Alistair broke in. "We saw it, those of us that weren't running, when ya faced the dragon."

"Aye," Lachlan said. "And there are others. If ya watch close, you'll see it."

"Have ya someone particular in mind, Lachlan?" Knox asked. "It wouldn't be that flame-haired beauty, would it?"

Hallam laughed. "Does 'er skin truly shine, or do yer eyes just forget what they're about when she looks yer way?"

Evander and the others chuckled. Only Chase didn't laugh. He studied Evander closely.

"Alright, men," Evander said, "we've a long journey tomorrow. I'll take first watch."

There were grunts of frustration, and some nods of agreement, but, one by one, they stretched out around the campfire, rested their heads on their arms or their packs, and slept.

Valour rolled her head back on her shoulders and stretched and yawned. The early mornings were beginning to wear on her, though she would not trade her new knowledge and skill for any amount of sleep. Errol had already shown her how to prepare and combine the ingredients for a batch of clear glass, taught her how to distinguish among the ores used for dyeing the glass, and shown her the basic uses of each of his tools. She had yet to remove any molten glass from the oven or pour it into molds or handle the cooled panes. But she was growing accustomed to the feel of the thick gloves that covered her hands and her arms past her elbows. And the heat of the raging furnace bothered her less. A little less. She wiped a wayward wave of damp hair from her forehead. *Is there no place in this cursed country where my braid is safe?* she thought. *If the heat of the furnace doesn't melt the hair from its place, then the winds from the mountains will pull it free.*

On this morning, Valour was caring for the fire, adding logs and poking them into place with an iron rod. She'd asked Errol about this strange ritual not long after her apprenticeship had begun.

"If the dragon fire burns hotter and longer than any other fire, why do we need ta stoke the furnace? Why add fuel at all?"

Errol had rubbed his hands together and spoken low. "If one o' the craftsmen saw the furnace blazing with hardly a log in place, he'd start ta ask questions, and then my secret would be out. We treat this furnace as we would any other."

"But why don't the craftsmen wonder at the unusual heat o' the furnace? Has none o' them ever questioned it?" Valour had asked.

Errol had smiled. "My girl, you'll find few men who've any burning desire ta question prosperity."

When she finished her work, she removed her gloves and the heavy leather apron she wore over her shift. She wiped the sweat from her face with a cloth, rearranged her hair as best she could, and set out. She took care not to be seen, slipping in and out of the craftsmen's huts, and making her way to the northwest corner of the village, where the Cutting disappeared behind the hill. On some mornings, she jumped right into the stream fully dressed, for her clothing was so filthy that she had no other choice. More often, she removed her shift and boots and plunged into the biting water, allowing the rushing current to remove all traces of the sweat and grime she'd accumulated that morning. She unwound her braids and ran her fingers through her hair to wash and untangle it. And when she climbed back onto the bank, pulled her shift over her head, and made her way home, she told her father and mother that she'd grown very fond of a morning bath.

They hadn't pressed the matter. Valour knew her parents worried about how she was adjusting to life in Holt, knew they wanted her happiness above all else. If a morning bath lifted her spirits, they were happy to oblige her. Most mornings, Da would kiss her cheek on his way out to the workshop, leaving Valour and her mother to their breakfast. Afterward, they sat by the fire, while her mother brushed her hair dry and braided it.

"Ma," Valour asked one morning, "do ya think of 'er often?"

The room was very still. The steady rhythm of the brush strokes faltered. "Sometimes."

"Her hair and eyes were the same," Valour said, absently.

"Aye."

Ada gathered small sections of red hair between her fingers and worked them into an elaborate braid. It began at Valour's left temple and passed over her forehead, picking up more and more hair as it went. "What's got ya thinking of 'er today, Valour?"

"I think of 'er most when I'm lonely. I wonder if she'd have thought as I think, if she'd have laughed at the same stories, if we could've talked."

Valour could hear her mother sniffing behind her. She began to hope that the two of them might talk, right then, of the things that were lost, of the shadows of the past. But Ada would venture no nearer the door of that deep pain. Valour had watched her shy away from it time and again. Instead, she tied Valour's braid with a leather cord. "There. Lovely as always."

Valour ran a hand lightly over her hair. When she felt the strands that hung loose, sweeping over her left shoulder with the end of the braid, she smiled. Valour was not vain. But she understood the power of her beauty, understood the effect it had on both men and women. Her hope was that it would serve her well, that it would open to her the possibility of real love and of an easy and comfortable future. If she had been merely beautiful, her beauty would have been a danger to her. But because she was so rare, so obviously blessed by the gods, it was unlikely that any man would lay a hand on her. Her brows knit suddenly at the memory of Cormac, here in this room, pushing her into a chair.

"Are there any girls in the village ya might talk with? Any that might become friends?" her mother asked.

"Emmeline is kind," Valour said. "But she mostly talks of 'er coming babies." Hallam's young wife spoke of little else, and the fact that the girl carried twins made their conversations that much more difficult for Valour.

"What o' the magistrate's daughter? She's come of age, has she not? What was 'er name?"

"Aster," Valour replied.

"Well then." Her mother smiled at her as though something had been settled. "You'll be back by midday?"

Valour nodded, kissed her mother's cheek, and walked out into the village. It had come alive by this time. Torches still blazed on the outer walls of the cottages, and lanterns and fires lit them within, but the dark was letting up, the day ripening from black to gray. Children played in the lanes between the cottages, hiding and yelling and chasing one another in turns. Some of them squealed and giggled when they saw the "flame-haired girl," and she winked at them. Women beat rugs against the walls and tended their gardens, some nodding and smiling as she passed. From behind her came the sounds of the rushing stream and the rhythmic clanging of hammers on anvils. To her left, the sound of hammers and saws reminded her of the coming market day. Some of the craftsmen were repairing tables and booths in preparation, and Valour wondered vaguely if anyone would come.

When she reached the center of the village, she hesitated, unsure of where to go. In the cave, with Errol, she felt a sense of belonging. But out here she was reminded of all the things she missed about Fleete. At length, she drifted into Moss's shop.

"Valour," Moss said, and inclined her head toward her customer.

Valour nodded in return, and looked over the shelves, now burdened with pots and glass phials and bundles of herbs. Valour smiled at the multitudinous powders, thanking the gods she didn't have to learn the names and uses for all of these as well. She inhaled the mingled aromas of the apothecary's shop, the sweet and bitter, the earthy and smoky. The combination was pleasant and green, very unlike the smell of the furnace, but she liked it. Valour was lifting a bundle down from its hook in the rafters when someone else entered the shop.

"Mina," Moss said. "I thought you'd never come!"

The girl with the crushed wreaths, the plain one who came to visit when we first arrived in Holt. Mina. She felt a pang that she'd forgotten the girl's name, for they were near in age and might have been friends. But this girl seemed to have a knack for making herself invisible. Valour couldn't think how to address her, for they'd met before. At last she decided to greet her formally, in the usual manner of the clansmen and women.

"A fair morning to ya, daughter o' the Clan o' the White Tree," she said. She felt like a fool the next instant.

Mina stared at her, and blinked. The words came slowly. "And ta you, daughter o' the Clan o' the White Tree," she said. She gave Valour a little nod and turned to Moss. "I knew you'd fret about the flowering tobacco, but I couldn't get ta the Fayrewood yesterday."

"It's no matter, Mina. Emmeline gave me a fright, storming inta the shop and telling me 'er pains had started. Thought I'd need those leaves right away, but it's not 'er time yet. She's just making ready is all." Moss didn't move from her chair, and Mina seemed to know what to do with the tobacco leaves. Valour stood with her bundle, watching as Mina crushed the leaves with a mortar and pestle, scraped the powder into a jar of just the right size, and deposited it in a tidy nook on a shelf.

She's so capable, so at ease with herself, Valour thought.

When Mina had finished, there was a pause. She glanced at Valour, waiting.

"Will ya tell me about the Midsummer Festival?" Valour asked. "No one's come of age in, well, an age, and I'm longing ta dance."

"The Dance o' the Lantern Light," Moss said. "It's a night like no other. You've heard of it?"

"Aye," Valour replied.

"It's not long coming," Moss continued. "Winds'll change soon enough, and then ya can dance the night away if ya like." She rubbed her knees and gave Valour a wistful smile. "There was a time when I caught a few eyes at the Dance o' the Lantern Light. Now days I just drink the honey ale and watch. You girls'll be lovely. You'll wear yer best and the young men'll be enchanted."

Mina snorted, and Valour's eyes snapped toward her, but she had already recovered herself.

"With whom will you be dancing, Valour?" Moss asked, ignoring Mina.

"I . . . well . . ."

"Ah, you'll have yer pick on Midsummer's night, I've no doubt. Now," she eased herself out of her chair and slowly stretched to her full height, "I've work ta do. You two get along with yerselves." As she shooed the girls out the door, she slipped a coin into Mina's hand and thanked her. Then, suddenly, Valour and Mina were standing in the lane, uncertain how to part or what to do next.

Valour dreaded the thought of returning home, and there was nowhere else to go. She fumbled for an excuse to stay with Mina. "Will ya take me ta see the sheep? I haven't been much on the south side o' the village."

Mina looked at her, as if to be certain that she was sincere, before nodding and leading her toward the sheepfold.

"I heard some of the ewes were injured in the attack."

"Aye," Mina said. "If they weren't so stupid, they'd be perfectly well. But they panic when they see the dragons, and they do themselves harm trying ta get out o' the fold."

"Who tends them?"

"I do. And some o' the other women. We all do our part."

"In Fleete, most families kept their own sheep, in pens near their cottages," Valour said. "Is it because o' the dragons ya keep 'em together?"

"Aye. They're not what the dragons are after, but it helps."

"As far as possible from the Peaks, and easier ta defend," Valour said, understanding.

"Aye," Mina said again.

They continued their stroll through the center of the village. Valour was in no hurry, but Mina seemed constantly to check herself, slowing her steps to match Valour's easy pace. The silence stretched. Then a question occurred to Valour, something that had plagued her since she arrived in Holt. She felt sure that Mina would know the answer. "Why are the lanterns wrong?" she asked. "If each pane o' the Fayrewood lanterns is meant ta mimic a season, then one pane is wrong. The blossoms are pink, not purple."

Mina turned. There was a faint line between her brows. Valour thought she looked as though she had other work to do, as though this little excursion was an irritating interruption.

"They've yet ta find an ore that'll dye the glass pink. Amethyst is as near as they can come," Mina explained.

"Oh." Valour could've kicked herself. She ought to have asked Errol about the Fayrewood lanterns. Her father would surely have known, too. Why had she asked Mina? The girl seemed to know everything, to need nothing. No doubt her days were filled to bursting with useful activities. She was probably constructing her own cottage with her bare hands while Valour idled about the village. As they neared the southern edge of Holt, Valour felt foolish, and small, and alone.

A cluster of torches appeared on the hillside, a hundred paces or so beyond the sheepfold. Valour heard the pounding of horses' hooves on the wooden planks of the bridge and the voices of hunters. One of the hunting parties had returned.

Evander came first, followed closely by Chase and Hallam, Lachlan and Knox. Lorne and Alistair brought up the rear. Valour saw the change in their expressions when they noticed her. There was a kind of fatherly tenderness in the eyes of the older men. But the younger men looked at her differently. Their eyes held wonder and hunger and fear. She knew those looks well. Only Evander looked at her as if she were any other girl in Shiloh, as if there were other things on his mind.

Valour smiled and nodded to the hunters, returning their greetings as they made their way into the village. She tried to catch Evander's eye as he took the reins of some of the horses from his companions. But she could not. She stood with her hand resting on the fence and the sheep grazing and bleating at her feet, watching him.

Evander confused her and fascinated her. He was not a particularly beautiful man. His hair and eyes were brown. His arms, his neck, his chin, were scarred. His clothing was plain and worn. But there was something about him that was unlike any man she had ever seen. He carried himself confidently, but without arrogance. He spoke with authority, but without ambition. She'd seen little girls offer him flowers, blushing and fleeing when he smiled and thanked them. She'd seen boys leap in front of him, challenging him to a duel with wooden daggers or begging him to teach them to improve their aim. When he could, Evander did so. Sometimes he flipped the boys over his shoulder and carried them home. Then there was the girl. He'd taken in the little orphan girl, Grey. And there was his mother, who by all accounts was mad. He cared for her as well.

On market day, Valour had only just seen him turning in his saddle to face the dragon before she'd fled. If she hadn't been so afraid for her own life, she couldn't possibly have torn her eyes from

Evander. This was not the kind of man who would guarantee her a life of ease. He would never be able to give her beautiful things. He would never pass his days in quiet labor in a workshop. Evander was the kind of man who would die young. He would die bravely in battle against the dragons or the wolves. He would save lives and sacrifice himself. But he would die all the same. And he would leave behind a broken, grieving wife and who knew how many hungry children. Her father would never approve of such a husband.

Still. Still, she wanted very much to catch Evander's eye.

When he disappeared into the stable with the horses, Valour looked around her, remembering Mina. But Mina was nowhere in sight.

Twelve

Next market day was a great success. Cole remarked on it again and again. He was shocked that so many visitors would return and that others would come, having heard of the attack. One man from the village of Dunn, on the edge of the Whispering Wood, laughed at Cole's surprise.

"Not one man lost in the attack? Yer visitors were in greater danger from the wolves on their homeward journeys than they were here with the dragons! Besides, where else in Shiloh can a man see such beauty as this?" He lifted one of the Fayrewood lanterns and studied the filigree work around the edges of the glass. He examined each pane, the green, the gold, the purple, and the clear, hinged pane reminiscent of winter ice that served as a door. "What price fer this?" he asked. When Cole named his price, the man whistled through his teeth and shook his head. "It's more than I can pay," he said. He bought only a small edanna charm, but another came and purchased the lantern. Cole was very pleased. Already that morning he'd bartered for a piece of fine wool, a basket of candles, and a sack of dried venison. His purse was filling with coins, and this was not even his best work. The special lantern he'd been crafting was almost complete. Before the season was out, if anyone could afford it, it would fetch a fabulous price.

Mina had not given up. The second Market of the year saw her table covered with newly fashioned wreaths. She sold several early in the day, pocketing the coins for later.

Valour came to her table, seemingly eager to talk. She skipped the formal greeting this time; that was something. But Mina was inclined towards coldness. She'd never been sought out by anyone before, and her first instinct was to question Valour's motives. As the morning passed, however, Mina grew more and more convinced of Valour's genuine friendliness. She was lonely, too, Mina realized, and a little homesick. Mina might have begun to enjoy their conversation if it hadn't been for the looks and comments Valour was constantly receiving. Sitting so close to Valour, Mina felt as if every eye in Holt was turned toward her. It made her skin crawl. She fought the urge to hide under the table, and it struck her for the first time that Valour's overwhelming beauty might be something of a curse.

"Are ya ever able ta get away from here, Mina?" Valour asked, after an especially forward proposition. "There was a place in Fleete, on the very top o' the hill, where I used ta go. I could sit there fer ages, with the winds roaring past, tearing at my hair. It was easy ta breathe there."

"Aye," Mina replied, understanding fully. She hesitated to tell Valour of her own sanctuary. It was a sacred, a hallowed place. She almost thought that she couldn't share it with this astonishing newcomer. But in the end she decided that such a thought was selfish, that it was a poor way to repay Valour's candor.

"I go ta the Fayrewood," she confessed.

"You're not afraid?" Valour asked. "Chase told me ta go, of course, but all I hear are warnings about the Turn and the dark things waiting beyond it."

"There's a whole world o' beauty untouched by the evil things beyond the Turn," Mina said.

Valour gazed at her with new admiration, as if seeing her for the first time. "You're not what ya seem, Mina. You're nothing like."

Mina shook her head, brushing off the compliment, if that was what it was.

"Would ya take me there?" Valour asked. "I won't ... I wouldn't ..." She sighed, her shoulders sinking.

"No, it's alright," Mina said. She called Reed to watch her table, knowing that he'd be distracted within half a moment and her wreaths would be left unguarded. But she had earned several coins already, and there were more than enough flowers in the Fayrewood to provide her with wreaths for the rest of the summer.

"We can go now?" Valour asked, and Mina laughed at her childlike enthusiasm.

They struck out, weaving their way through the crowds. With Valour in tow, it was impossible to make quick progress. Everyone wanted to gawk at her, talk with her, question her about her unusual hair and eyes. *Perhaps this is why Maeve stopped coming to Market*, Mina thought. It must be very tiresome, even for such beauties as Maeve and Valour, to be noticed by everyone all the time. For Mina, it would have been a torment.

There was a long delay while Valour endured the endless questions of an old woman from Thayer. As she waited at Valour's side, Mina noted one man who followed Valour's every move. Cormac. She'd never cared much for the magistrate's son, but what she saw in his eyes now unnerved her. She turned, clutching Valour's hand and dragging her away from the stunned and indignant old woman, around the corner of a cottage and into a narrow lane. Mina knew how to avoid being seen in Holt. She followed lesser-used paths, overgrown with nightshade, racing from shadow to shadow.

When they broke from the cover of the last cottage on the south side of the village, they turned east, following the Cutting until they came to the entrance to the Fayrewood. Valour gasped. The trunks of two great trees stood together, leaning inward as they rose and forming a kind of arched doorway. Mina stretched out her hands and brushed the tips of her fingers over the bark as she passed through. Valour followed, her gaze sweeping over the stones covered in feathery mosses, the bright blossoms on vines and shrubs, the clear green leaves that rustled in the wind, the branches that groaned and swayed.

"Oh, Mina." Valour's eyes were wide with wonder and disbelief. "We don't need lanterns!"

"Aye," Mina whispered. She felt the magic of the wood seeping into her. "The Fayrewood has its own light. The Shadow doesn't come here."

Valour craned her neck, searching the treetops for some sign of descending darkness. There was none.

"Oh, Mina," she said again. "I thought the lanterns were a wonder. And people come from all over Shiloh. They buy the colored lanterns and carry them home without ever seeing this place." She took Mina's hand. "It breaks my heart."

Mina nodded understanding. She hadn't wanted to know Valour at all. And here she was finding that she loved her.

"I'll show ya my favorite tree if ya like," she offered.

Valour grinned in reply and followed her down the path.

They'd walked nearly halfway to the Turn when Mina stopped. Just ahead, off the path to the left, was her tree. She looked around, reviewing the familiar landmarks one by one. There was the trunk covered in moonflower vine, the big moss-blanketed stone that jutted into the path. But one tree looked unfamiliar and strange. Its leaves matched those of the other Fayrewood trees. The grain of its trunk followed the same pattern. But Mina could swear that she had never seen it before. She stared at the new tree, thinking.

"Mina?" Valour said. "What is it?"

She shook her head, as if to knock something loose. "It's nothing," she answered, and turned off the path. She relaxed when she saw her tree. She shimmied up the trunk in her soft, well-worn boots and settled on her branch. Valour's boots were newer, finer, and not nearly so suited to climbing trees. Her labored voice rose up to Mina as she struggled.

"Is there anything ya can't do? Ya nurse wounded sheep and weave tobacco wreaths, ya know every leaf and branch in the Fayrewood, and ya climb like a cat. I'll bet yer stews are the stuff of legend."

Mina laughed and caught Valour's arm when it popped into view. She pulled her to a seat on the wide, smooth branch, and the two of them sat without speaking, side by side, captivated by the color and motion of the wood.

It was the first of many such days. Valour and Mina slipped away to the Fayrewood as often as they could, to sit in Mina's tree and talk and watch and listen. Valour helped Mina gather flowers for her wreaths and sat beside her at her table on market days. Mina learned that if she promised Reed half her earnings, he'd take charge of her table and stick to his post. So, when the press of the crowd became too much, she and Valour retreated to the quiet of the colored wood.

One market day, while Holt swarmed with visitors, Valour and Mina were sprawled out on their branch. They were wondering if the leaves could possibly be greener or the flowers brighter when the winds changed. One moment, they whipped down from the north, cold and fierce. There was a lull, and the next moment, the winds came from the south. They were warmer. They smelled of water and grass and distant fires.

Valour sat bolt upright. "Will the dance be held tonight?"

Mina laughed. "Nolan will say when. He'll wait until all the hunters have returned."

The two lingered as long as they could and longer, knowing they were missed and that they must return and yet resisting. When they climbed down from their perch and returned to Holt, the mood of the villagers had changed. Voices were lighter, smiles given more freely. And not a few of the craftsmen let an axe or a lantern go for rather less than his desired price. There was cause for celebration. Midsummer had come.

Thirteen

Nolan set the festival for the following night, and the people of Holt busied themselves with preparations. Those men in the village who played drums and pipes and reed flutes dusted off their instruments and tried their hands at a few old tunes. Others cut logs for the bonfire, cleaned their kills in preparation for cooking, and carried tables and chairs down to the pool. The women gathered berries, made cheese, and harvested the best their gardens had to offer. They pulled their finest aprons and shifts from their trunks and washed and dried them. A few of the villagers caught up on long-overdue baths, and all of them brought out extra stores of candles and tallow. Every lantern would be needed, and as much fuel as they could spare.

Evander had never cared much for the Midsummer Festival, though his mother had delivered him while the people of Holt danced in the lantern light on Midsummer's night. He wasn't much for dancing, and since he didn't partake of the beer and cherry ale and honey ale, he never quite caught the unhindered joy of the celebration. The only thing that struck him about the Dance of the Lantern Light was the beauty of it. He went, every year, and watched the fireflies rise out of the grasses like so many flickering candle flames. He watched the light of the lanterns breathe life into the dark water of the pool. And he watched the radiant faces of the villagers, of his people, as they feasted and danced in the darkness.

Late in the afternoon, there was a sudden break in the furious motion of the village, and the lanes grew still. The tables were set, the feast spread, the bonfire lit. Evander strolled to the center of Holt, waiting while the villagers donned their finest, or their cleanest, at least. Then, in twos and threes, in family groups and clusters of friends, they emerged from their cottages and assembled, carrying lanterns fixed to little wooden rafts. The girls wore flowers in their hair, and those who had come of age wore embroidered shifts and belts. The boys bounced and laughed, doing their utmost to overturn their lanterns. The women had taken extra care with their braids, and the men were clean and merry. They were all of them luminous, joyful. Evander smiled in spite of himself. Nolan said a few words. Lachlan took up his pipe and started to play. The Dance of the Lantern Light had begun.

It was a gladsome procession down to the pool, with the lights and the laughter and the chattering of the children. The little girls drifted from their parents, skipping and twirling on the fringe of the procession. The boys captured fireflies with their free hands. When the company reached the pool, they set their lighted lanterns on the water, allowing the currents to carry them off, bobbing and spinning and bumping gently against one another. Soon the surface of the pool was lit with a shifting sheen of blue and green, purple and gold, and the villagers waited, hushed, watching the lantern light dance on the dark water. For Evander, the moment was never long enough. He felt as though the lighted lanterns and the lapping water whispered some indispensable truth. He could almost catch it, could almost understand their language, if only he

Seeker

listened long enough. But then the music began in earnest, and the moment was lost.

The villagers dispersed, some heading straight for the feast, and others to find dancing partners. Evander held back, standing near the entrance to the Fayrewood and observing. He smiled when he saw Knox and Chase piling their plates with roast venison and potatoes and filling their mugs with sweet honey ale. They'd need the ale to give them courage to find partners for the dances. He saw Nolan and his daughter, Aster, talking with Cole and Ada. Jameson was chatting with his own band of hunters and their families, while Tilly and Mina stood together and sipped from their mugs. Reed was crouching on the edge of the pool with a group of boys, plunging a long stick into the deep water and planning some mischief, no doubt. Moss was seated on the other side of the dancers. She seemed to be pairing hesitant young people and shooing them into the midst of the dance.

Maeve hadn't come. That much he'd expected. But he'd encouraged Grey to come and dance with the other girls, or at least enjoy the food. She had refused. "It's too far," she'd said, and Evander hadn't pressed her.

"Evander!" Hallam extended his arm as he approached, and Evander took it. Behind Hallam was his young wife, Emmeline. She gave Evander a tired smile. Evander noticed her bulging belly and wondered how long she could possibly go on before having those babies. He nodded to her and smiled.

"I've thought on what ya said when we camped the other night," Hallam began. "Truth be told, it's what Lorne said that's plagued me. He said he doesn't tell his little ones any o' the stories his da told 'im."

"Aye," Evander said. "I remember."

A shadow passed over Hallam's face, and he looked away. "I know why my da stopped telling those tales ta my brother and me. It was hard on 'im, losing my sis." When he looked up at Evander, his eyes were fiery. "But I want my sons and daughters ta know the stories. They're beautiful stories, Evander, and they gave me hope when I was a boy. I remember how I felt when I heard 'em. I want my children ta know the stories even if there's nothing but Shadow in this world, even if there was never anything else."

Hallam swallowed and stepped back, and Evander was gripped by the young man's passion, his conviction. He wondered what it might have been like if his father had lived, if bright images apart from his mother's maddening, incessant visions of the sun had cast their light over his years. He wondered what hope he would have to offer if ever he looked into the shining face of his own son. Could he muster the courage to speak of light when all around was darkness?

Evander took his friend's arm with one hand and squeezed his shoulder with the other. "That's well said, Hallam," he managed, and pulled away. He wanted to encourage this young hunter and his young wife. But Evander always straddled the narrow line between desire and despair, and tonight despair had the upper hand.

Hallam hesitated a moment, waiting for something more. When it didn't come, he nodded and took Emmeline's hand and led her away.

Evander sank against a tree and sighed. This was the Dance of the Lantern Light. The food was rich and the ale sweet. The warmth and light of the fires and lanterns was breathtaking. The music was intoxicating. Evander wanted to find pleasure in it, if not for his own sake, then for the sake of the people he loved and the joy it brought to them. Their lives were hard, beset by wolves and dragons, by wind and snow, by hunger and loss. What they all needed, surely, was a night of celebration, a night to feast and dance and forget the cares that would crowd in tomorrow.

Tomorrow. In the heart of summer, surrounded by warmth and beauty and extravagant fare, winter seemed worlds away. But it was not. His band would have to set out again, and soon. Evander's eyes fell on Reed. He would be a hunter, like his brother and his father. How many times would that boy go out in search of meat before the wolves got the better of him? He noticed Errol, the old white-haired craftsman, waving a four-fingered hand in the air as he recounted some tale or other. Even the craftsmen were not exempt. The fires of the furnace showed no mercy. And hunger and starvation could come for any man, when the winters were long and food was scarce.

But the people of Holt feasted and danced as if none of those perils loomed. This was the Dance of the Lantern Light, a single night of perfect, unspoiled beauty in all the long, bitter year. *And this*, Evander thought, *is the best we have to offer*. He couldn't stand and watch anymore. He snatched a lantern from one of the tables and stepped into the refuge of the Fayrewood.

It was never fully dark inside the wood. When the oppressive dark of night descended on Holt, the Fayrewood still shone faintly at the bottom of the hill. Wherever the light began or whatever its source, the leaves took it and tossed it among them before letting it fall to the floor of the wood. Then shrubs and stones tossed it back, sending it soaring into the topmost branches where it began another slow and joyful descent. Evander walked beneath a muted canopy of shimmering green, and the tense knot in his chest loosened and uncoiled. He breathed the air of the colored wood. It was so rich, so fragrant, it seemed as though a man might live off of that alone, forgetting the need for food and water. Truly, the Dance of the Lantern Light was not the best the world had to offer them. The Fayrewood was.

He stumbled over something in the path. When it cried out, he nearly dropped his lantern.

"By the gods, who's there?" He knelt and leaned in until the lantern light revealed her. Her blue eyes were bright and brimming with tears. A single braid circled her head like a crown, and the rest of her hair flowed over her shoulders in red waves. Her white shift, covered in an intricately embroidered tree, glowed in the dim wood. Valour.

"I didn't see ya coming," she said, wiping her eyes. "I'm sorry."

"You've no light?" Evander asked.

"No, I can see well enough. The Fayrewood has its own light."

"I know the Fayrewood," Evander said, and found himself recalling the figure he'd seen emerging from the wood months before, when Valour first came to the village. "Perhaps you know it as well, but it's wise ta carry a light, at night especially. If ya walked along far enough, you'd find more than birds and flowering vines."

She nodded, and Evander abandoned his lecture.

"Why aren't ya dancing with the others? Surely you'd have no lack of partners."

Valour didn't answer. Instead, she scooted to the side of the broad, flat stone where she sat. "You're welcome ta join me," she said. "There's room enough fer another."

"I know. I've sat here, and thought, many times." Evander sat down, resting the lantern on the floor of the wood and waiting for her to speak.

"It's a lovely night, a lovely tradition," Valour said. "I don't know why it should make me sad."

"Ya don't?"

Valour released a trembling breath and spoke low, as if remembering.

"My mother carried twins in 'er belly," she said. "When the time came fer the babies ta be born, the first would not come. The midwife in Fleete did everything she knew ta do. She tried every herb, every birthing position, every trick she'd ever used. Hours passed, and everyone feared that my mother would be lost, and 'er babies with 'er. But the first finally came." Valour stopped, and Evander could not turn to look at her face. He stared out into the soft light of the wood.

"After she was born inta the world," Valour continued, "that first baby didn't cry or struggle. The midwife slapped 'er back, massaged 'er little arms and legs, but she was gone."

"And the second baby?" Evander asked, his voice low and tender.

Valour hesitated before answering. "The second came easily, without a struggle; the first had opened the way."

"What was yer sister's name?"

Valour's voice caught on the word. "Honour."

"She looked like you?"

"Aye. Red hair and blue eyes. My mother broke tradition. She wouldn't let 'em burn the body. She buried Honour under the cherry trees in the valley."

They sat without speaking, allowing the rush of the wind and the scent of the wood to wash over them. When Valour spoke again, it was little more than a whisper.

"I never saw 'er, never knew 'er. But I miss 'er. When Da saw me tonight, dressed fer the dance, he said, 'You'd have made quite a pair, the two of ya.'" Valour stopped once more, waiting until her voice was steady. "On nights like these, I wonder what it would have been like ta dress fer the dance together, ta walk in the Fayrewood with 'er. It sounds mad, I know. How could I miss a sister I never met? How can I long fer something I never had?"

Evander's head jerked toward her, as if someone had struck him. *How can I long for something I never had?* Valour turned and looked into his eyes. And before any other thought came into his mind, Evander reached out and touched her face. His fingers disappeared in the waves of her hair. He brushed away her tears with his thumb. The two of them remained, for a moment, just like that. The wind softened, and the noise of distant music drifted through the wood. There was something in her eyes, in her beauty, in her words, that stirred Evander deeply. Without warning, despair gave way to desire.

He felt the rising heat in her face and neck, and he dropped his hand, remembering himself. "Fergive me. I'm sorry."

Valour raised her fingers to her cheek and looked at Evander with wide eyes.

"Keep the lantern, please," he said, jumping to his feet and backing away. "Fergive me." He hurried out of the Fayrewood, past the dancing villagers, and up the hill to his cottage.

He leaned against the outside wall, not yet ready to see his mother and Grey. He was stunned by what he'd done. He had always, always thought carefully before acting, whether he was hunting or caring for an injured horse or making repairs to the roof. What he'd done in the Fayrewood was so . . . impulsive.

He went to the stable, stopping to splash his face with cold water from the barrel before going inside to check on Rogue. The stalls were full, and most of the horses, Evander's black stallion among them, were asleep on their feet. There was nothing for him to do but breathe in the scent of the stable and try to slow his racing mind and racing pulse. It was a good strategy. Evander left after a few minutes, feeling more like himself.

The cottage was warm and welcoming when he entered. Grey was expert at feeding and tending the hearth fires. She jumped from her place at the table and ran to him, leaving a scrap of rough embroidery behind. Evander lifted her and swung her in a circle before setting her down again, and the two took seats by the fire.

They'd established a sort of routine for those nights when Evander was home. Grey had spent enough time watching Maeve that she'd picked up some basic embroidery skills, so she would sit in her rocking chair before the fire and fumble with a bit of work. Evander would sit beside her, oiling his bow or his saddle, sharpening his dagger, or fashioning arrows. Most often they sat in contented silence, but on occasion, Grey asked Evander questions. On this night, she was full of them.

"Did the lanterns really float on the water?" she asked.

"Aye," Evander answered. "You'd have liked ta see the pool all lit up, I think."

"Did the girls wear flowers in their hair?"

"They did."

"Was there roast venison?"

"Roast venison in heaps."

Grey looked into the fire, considering this. Evander marveled at the unusual way the light reflected in her eyes. Her next question surprised him.

"Will ya tell me a story?"

"A story?" he asked.

"The Tale of Grosvenor?"

Evander smiled. After a child learned to say his name, he learned the names of his father and mother and the name of his clan. After that, he learned The Tale of Grosvenor, and if he was still unsure about the names of his brothers and sisters, it was no matter. The Tale told the story of the Father of their clan, of the founding of the Clan of the White Tree. Evander knew it well.

"Alright then," he said. "But if I'm ta tell a tale, then you'll have ta sit in my lap." He sheathed his dagger and set it aside. Grey set her embroidery on the hearth and curled up in his lap, resting her head against his chest.

"Hearken, my children, come gather ye 'round
Ta hear o' the Hunter of greatest renown.
No traveler bolder, no warrior more fell
Than Grosvenor. List, and fall under the spell."

Evander fell easily into the rhythm of the tale, relaxing as the story progressed, and marveling at the keen sense of delight he felt in sharing it with Grey. By the time the Hunter had returned from his adventures, Grey was asleep, and Evander carried her to her cot and tucked her in.

He went to see about his mother, moving quietly into the back room and looking first toward the window. She was there, hovering over a new batch of bleeding flowers. The flowers on the hill had long since shriveled and fallen, but Maeve's were still dropping their precious nectar. Evander had never understood it. It was as if Maeve willed them to live.

"Ma?"

He sat down on her cot and tried again. "Ma, are ya alright?"

When she turned to him, the look in her eyes was confused and urgent. "I don't like that child, Evander."

"What's happened, Ma? Did Grey do something?" He worried that she might have damaged one of the bleeding flower blossoms or stained one of Maeve's fine cloths. But Maeve shook her head.

"She watches me. I don't like it. I don't like the way she watches me, Evander."

Evander took his mother's hand in both of his. "She's just a child, Ma. She watches ta learn from ya. No doubt she feels the loss of 'er mother, and she's still afraid. She missed the feast tonight fer fear of going too far from the cottage. Please, Ma, as much as ya can, be patient with 'er."

"She's not afraid. There are nights she doesn't come home, when you're out hunting. I don't know where she goes."

"It's likely she sleeps in the stable, waiting fer me. She's done it before."

It was awful to watch Maeve's face as she struggled with Evander's words. Her eyes moved erratically, as if following a firefly that drifted through the room, its light disappearing and appearing again in another corner. She clutched Evander's hand, held on as though the floor might collapse and the dark hill beneath swallow her whole. In the end, she could find no words, so lost was she in her tangle of thoughts. Evander pulled her close and kissed her head and stroked her hair and rocked her like a child until she, too, fell asleep.

Fourteen

Evander was restless, and more than usually eager to be out of Holt. He felt the winter looming. He was troubled by thoughts of the coming snows, the biting cold, the long, still, hungry hours when the walls of the cottage caged him in. He was haunted, too, by his mother's face, by Grey's questioning eyes. They were counting on him. He gave his men one day to recover from their indulgences during the festival before leading them south of Holt, out of the foothills, and into the broad, flat land north of the Whispering Wood. This was dangerous country. It teemed with deer and elk, and wolves. Evander was ready to risk it.

They had just forded a narrow branch of the River Meander when they spotted a large herd of elk, already running. In that murky light, the elk heard the approaching horses long before the hunters caught sight of them. Evander's men pursued, releasing a volley of arrows.

Evander leaned forward, stringing another arrow as Rogue charged ahead. The gray-brown hides of the animals blended too well into the landscape. It was difficult to distinguish one from the next, or to discern between the animals and the swath of darkness that swallowed up the light just ahead of them.

His arrow flew and missed, lodging in the ground as his racing target veered off to the left. The elk made a strange, hoarse bleating sound as it turned, and Evander saw them. A pack of wolves broke from the northernmost line of trees in the Whispering Wood, fanning out as they neared the little band of hunters. Evander called out to his men, but his voice was lost in a chaos of cries as Alistair and Chase warned of wolves approaching from the east. For one terrible moment, all the hunters stopped. They gripped their bows. They held their horses' reins, awaiting their leader's command.

Evander scanned their surroundings, his eyes straining into the gloom. He could see nothing clearly except eyes, scores of eyes, like orange candle flames fast approaching. He could hear their muted footfalls. He could feel them closing in, feel the darkness they carried with them.

There were too many. The Wheel would not serve. To the east, the enemy was almost upon them. To the west, the Meander deepened and broadened, cutting off their escape. There was nothing to do but retreat.

"Back!" he cried, and the hunters rode hard for the ford. The blood rushed through Evander's head, pounding out a slow beat. One. Two. A horse screamed behind him, and he looked back. Alistair was down. The two packs had come together on his very heels, and one wolf had leaped, its claws gouging into his horse's hindquarters.

Lorne and Evander slowed, in an agony of indecision. If they stopped and faced the wolves, they would not survive. But how could they leave one of their own?

Evander jerked the reins, turning Rogue around.

Alistair screamed, "Go!" It was not a request. There was nothing noble in that scream. It was a command, and it was desperate. Evander gritted his teeth and turned his horse. Rogue surged ahead, fording the Meander while Evander called to his men.

Knox answered, and Lachlan, but he could see nothing of Lorne or Hallam or Chase. They did not answer his call. He kept Knox and Lachlan in his sights as he rode, begging the gods to spare them. He pushed Rogue until their small company came to a low hill. The horses were near the end of their endurance. He shouted instructions to Knox and Lachlan, and they huddled together, thrusting the oiled tips of their arrows into Lachlan's torch and firing into the line of wolves. Their arrows flew sure. They fired them one at a time, then two together, and the wolves vanished in clouds of vapor and smoke. The line of enemies thinned, and several turned eastward and disappeared. When he saw the blazing eyes and shadowy forms moving away, Evander was afraid, more afraid than if the animals had advanced on him alone. If they were moving toward Chase and Lorne and Hallam, he could do nothing.

Knox fired two more arrows, felling a wolf with each. Now only one remained. Its eyes were trained on Evander, and it picked up speed as it came. Evander reached for his quiver, paused, dropped his hand. He would not waste an arrow on this beast. Fear and rage mingled in him as the wolf's eyes grew larger and brighter. He snatched the torch from Lachlan's grip. He drew the dagger from his belt and ran, straight for the wolf. At the last moment, the animal lunged. Evander dropped to his knees. With his left hand, he drove the torch into the wolf's open jaws. With his right, he drove his dagger into its belly.

Fire and smoke broke out. Waves of heat swept over his arms. And then the wolf was gone. But for the labored breathing of men and horses, the world was still.

Knox offered Evander his hand and pulled him to his feet. He wrapped an arm around Evander and hugged him, pounding his back.

"You've spoiled our torch," Knox said.

"We've got our flints. What say we give the horses a rest before setting out ta find the others?" Knox and Lachlan agreed.

There was no more talk for a time. They let the horses graze and recover. They drank from their water skins and sat, each in his own silent torment, waging war against the memory of Alistair's fall and the lingering echo of his screams.

Mina woke to the sound of knocking. It was full dark, an inky, liquid night, and she could see nothing through the window. She hurried to the door and cracked it open, squinting in the light. One of Knox's little brothers was there, holding a lantern high.

"Moss needs ya!" he hissed.

"Now?" Mina whispered.

"Aye, right away. I'm not ta go home until I get ya."

"Alright," Mina said. She slipped into her boots and closed the door behind her, shushing Reed back to sleep as she left.

"Our cottage is close enough, we could hear the moaning," the boy explained, as they rushed to the apothecary's shop. "Ma told me ta go and see about it, and when Moss caught sight o' me, she sent me ta get ya."

Mina nodded, absently.

"What's wrong with 'er?" the boy asked.

"Who?" Mina asked. "It's not Moss that's ill?"

"Emmeline," the boy said.

Mina knew what must be happening, and why she'd been called. The lights inside Moss's cottage spilled out the windows and onto the lane, splashing against the walls of the surrounding cottages. The messenger hurried off, and Mina went in. The fire was blazing, the room stifling. Water boiled in the iron kettle on the fire, and Emmeline was flushed and sweating, her eyes unnaturally bright. She was bent over, leaning her weight into her hips, gripping the edge of Moss's table and swaying.

"I can't support 'er weight, Mina, not with my knees. If ya could just help 'er move about a bit, give 'er something ta lean against . . ." Moss motioned her toward Emmeline.

Mina approached, laying a hand lightly on Emmeline's back. The girl looked up at her, eyes large and pleading. "I don't want ta lay down," she said. "I don't want ta rest. I . . . Oooooooh!" Emmeline moaned, giving voice to some deep, unstoppable wave of pain. She clasped Mina's hand in a crushing grip, and Mina swallowed her own cry of pain.

Emmeline's grip eased, and her face relaxed. She slumped against the table, resting her head on her arms and panting. Moss shuffled to the hearth and scooted the kettle away from the hottest part of the fire. "There's hay out back, Mina. Bring in a big armload before her pains come again. Everything else is ready."

Mina wasted no time, rushing behind the cottage, hitching up the hem of her shift and filling it with hay, and rushing back inside. But Emmeline was already crying out.

"Right here, Mina!" Moss said. "Spread it here!" Mina did, taking Emmeline's arms as soon as the task was finished and allowing the girl to press her forehead against Mina's shoulder as she swayed.

"Ooooooh!" Emmeline moaned again. Mina found the sound hard to bear. She held on to Emmeline's elbows, supporting her as best she could, until the next pain came, and the next. Soon, Mina could not tell one from another. Emmeline's cries grew to an unbroken wail. Her grip was like iron, her face strained and contorted.

Moss crouched beneath them and Emmeline leaned into her pain, and all of a sudden there was a tiny cry.

"Emmeline, you've a little daughter!" Moss said. She snipped the cord that bound mother and child, and hurried the baby away. Emmeline looked at Mina, panicked.

"It's alright. It's alright. Moss is only cleaning 'er," Mina said. "One more ta go, now. You're nearly there."

The second child came quickly, and Emmeline collapsed to her knees immediately after. Mina managed to scoop the child up and examine it as Emmeline eased herself down onto the bed of hay.

"Emmeline," she said. "You've a little son as well."

Moss returned, the baby girl wrapped tightly in a soft cloth. Mina took the girl while Moss took the boy and cleaned and swaddled him. Then, while Moss tended to Emmeline, she sat in front of the fire and held both babies in her lap. She'd never before seen the precise moment when a child entered the world. To witness such a thing twice in the same night was stunning. Their faces were so bright, so luminous, Mina thought their coming should have shaken the world to its foundations and put the Shadow to flight. She gazed at them and smiled, and wept. And when the time came, she laid them in their mother's arms.

Mina was exhausted. She chided herself for admitting as much after what she'd just seen Emmeline endure. She stayed a little longer, watching the weary, lovely young mother with her new babies. "What'll ya call them?" Mina asked.

Emmeline smiled. "The girl'll be called 'Fayre,' after the Fayrewood. And the boy'll be called 'True,' after 'is father, for I know of no truer man than my Hallam." Mina thought the girl's skin might kindle a fire in her blankets, so bright was the light around her in that moment.

"I hope he'll return soon, then, ta see his perfect little boy and girl," Mina said.

Hallam did return, the very next day, but his body was slung over the back of his Fell horse and his blood marked the homeward path of the five remaining hunters in Evander's band.

Fifteen

Maeve regarded the window and the Shadow beyond. Torches and lanterns streamed toward the southwest corner of the village, their bearers gathering around two stone pyres. On one of the pyres, Hallam's body rested. On the other, bare logs and chunks of turf were topped with flowers, in memory of Alistair. His widow had made no complaint when Evander told her that her husband's body could not be retrieved. She'd given Evander a brief nod and closed the door against him. Evander had said as much when he'd tried to convince his mother to attend the burning. She'd promised to try, in honor of the man who'd ridden and fought beside her beloved, in honor of the man who'd brought her husband's body back to Holt, in honor of his widow. That woman had been her friend once, in the days before the light of her life, the one she could see with her waking eyes, the one she could touch and embrace, talk with and laugh with, had been replaced by visions of an unreachable Light. That woman had been her friend, and Maeve knew well what heartache awaited her. It was right that Maeve should hold her hand while the fire burned.

She opened the door. One hand rested on the latch while she stepped over the threshold. She heard music, the beginnings of a mournful tune, but it fell away as the pyres were lit and the flames spread. Sobs cut through the roar of wind and fire. That would be the younger widow. Maeve shut her eyes against the sound, and light bloomed at once. The air was clear, the sky broad and blue. The sun rode over all. She opened her eyes on darkness and death, on fires stretching endlessly up into Shadow. She heard the snapping jaws of a wolf, heard the low rumbling in its belly, heard it as clearly as if it waited round the very corner of the cottage. Her knuckles whitened on the latch.

She stepped inside and closed the door.

Evander's band set out again on the day after the burning, and the hunters' faces, as they rode and tracked, were shadowed. No songs were sung around their campfires for many nights. They met with some success at last, bringing down two large elk in the hills west of Holt, but still the men were grave. They saw absent faces, heard absent voices. They could not bear to speak over the hollow screaming of the empty places around the campfire. Until one night, when Lorne asked if Evander would tell them all he knew of Maeve's dreams. Evander did, and his men listened hungrily.

"It's strange," Lorne remarked, "but some o' these visions you describe remind me of stories my da used ta tell." And Lorne sang half-remembered snatches of old songs and told tales of gods and immortals, of lights small and great, of wars and cataclysms. The hunters were amazed, and captured by his words.

"Why did ya never share these stories before, Lorne?" Evander asked. "And why should you remember them now?"

"I didn't have the heart ta tell 'em before," Lorne answered. "I hardly have it now. But Hallam would've liked 'em."

Evander thought of Hallam's words during the Dance of the Lantern Light, and he grieved anew, wondering who would share these tales with Fayre and True.

"Alistair as well," Lorne continued. "He knew more stories and songs than I." He turned to Evander. "Yer father and Alistair were always passing 'em back and forth around the fires, when we were younger."

Lorne's revelation unleashed a flood of emotion in Evander. He had not known that his father was a teller of tales. How he wished he could have known him, and every last word of every last story, and the rise and fall of his father's voice as he related each one. There was quiet around the fire for a time. Evander mourned for Hallam and Emmeline and the babies. He mourned for Alistair and his widow and their children. He mourned for his father, for memories never made, and stories never told.

"Would ya sing the song again, Evander? The one about the mountains?" Chase asked.

Evander nodded, and when he found his voice, he sang. No more words were spoken that night.

The hunters returned to Holt and set out again, but the brooding quiet of their days and nights slowly filled with story and song. Talk of what lay beyond the Shadow became common, and in that manner, among five weary hunters, the Sun Clan was born.

Valour was struck by the sudden loss of Hallam, not because she'd known the man well enough to grieve for him deeply, but because she couldn't shake the thought of Emmeline, alone in her cottage with her tiny babies. Valour wondered if Fayre and True would survive the coming winter, if they would survive enough winters to feel the loss of their father. And what of the young widow? Would she marry again, or would she spend her days watching the road, pining for a man who would never return? Had it been worth it, Valour wondered, to love a man and bear his children only to lose him to the Shadow within the year? She knew what her father would say. She suspected Errol would agree. The old man was pouring molten glass into an iron mold. The thick, orange-gold liquid would cool and harden into a sheet of clear green.

"Why did *you* never marry, Errol?" she asked.

"Marry?" he said, his brows nearly reaching his hair.

"Aye. You could've supported a wife and children, surely."

"Oh, yes. I did well enough even as a young man, for my da taught me the secret o' the dragon fire when I was a boy." He stepped away from his work and set his tools on the worktable. "Suppose I've been content with my craft. It's always pleased me as much as any wife could." He removed his gloves and handed them to Valour. "Course, if there was a girl as pretty as you who'd come along at the right time, I might've thought a bit different." He winked. "Now, I hope you've been watching and not just fretting. It's your turn." He handed the tools to Valour and motioned her toward the mouth of the furnace.

She pulled the gloves up over her arms. "But if you'd married, and yer wife died within the year, do ya think it would've been worth it?"

"Hard ta say," Errol answered. "If I had naught but a year ta fill with anything, and I could fill it with what I liked, I suppose I'd be content."

"Even if it was taken away? Even if ya felt the loss of it fer the rest o' yer days?"

"Aye, even then. A year working at this furnace, shaping and coloring the glass, would give me joy even if I had ta go and hunt forever after. Now, enough talk. Take the scoop . . . aye, that's right. Easy, not too much. Alright . . ." He guided Valour as she moved the molten glass toward the molds. She stumbled, spilling a few drops onto the floor of the cavern. "Whoa! Easy, Valour. Watch what you're about!"

She made it to the mold, emptied the bowl, and set the tools aside.

"Ya can't lose yer focus, my girl. The furnace'll show ya no mercy."

"I know, I know. I'm sorry, Errol," Valour said, removing her gloves and cursing herself for her clumsiness.

"You're not good fer much, today, Valour. What's on yer mind?"

She shook her head. "It's nothing."

But it was the memory of Evander's touch that had caused her to stumble, and the thought that he might fall prey to the wolves at any moment. Valour mumbled a farewell and fled from the cave, hoping that the frigid waters of the Cutting would push all thoughts of Evander from her mind.

Mina was mending in her chair by the south-facing window when a lantern came into view. Its light fell on Chase's face as he crested the hill. She held her breath, waiting. Lachlan appeared and spoke to Chase. Then Lorne and Knox, each leading a horse with an elk over its back. Another long moment passed, and Mina clenched the frayed hem of the tunic in her lap. Then she saw him. Evander. He was home, and talking easily with his men. They slapped him on the back as they dispersed. She filled her lungs with air and sighed, resting her head against the chair. Evander was safe.

Chase came through the door and dumped his gear on the table. "Hello, Mina," he said. She could see that he was cheerful, remarkably so considering their recent losses.

"Ya had a good haul?" she asked.

"Aye, good enough," he answered.

She watched him hang his quiver on its hook and lean his bow against the wall by the door. He smiled as he unpacked, smiled for no reason at all, and at no one in particular. She wondered if some girl might have caught his eye and hoped that it was not Valour. He'd been keen to see her when she'd first come to the village, but Mina thought that initial fascination had passed.

"What is it, Chase?" she asked. "You're not yerself."

Instead of replying, Chase scanned the room. "Where's Ma?"

"Visiting Moss."

"Da's band still out?"

"Aye."

"What's Reed up to?"

"Said he's off ta practice 'is marksmanship," Mina replied, exchanging a knowing glance with Chase. He laughed. Reed had gotten into all manner of trouble under the guise of "practicing his marksmanship."

Chase came to sit beside her and looked at her steadily before beginning. "Mina, you've heard that Evander's mother has visions, while she sleeps?"

"Aye."

"Do ya know what she sees?"

"Lights, isn't it? Or one light, in the sky?"

"Aye, she calls it the sun. Evander's told us as much as he knows about Maeve's visions, and Lorne, he knows tales . . ." Chase stopped, struggling for words. "I hardly know where ta begin. Mina, you've never heard tales like this. Da's mentioned a few things, here and there, but Lorne speaks of a time before the Shadow fell over this land, a time when Shiloh was different. He says this wasn't always the Shadow Realm."

Mina listened eagerly to all that Chase said. He shared portions of dozens of stories and songs, pointing out images and ideas that appeared over and over. Something quickened in Mina's heart. Chase's words were beautiful, overwhelming, impossible. And yet . . .

"The more the men talk, the more we'd like ta know if there's any truth in the stories, if there's any purpose in Maeve's visions," Chase was saying.

"Does Maeve know where ta find this great light? Does she see that much?" Mina asked.

"No. The best Evander can tell is that it lies somewhere beyond the mountains."

"The Peaks or the Black Mountains?"

"Don't know," Chase said.

"But Evander thinks this sun is real? *He* believes the tales?" Mina asked.

She felt very naked before the gaze her brother gave her in reply. "Aye, Mina. Evander does. Or rather, Evander wants it ta be so, as we do."

Mina could say no more. An unbearable ache filled her and she could only nod to Chase. She struggled to imagine food without wolves, lanterns without dragons, the Fayrewood without the Turn. She tried to imagine a world without Shadow. She knew she would pass the night in the attempt, wrestling with the familiar darkness and the terrible promise of hope. She'd sift through those thoughts and feelings later, when the house was quiet. But for now, one thought made itself heard over all the others. *Evander believes.*

"Evander means ta speak to the villagers, next market day," Chase said, and laughed. "And they called 'im mad when 'e faced the dragon."

Cole was no fool. He waited for just the right moment, when the crowds who'd come to buy and trade were filling Market Circle. A man from the village of Thayer asked him if these were all his pieces, and Cole smiled. It was clear the man had some wealth, and he wanted to return home with something extraordinary. Cole reached beneath the table and unwrapped a bundle, lighting it before lifting it to show to his customer. The man gasped and cursed, and the people around him turned to see. A hush fell over them all, a stillness that radiated to the very edges of Holt. In a sea of colored light, with chains and belts and charms and wreaths of flowers and fine embroidery spread out around them, the people of Holt fell silent at the sight of this lantern. The green and gold and amethyst panes seemed to breathe, inhaling and exhaling pale flame. Fragile bands of red-gold filigree glinted in the dancing light.

The man from Thayer finally found his voice. "How much?"

Cole gave him a price. It was extravagant. A fortunate man could earn as much in a year, perhaps.

The man's face fell. "I can't fault ya fer asking so much. It's a marvel, truly." He tore his eyes from the lantern and moved on.

Others came to admire the lantern, but no one could pay so high a price. Cole was content. He still sold several pieces and fared very well, as he always did, for his work was exquisite. He tucked the lantern away for another time.

When the tables were dismantled or returned to their proper homes and the last of the visitors had ridden out of Holt, Evander spoke with a few dozen men in Nolan's cottage.

Cormac didn't take his usual place at the front of the room. It irked him that Evander had called a meeting. That privilege only ever fell to the magistrate. Yet here were the men of the village, assembled and expectant.

Cormac slumped against the back wall and waited. He let his mind fall into its comfortable ruts, imagining all the ways Evander would contrive to take power in Holt. The fires of hatred and jealousy and impotent rage burned hot in him. His blood roared in his ears; his breathing quickened. It was as if he stood in the bog

Seeker

in deepest darkness. The bog creatures shrieked and moaned, and his feet sank in the mire. He could almost feel the thick, squelching mud sucking him down and down. It was useless to struggle. Evander would have Valour. Evander would have Holt. Evander would win.

He took a deep breath and shifted his weight. He caught his father watching him from his seat near Evander. Nolan loved the people of Holt, and he served them well. He was a good magistrate and a good man. But for many years Cormac had read his father's disappointment in every look, heard it in every word of admonition. He'd burned with shame every time he came into his father's presence, so, little by little, he had severed their bond. Over time, Nolan came less and less into his mind, and his thoughts were bent instead on his adversary. When Evander began to speak, every other face faded from Cormac's vision.

At first he doubted his ears. Evander spoke to hardened hunters and seasoned craftsmen about children's tales and a mad woman's sleeping visions. He made no grand proposals, no promises. Evander didn't go that far. He merely suggested the possibility that there was more to the world than what they'd seen.

Cormac's back straightened. He lifted his head. He felt suddenly very light. He couldn't recall when the smile had first broken over his face. Wisely, he said nothing. When Evander asked the men to share any shred of knowledge, any memory passed down from father or mother, any song or tale, anything that might suggest that others had known something of the sun, or of a world beyond the Shadow, Cormac tore his focus from Evander and watched the villagers, gauging their reactions.

Some of the men offered Evander snatches of old rhymes. Others eyed him warily. Some shouted opposition. The craftsmen voiced their doubts with the most force. They feared that Evander would stir up trouble with the other clansmen, or worse, draw the attention of the Shadow Lord. Though the people of Shiloh had no clear understanding of Ulff and his ways, the idea of seeking a world outside his dominion sounded much like rebellion. The craftsmen especially, whose lives were comfortable by comparison with most of Shiloh's inhabitants, were horrified at the thought of such a risk.

Some of the hunters had weathered too many winters and been hunted for too long to give Evander's words much credence. For them, the Shadow had become their only certainty. But Cormac saw how light was kindled in the eyes of the younger men. A strange fear fell over him at the sight of those bright faces, but he dismissed it, and it passed.

There was not a man in Holt who didn't respect Evander. Cormac had heard men boast that Evander might one day rise to become Father of their clan. He had always seethed at the thought, until this night. He watched the men of Holt leave the cottage in a state of confusion, anxious and divided. Evander's words had been hard. The summer winds were warm. And there was food on every table, and the Market was booming, and coins jingled in their purses. If Evander was seeking to unite the men of Holt, and to lead them, he'd chosen a very curious time, a very strange approach.

Cormac smiled as he closed up the front room and snuffed out the lights. Perhaps Evander would not win after all.

Sixteen

"I've not seen 'er today, not since ya left this morning," Maeve said.

Evander had just come home to find Grey gone and Maeve hovering over her flowers. He ran to the stable, but only the Fell horses were there. He rushed back through the center of the village, checking the lanes between the cottages, poking his head into doorways and asking after Grey. No one had seen her. He went to the huts and workshops, to the cavern in the hillside, to the sheepfold. Nothing.

He checked the cottage again, to be sure she hadn't returned, before racing out to the Fayrewood. The images rose unbidden, of Grey in the jaws of a wolf, or dragged along the rushing currents of the Cutting. He reminded himself to breathe, to think. She had gone out before. Maeve had told him so. Clearly, Grey was overcoming her fear. She was recovering. It was only natural that the child should tire of being cooped up, that she should long to stretch her legs and explore. *That must be it*, Evander thought. *She's just learning the lay of the land, settling into her new home. She must've* gone to the Fayrewood. What little girl wouldn't love to see the bright flowers and the canopy of green leaves?*

Evander rushed in, calling her name. *She'll come*, he assured himself. *When she hears my voice, she'll come. There's no need to upend every stone or uproot every shrub, no need to climb every tree. She'll come.* But these thoughts brought him no peace. They could not silence the panic that rose in his breast. He ran through the Fayrewood, still calling, until he neared the Turn. He slowed and stopped, his eyes adjusting to the thickening dark and the shifting motion of the trees.

"Grey!" he shouted, for she was there, just beyond the Turn, and something stood over her, something that shone with an eerie, fitful radiance.

Evander drew his dagger and surged forward. The dark figure retreated, disappeared. Grey looked in surprise at Evander. He snatched her up in his arms and ran into the heart of the wood, past the rustling leaves and out through the arching entrance. He did not rest until the wood was far behind and warm light from the stable cascaded over his shoulders and shone in Grey's eyes.

"Grey!" he said, hugging her and wanting to shake her and hardly knowing what to say. "What happened?"

"I wanted ta see the Fayrewood," she said. "The lanterns are so lovely, and I wanted ta see the trees."

Evander sighed. "Ya wandered too far, little one. Too far. The Fayrewood's not safe beyond the Turn." And then he remembered and held her at arm's length and looked hard into her eyes. "Did something . . . was someone . . . what did ya see beyond the Turn? Did someone speak to ya?"

"There was a man," Grey said. "He had blue eyes like Maeve's, only much brighter. They were very beautiful ta look at, but he didn't speak."

A chill ran down Evander's spine, and he held Grey close. "Please, Grey. Please! Don't go back there. It's no place fer a warrior, much less a child."

When Grey was asleep in her cot, and Evander had told Maeve as much as he thought she should hear, he returned to the stable and leaned against the low wall of Rogue's stall. He brushed the horse's black coat and stroked his neck and muzzle. When the morning glories were just a few hours from showing their faces, Evander crept back to his cot. But he was haunted by the memory of the dark form towering over Grey, and sleep eluded him.

Valour had not seen Evander for many days, and she'd told no one of what had passed between them. Instead, she sank into a maelstrom of secret fears and doubts and desires. Her thoughts were muddled, her emotions unpredictable. She might have run mad if she hadn't had so much to fill her time. Emmeline was desperate, and Valour and Mina had offered their help. They brought food, tended her garden, swept the floors of her cottage, and beat the rugs. Occasionally they watched Fayre and True while Emmeline went out. Valour would have chosen any task above this last, not because the babies were any trouble, but because Emmeline inevitably returned with red, swollen eyes, and the sight tore at Valour's heart.

On some days, Valour went with Mina into the Fayrewood to gather herbs and roots for Moss. Sometimes they sat in Mina's tree, and sometimes they talked. But Valour could not speak to Mina about Evander. She knew it was foolish to waste any thought on the man, much less speak of him. Evander had hardly looked her way before the Dance of the Lantern Light. He must have suffered some failure of judgment, some temporary madness, when he spoke to her in the Fayrewood. And she'd seen nothing of him since. She despised herself for thinking of him, for remembering his touch. It was ridiculous. It was childish. Besides, her father would never allow him to come near her. She was certain of it, until one evening at supper, when her family's conversation turned to Evander.

"He's not like the other hunters I've known," her father said. "That's fer sure."

Valour looked up from her meal and tucked a wayward strand of hair back into its braid. "Who's not?" she asked.

"Evander."

"He's worse, surely," her mother said. "Seems all I hear are tales of how Evander faced the dragon, how Evander charged inta the ranks o' the wolves, how Evander would set out ta find a country *beyond* the Shadow."

Cole's brow furrowed in thought. "Aye, true enough, but 'e has a way about 'im. He's the kind of man who earns another man's respect almost from the first moment. He's a leader of men."

"And what would 'e lead them to?" Ada asked. "It sounds like madness ta me!"

"No doubt," Cole replied, taking another bite. "It's only, well, Evander's the kind of man who kindles fires in other men, and if 'e can manage ta stay alive long enough, he could end up as Father o' the clan."

"Well, he won't live ta see the first frost if 'e keeps on as he's been going," Ada said. "Leaping inta the mouths o' the dragons . . ." She shook her head and muttered her indignation as she cleared the supper dishes.

Valour hardly slept that night. When the time came to meet Errol, she was foggy with exhaustion. She stumbled into the hillside cavern yawning, and added fuel to the furnace. The little clay pots bumped and clattered as Valour fumbled to gather the ingredients for a new batch of glass. Errol scolded her. With twinkling eyes, he threatened to find a new apprentice. She laughed and yawned and checked the consistency of the batch in the oven. Then a man's voice broke into the well-worn rhythm of her morning routine.

"Fergive me, Errol."

Valour whirled around, almost knocking Errol down with the iron rod she held in her hands. Evander stood in the cave, close enough that she could stretch out a clumsy gloved hand and touch him. His face shone in the light of the furnace as he looked from Valour to Errol and back again. He saw the rod, the apron, the gloves. It would be clear to anyone what Valour was doing, clear that she did it in secret. Evander gave her a little surprised smile before his eyes fell away in... regret? Embarrassment? Valour couldn't say.

"I've come to ask a favor, Errol," he said.

"Let's have it then, Evander. We've work ta do," Errol replied, and winked.

"I know blacksmithing isn't yer main work, but I'd like a new brand made."

"I've done a fair measure o' smithing in my day, my boy. What sort o' brand would ya like?"

"Just one symbol," he said, pulling a scrap of cloth from his belt. The cloth was embroidered with an intricate design that chiefly consisted of circles. They were joined by a series of lines, long and short, straight and curved. Evander stretched the scrap between his hands, using his thumbs to mark off the boundaries of the symbol. "Like this," he said.

Errol nodded. "May take a few days," he said. He took the scrap of cloth from Evander and tucked it into his apron.

"My men set out again tomorrow. I'll come fer it when we return." He extended his arm, and Errol took it.

"Valour," Evander said, nodding toward her as he left. Her mouth was too dry to swallow, too dry to speak. She thought, or perhaps she imagined, that his eyes lingered on her a little longer than they once had. But whether he thought of her with longing or disgust or indifference, she could not tell.

"Ya could do much worse, my girl," Errol said, making no attempt to hide his smile. "Much worse."

That night Evander woke to the sound of screams and the pulsing beat of enormous wings. Before his feet touched the floor, he understood. *The dragons.* He snatched up quiver and bow, looked sternly into Grey's wide, staring eyes. "Not one step outside the cottage, Grey!" She nodded in reply.

Outside, the village was alive. A current of terror coursed between the cottages and spilled out the doorways. The hunters were the first to come, bows and arrows at the ready. The craftsmen stumbled out behind them, and women and children kept out of sight.

Evander looked up. The torches fixed to the rooftops at the northern end of the village were blazing with blue fire. They cast an eerie light over the village. Beyond them, something small and bright faded into the darkness, carried in the claws of a retreating dragon. One enemy come and gone. But two more were closing in, fire billowing from their jaws. Their croaking screams split the air. Evander ran for the stable. The air around him grew hotter, thicker. He gasped and choked in the fume.

A single torch, perched on the corner of the stable roof, burned clear and blue. In its light, Evander saw the dragon descend. It hovered behind the stable, waiting. He drew an arrow, raised his bow, fired. The arrow caught the blue flame as it flew and landed in the shoulder of the beast. It roared and thrashed, its tail convulsing and smashing the stable wall. Evander heard the screams of the horses as the dragon turned and spewed fire into the stable.

"No!" he roared, and ran toward the dragon.

Mina was familiar with the coming of the dragons. Like Evander, she understood what was happening before she was even fully awake. Quick as lightning, she grabbed a cold torch and ran behind the cottage. She took a ladder from the ground and leaned it against the roof. She climbed to the top and waited, breathless and afraid, as hunters called and arrows flew and blue flames appeared on rooftops all over the village.

She saw Evander's arrow land, saw the dragon turn its fury on the stable, saw Evander run to meet it. The second dragon swooped down, belching flame, its talons grazing the slate tiles of the roof not three paces from where she stood. The torch in front of her caught fire. Mina trembled in terror of the dragon's passing. For a long moment, she clung to the ladder. Then she fixed her eyes on Evander, and her mind cleared. She looked up. The torch above her burned bright. She thrust her own torch into the flame, and scrambled down the ladder. She would take the precious blue fire to Evander.

There was a woman wailing. And with her wailing a smaller cry was mingled. The sounds shattered Mina's singular focus. She turned back toward the heart of the village, saw the armored legs of the second dragon tear into the roof of a cottage. A woman ran to meet her. She carried a bundle in her arms.

Emmeline. Mina groaned. She stole one anguished glance at Evander before running to meet the young mother.

"Mina!" Emmeline cried, as she recognized Mina's face in the flickering blue light. The dragon rose up behind her, its black talons reappearing above the roof of the cottage. "I couldn't reach 'er! I couldn't reach Fayre!"

By the gods, Mina thought, *she's only got one baby in her arms.*

Mina took off, running toward the dragon as Emmeline ran from it. She heard shouting, and the hissing flight of many arrows. There were men, she realized, moving through the village. They were trying to bring down the dragons, *this* dragon. But there was no time. On its next descent, the dragon would take Fayre in its grip, and something innocent and lovely, something beyond price, would be lost forever.

She did not see how the light seeped off of her and bathed the walls of the cottages in the center of Holt. She could see nothing but the dragon's eyes. She could do nothing but run.

The dragon turned from its prey and faced her. She was luminous now. The dragon's head reared back. It let out a roar that shook the village. Mina ran faster. At the last moment, the dragon lowered its head. Its claws settled into the dust of the road. Mina shouted her battle cry and thrust her torch into the dragon's eye as flaming arrows hit the beast from left and right. She stumbled to a halt, dropped her torch, rushed into Emmeline's cottage. Against the back wall, in a little basket, Fayre was flailing arms and legs and sobbing.

Mina gathered the baby into her arms and calmed her, while the last of the dragons wheeled overhead and retreated to its lair in the Pallid Peaks. When the baby was quiet, and sleeping in Mina's arms, she went to find Emmeline.

All over the village, women and children crept from their cottages to survey the damage. More than a few of the hunters who stood nearby regarded Mina with wonder and mumbled to each other about what they'd seen. Chase embraced her, and her father, and soon Emmeline was scooping Fayre out of her arms and weeping and thanking Mina again and again. She nodded to Emmeline and gave her a weak smile. But as Emmeline and Fayre dropped out of the forefront of her mind, she remembered. She saw men moving toward the stable and she was afraid. She followed, searching the faces ahead of her for some sign of Evander. Her heart stopped its beating, and waited.

He was alive. She noticed his face first. His expression was tight, pained. In the ghastly blue light, he looked older than his years, and unspeakably weary. Lachlan was putting Evander's arm over his shoulder, supporting him on his right side. Knox took his left arm, his wounded arm. When she saw the blood oozing from three deep gashes in his forearm, she put her hand against a wall to steady herself. Evander winced as he leaned into Lachlan and Knox. Knox was taking great care, not only of the forearm, but of Evander's shoulder. There, the tunic had been scorched, and the skin beneath was red and liquid.

The three hunters stumbled off in the direction of the apothecary's shop, and others set to work extinguishing the torches. Some of the villagers went in search of the wounded, others to check on the horses, and a whole crew of men took axes to the carcass of the dragon.

Mina came to herself slowly. She was staring at the corner of the stable, at the place where Evander had been. But he was gone, and the rest of the villagers had moved on.

"Mina!" Her mother ran to her, weeping, and hugged her fiercely. "I was so afraid," she whispered. "I was so afraid I'd lost ya."

Mina rested her head against her mother's shoulder and cried like a child.

Seventeen

Within ten days, cottages and stables were repaired and nearly all traces of the attack washed clean. But the people of Holt were changed. Moss mused on it while she rocked in her chair and massaged her aching knees. Errol remarked on it as he shuffled around the furnace. Cormac noticed it as he strolled through the lanes, shadowing Valour. The villagers talked of it down in the bog, as they sliced dark turf into neat blocks and stacked the blocks to dry. Something was different.

The attack on Emmeline and her babies was doubtless responsible for some of the disquiet that had settled over the village. The dragons came for bright things. There was no mystery in that. But it's one matter to know a thing is possible and another matter to see it done. One moment a baby girl slept in radiant contentment. The next moment, the dragon came for her. Black talons tore away the roof that covered her tiny head. It was not a thing to be forgotten.

Evander's injury was another factor. There wasn't a man in Holt, apart from Cormac, who liked to see Evander wounded. The hunters in particular felt it sorely. During the days he spent on his cot, his arm and shoulder wrapped with bandages, the villagers left no end of food on his doorstep. Grey piled the vegetables in baskets until they overflowed, and she hid a few precious bundles of salted meat in secret places around the cottage.

Then, there was Mina. Her fiery charge toward the dragon had filled the hearts of her people with astonishment and a terrible, long-forgotten hope. Men who'd looked too often into the eyes of the wolves turned it over in their minds. Women who stirred the kettles over their hearth fires remembered verses of songs their mothers had sung when they were still in their cradles. And those who had lost husbands and brothers and sons and daughters wondered if it might, perhaps, be possible to run unafraid into the jaws of the enemy and live to tell the tale. The people of Holt began to ponder the legend of the sun, and to wonder and hope as never before.

Valour knocked at the door and waited, chewing her lip and running her fingers over her hair to be sure every strand was in its place. The door cracked open, and a huge pair of eyes emerged.

"Hello," Valour said.

Grey stared back.

"I've something fer Evander, if it's alright," Valour stammered. "I know he's not yet recovered, but it's something he wanted . . . needed. It's important."

The eyes disappeared and the door swung open. Valour took a step inside.

"He's in the back room," Grey said.

Valour passed the overflowing table, went into the back room, and saw Maeve embroidering in front of the fire. The woman made no move to greet her, so Valour turned toward the cot in the opposite corner. Evander was sitting up, his back against the wall. He was staring out the window, absently brushing his knuckles against the scar under his chin.

"Evander," she said, and fire shot through her. She wondered if she had ever spoken his name aloud. It felt so strange and beautiful on her tongue.

He turned slowly, as if returning to himself. When he saw her, he jumped and winced at the sudden movement. He took a breath, relaxed.

"Valour," he said.

How she wished she could read his face, his eyes. She wondered if her presence made him uncomfortable, if she had violated his privacy, if he was embarrassed. It could be that his wounds pained him, and he wished to be left alone. Valour's head spun with possibilities and she wondered, suddenly, how long she'd been standing in that room, staring at Evander with her mouth open. The fire crackled. The fabric in Maeve's hands rustled against her shift. Valour thought the sound of her own breathing was thunderous. She was mortified. Evander's eyes were on her.

"This is from Errol," she said at last, and approached the cot. She gave Evander a small bundle and retreated, watching him from the center of the room.

Evander unwrapped the bundle with one hand. When he saw the brand, molded to mimic Maeve's symbol for the sun, the hard lines in his face softened. He smiled.

"What'll ya do with it?" Valour asked.

"Don't know yet," he answered. He looked at the brand from several angles, admiring it.

Valour nodded. "How's yer arm?"

"Feels like a dragon tried ta claw it ta shreds and burn it to ash."

Valour grimaced and glanced over her shoulder, toward the door. She really ought to leave. She was taking a breath to say her farewells when Evander spoke.

"They say yer hair is red as flame," he said, studying her. "But that's not quite right, is it?"

She touched her hair and looked down at her boots.

"It's darker, more like the color o' the tobacco blossoms," he said.

The blossoms grew mostly in the Fayrewood, and the mention of them brought Valour inescapably back to the Dance of the Lantern Light.

"Do ya go often ta the Fayrewood?" she asked, looking at Evander's forehead instead of his eyes.

"Not often enough," he answered. "You?"

"A little."

"Valour," Evander said, and he searched her face until he caught hold of her eyes, until he had her full attention. "Would ya meet me there, in the Fayrewood?"

Valour couldn't think of a response. She couldn't think of anything.

"We leave in two days, my men and I. Would ya meet me at midday tomorrow? Where we met before?"

Valour's mouth was dry. She made a futile attempt to swallow before managing, "Aye."

Evander relaxed against the wall. Valour hadn't noticed that he'd been tense until his muscles eased into the curving stones behind him. His face shone. "Tomorrow, then."

"Tomorrow," Valour said. She hurried into the front room, passed a curious Grey, and left.

Chase and Jameson were arguing again.

"There's nothing ta be gained by such a venture, Chase. It sounds well and good, and if I were a boy of yer age, I might just risk it. But I won't leave a prosperous village and tempt the armies o' the Shadow Lord in search of a legend."

"What has age ta do with it? Lorne's older than you are, and he's already said he'd risk it."

Seeker

"Age has much ta do with it. You've no wife o' yer own, no babies ta feed. Ya risk yer own neck, and that's all."

Mina was mending in her chair by the window. She noticed the sharp look her mother gave her father when he spoke so flippantly about her firstborn's neck.

"What of it?" Chase said. "We set out in search o' this new land, and we return fer our wives and children when we're sure o' the way."

Jameson shook his head in frustration. "This is the best bit o' land in all Shiloh, Chase. We're scooping wealth out o' the water with our bare hands."

"No, we're not! You're not, and I'm not. We'd drag our meat out o' the jaws o' the wolves no matter what corner o' Shiloh we were settled in. It's the craftsmen who depend on the Peaks and the Cutting, not the hunters."

"We're a part o' this village as much as they! Our fathers' fathers settled here, theirs *and* ours. Would ya leave it ta the dragons? Would ya have others come and take what's ours?"

While his father spoke, Chase paced the length of the cottage. Once, he looked to Mina in desperation, but she gave him nothing more than a quick shake of her head before returning to her work.

"Let's talk of dragons, then, Da. As the years pass, do ya suppose they'll lose the will ta torment us? And the wolves? On some fair morning, do ya think they'll retreat ta the Whispering Wood and never hunt again?" His voice rose as he spoke, until it echoed against the walls. "If it's not the dragons and the wolves, it's the hunger and the cold. If this is all that's ours, I'd give my right arm fer someone ta come and take it!"

"This is madness, boy. Ya waste my time!" Jameson rose from his chair and moved toward the door.

Chase pounded his fist against the table and shouted. "No, Da! It's you who waste mine! Two of our band are dead, Hallam and Alistair lost forever." Mina saw pain and memory darken his face. Then he dropped his hand and stood before their father looking weary and spent. "More will die. Perhaps tomorrow my time will come."

Tilly covered her mouth with her hand, stifling a whimper.

"Is that what our lives are ta be, Da? A game of waiting, waiting fer death? Is there nothing else ya want? Nothing more than this?"

Jameson paused on the threshold, and his eyes took on a new light. "Cole invited me ta stop by 'is workshop. Did ya see the lantern 'e had on display at the last Market? A craftsman with skills like that . . ." He shook his head, momentarily lost for words. "There's no telling what I might pick up. Ya never know, Chase."

He headed out to the stable to prepare his horse for the next hunt, leaving his son confounded and defeated. The tension hung in the air. Tilly chopped potatoes, her mouth set in a hard line. She didn't look up when Mina made an excuse about gathering supplies for Moss and hurried to the apothecary's shop.

"More mandrake," Moss said, and Mina fairly flew into the Fayrewood in search of it. She moved through the shrubs on the easternmost border of the wood, combing the ground for the broad green leaves with snow-white blossoms whose roots could ease so many ills. Her movements were graceful and silent. Whenever she came upon other herbs and berries that she knew Moss could use, she tucked them into one of the pouches that hung from her belt. But there was no mandrake on the eastern side of the wood.

She crossed the Fayrewood's central path not far from the Turn and scoured the western half of the wood. She was moving south again, back toward the entrance, when she spotted a little patch of mandrake among some stones and added it to her stash.

After that, there was no excuse to linger in the Fayrewood. Except . . . Mina closed her eyes and listened to the rustling of the leaves, the creaking and swaying of the trees, the snatches of birdsong that drifted down from the branches. The wind played with her hair and the hem of her shift. She felt the toes of her boots sink into the forest floor, felt her spine and shoulders sink down as well. It was so lovely here. She opened her eyes on a world of shimmering green. Soon, autumn would recast the leaves in blazing yellow-gold. The rich green canopy would be lost. Mina decided she wasn't quite ready to lose it. Her feet carried her home to her tree, and she climbed to her branch and breathed in the scent of the wood.

The voices took her by surprise. There were never voices here, not in the Fayrewood. Evander came, certainly, but his visits were infrequent, and he always came alone. Mina adjusted her position, peeking through the swaying foliage to the center of the wood, where a flat stone protruded into the path.

Evander. She could see the bandages on his forearm. A blot of red appeared between the leaves. It was deep red, redder than flame. Evander's hand moved over it and down along Valour's arm. He took her hand.

Mina froze, her fingers gripping the bark of the tree. Evander was taking Valour's hand. Evander, her Evander. She caught herself. He was not hers. Not hers. But he belonged to Holt. He belonged to the Fayrewood. He was part of this place, as she was. Valour was something else. She . . .

Oh. Mina's chest ached, as though the old crack had opened, and the bitter winds from the Peaks were raging through her again. She was hollow inside. She was nothing but empty, windswept space. She watched Evander and Valour, watched in agony, for she could not tear her eyes from the two of them. And when Evander drew Valour close and kissed her, Mina pressed her face to the trunk of the tree and cried. Her tears burned her cheeks, and she made no sound. The colors of the Fayrewood faded; the comforting noises fell away. She fumbled for a thought, any thought, to give her a foothold. She found none. There was nothing inside her but a hollow, echoing torment that refused to be diminished by words.

Hours later, when she climbed down from the tree, the mandrake slipped from her pouch. Mina didn't notice. She failed to check the path to be certain Evander and Valour had gone. She forgot about Moss. Mina was consumed by pain, and for once, she had no thought for anything else.

Eighteen

"How long, Valour?"

Valour was still dripping from her bath in the Cutting when she entered the workshop. Her father sat at his worktable, his back to her. He spoke without turning.

Valour took a deep breath, buying time while she guessed which of her secrets had been discovered. He couldn't know about Evander. No one had seen them together. They'd hardly been alone together at all. No. He must have found out about the apprenticeship. Judging by the timing of his question, it was a fair guess. She took another breath. If he'd found her out, it was best not to mince words or plead or speak as if she were in any way uncertain about her choice.

"Since the first market day," she said.

He nodded once, and said nothing until he'd finished bending a piece of edanna wire into place.

"Why Errol?"

"Errol offered."

"I told ya you'd no need of such training, Valour. The matter was settled," he said, rising from his seat and facing her.

"No, Da. It was settled that *you* wouldn't train me, that's all. Ya knew I enjoyed the work, knew I had some skill. Errol offered ta take me as apprentice, and I accepted."

"But, the secrecy, Valour. How early did ya have ta rise of a morning ta work with Errol before anyone else was stirring? Grown fond o' bathing in the stream, is that it?" His eyes fell to her arms and she yanked them back. There was no concealing her scars. She had half a dozen by this time, from the fires in the furnace, from the molten glass, from hot tools dropped in a moment of clumsiness.

"I knew the danger, Da. You'd never have allowed it," she said.

"What's ta be gained by it? Choose a man today, this very morning, and he'll thank the gods fer the chance ta marry so rare and beautiful a creature as you." Cole walked to the other side of the workshop, waving his arm as he spoke. "But, no! You'd rather creep out in deepest darkness and weary yerself wrestling with fire and drown yerself in the Cutting before breakfast! What's ta be gained by it, Valour? Some brute could've carried ya off into the hills. Anything could've happened."

Valour was angered by his words until she saw his face, saw the fear so deeply etched in the lines on his forehead and around his mouth. Cole couldn't bear to lose another daughter. She swallowed her bitter reply.

"Can't ya see the sense in it, Da? I've something that pleases me ta do, and a skill besides. I've knowledge I can take with me always, wherever I go. Now, if I choose ta marry, I don't have ta marry a craftsman. And if I lose my husband, I can feed myself and my little ones."

Cole breathed a weary sigh. "My lovely daughter," he said. He took her face in his hands and kissed her forehead. "Why could ya not be content ta sit with yer ma and sew?"

Valour grinned and kissed his cheek. "Does Ma know?" she asked.

"Not yet, but you'll have ta tell 'er."

"Alright." Valour stepped around the worktable and reached for the latch on the cottage door.

"Valour," Cole asked suddenly, stopping her. "Ya said ya don't have ta marry a craftsman. Has one o' the hunters caught yer eye?"

Valour's cheeks bloomed with color, but she went inside without a word, leaving her father to reach his own conclusions.

Evander took the brand with him on the next hunt. Their first and second days were unsuccessful, but the little band laughed as they sat around the campfire and all but Knox made grandiose plans for the future of the Sun Clan. Evander heated the brand until it glowed orange-gold before marking his belt, his quiver, and his saddle with the sign of the sun. Chase did the same, and Lachlan, while Lorne told the hunters how changed he was since he'd begun to tell his children some of the old tales.

"My boy will hardly go ta sleep nights, when I'm home." Lorne shook his head and smiled. "Keeps asking fer more stories. Can't get enough. And one o' my girls, the youngest, brought me a flower one morning. It was yellow, like candle flame, and she said, 'Da, look, it's like the sun.'" Lorne's eyes filled. He cleared his throat.

"Pass me that skin, Chase!" he said. Chase surrendered his water skin.

"No, the ale!" Lorne said, and Chase complied. Lorne tipped it to his lips and drank long, gulping the sweet ale until the skin was nearly empty. He stood and yanked off his tunic. The brand was resting with its tip thrust into the embers of their campfire. Lorne picked it up and, before anyone could stop him, branded his left shoulder.

Chaos erupted in the camp. Lorne bellowed. Evander came at him from the left, Chase and Lachlan from the right. Lorne held the brand like a weapon, waving it menacingly. The hunters closed in, ducking and sidestepping. The glowing tip of the brand burned little orange pathways through the black sky. Knox saved them all from any number of burns by tripping Lorne. The man fell hard. Evander wrested the brand from his grip, doused it with water, and put it out of sight.

They all laughed then, and slapped Lorne on the back. In return, he cursed the quality of the ale and threatened to throw them to the wolves with his own two hands. It was a good night.

The next day, Evander's men came upon a hunting party from Fleete. It was not an uncommon occurrence. The hunters would exchange bits of news from home or share the locations of the most recent sightings of deer and elk. This meeting unfolded like any other until one of the hunters from Fleete remarked on the strange sign branded on their belts and quivers. Evander answered him only briefly, but he invited all the men to a meeting in Holt on the next market day. They agreed to come.

As the hunters from Fleete rode out, still eyeing the new clan sign with curiosity, Evander thought of something he hadn't before. In all their talk of the sun and of seeking out a land where the Shadow was burned away by the light, they had never once considered how such a venture might affect the other clansmen. Generations before, Grosvenor had broken with the Fire Clan and formed the Clan of the White Tree. How had the Father of the Fire Clan reacted when Grosvenor made his intentions known? Had Grosvenor appeared arrogant? Rebellious? Mad?

Evander raised a hand to his forehead. If any of their plans took shape, he and his men would be breaking from the Clan of the White Tree and founding an altogether new clan. *He* would be the Father and Light of the Sun Clan.

Knox rode up next to him and, seeing his face, asked, "Are ya well?"

Evander nodded and told him what he'd been thinking.

"It's no small thing ya speak of doing, Evander," Knox said.

"Men fall prey ta the Shadow every day. They're devoured by wolves and dragons and hunger and despair, and there's naught ya can do ta stop it. But if it's *you* they follow inta the darkness, *you* they hang their hopes on, you'd best be sure there's something worth finding."

Summer was waning, and Maeve's dreams were changing. She walked through the Fayrewood, in the light of innumerable golden leaves. There was no sound, only a hushed expectancy. She would find it, she was certain. It was not so very far away. Her steps quickened, the leaves whispering a promise of coming beauty.

But the path did not grow brighter. The trees never opened on a clear, blue sky. With every step, the Shadow sifted further in among the branches of the Fayrewood trees. The golden leaves lost their splendor and faded to gray. The trees crowded together. Trunks and branches lost their clarity. They twitched and shivered.

The vague sense of delight that kept her captive to the world of her dreams was stolen away, and freezing terror took its place. There was no path to reach the sun. There was no escape. The Shadow held sway in Shiloh, and it did not let go.

Maeve woke screaming, and the lingering horror of the nightmare was slow to fade. When she was calm, she rose from her cot and fumbled through the embroidered cloths in her basket. She removed several pieces and put them on the edge of the hearth. She took more of her embroidery from the trunk in the front room and stacked those pieces on the hearth as well. She sat in her chair and ran one finger over the sun pattern on the sleeve of a white shift. Then she threw it on the fire, and with it, everything in the cottage marked with the sign of the sun. Gray and white wool withered, colored threads blackened, and Maeve sang:

Helena Sorensen

"Tiny drop
Clear as glass
Hold the light
When lanterns pass

Watch fer dawn
Wait fer sun
On the petal's
Velvet tongue

Fade ta red
Turn ta blood
Weep fer all
That once was good

Loose yer hold
Stain the ground
All is lost
That once was found"

Nineteen

Evander and his men returned from the hunt, and Evander met Valour in the Fayrewood. On the next day, heavy rain prevented the hunters' departure, so Evander brought Valour to the cottage and sat with her by the fire. He talked of many things, for Valour was full of questions and eager to know more of him. He told her of his love for Holt, of boyhood adventures with Knox, of narrow escapes from dragons and wolves. More than anything, Evander talked of the sun, of sundry stories that whispered the same promise, of hope rekindled. Valour listened with shining eyes.

Their time together was too brief by far. Never in his life had Evander known loveliness so complete. Here, beneath the Shadow, was beauty undimmed, beauty he could hold in his scarred and calloused hands. Valour fed his desire for bright worlds and mighty destinies and all things good and lasting.

The rain passed, and the hunters rode out. Evander was sorry to part from her.

"Welcome, daughter o' the Clan o' the White Tree," Errol said, and winked. "I know what you're thinking. You'd rather be curled beneath yer blankets than here with this smelly old man in a smelly old cave."

That was not what Mina was thinking. In fact, Mina was relentlessly clearing her mind of any thought except the next one, the one she must think in order to move and eat and work. In the last several days, she had sharpened her focus until it was pointed like an arrow. She aimed at the step in front of her, or the latch that had to be lifted, or the spoon that needed to reach her mouth. It was the best she could do, for now, but she was glad of it. And Valour's presence was threatening to undo all her careful work.

They'd met in Moss's shop the day before. Mina had wanted, on first sight of the dazzling redhead, to hate her. But after a moment of uncomfortable silence, Valour had come and taken her hand and asked her to visit the furnace early the next morning. Mina had been confused, but she couldn't resist the simple, openhearted request. She'd groaned inwardly before squeezing Valour's hand in return and agreeing.

She had pushed all thoughts of Valour from her mind until early this morning, when she woke from a fitful sleep and slipped out into the darkness with her lantern in hand. Standing next to Valour now was far more difficult than she'd anticipated, for Valour's breathless joy grated against her wounds.

"Look, Mina," Valour said, as she spread a collection of small bowls and jars across the worktable. She held one up for Mina to see and raised her brows. "What do ya suppose this is?"

Mina blinked. "I couldn't say." Those were the last words she spoke for some time. Valour was brimming with explanations about each of the ores and their uses. She showed Mina her tools, her apron and gloves, and then she stopped her chattering and stood in front of the table where the panes of glass were cooled. She faced her friend.

"I've ruined more panes than I can count," she began.

"More than that," Errol said, looking up from his work at the furnace. Valour ignored him. "But my last few batches have been very good, the color clear and uniform. No bubbles at all." She adjusted her braid and stood very tall, as if she were about to address all the members of her clan, and turned her back to Mina. When she faced her again, she was holding a small pane of yellow glass. She beamed.

Mina's eyes swam at the sight of the glass, warm and gold as the autumn leaves of the Fayrewood trees, and at Valour's childlike delight in her accomplishment. She understood then that this was Valour's gift to her, this visit to the furnace, this revelation of herself. Valour had missed Mina, and she was seeking to strengthen their bond.

"It's lovely, Valour, truly."

Valour replaced the glass pane and wrapped her arms around Mina, and Mina returned the embrace.

"What will yer da make o' this, Valour?" Mina asked, when Valour let her go.

"He knows already."

"I thought sure as the dark he'd come fer me," Errol said.

Mina's eyes grew wide. "Did 'e?"

Errol chuckled and Valour smiled. "No. I helped 'im see the sense in it." A mischievous grin spread over Valour's face. "But I've another secret," she said.

Mina stiffened.

"I've taken Da's best lantern," Valour continued, her voice low and laughing, "and replaced the panes. He hasn't noticed. It's 'is best work. And now, it's mine as well."

Mina breathed, a short burst of relieved laughter.

"He may well fetch 'is price this market day," Errol said.

"Do ya suppose he'll share the payment with me?" Valour asked.

"Only fair," Errol said.

Mina thanked Valour for bringing her and hurried out of the cave, leaving Valour and Errol to their work. Her lantern floated before her through the turbid dark of morning. She was determined to gather the last of the tobacco blossoms from the Fayrewood and make wreaths for the next market. With a few more coins, she might have enough to buy a bit of salted meat to set aside for the winter. And since she'd completed one impossible task already this morning, she thought she might as well tackle another.

She passed through the archway. At once, the Fayrewood trees took the light from her lantern and splintered it, passing it from leaf to leaf. The wood was luminous, alive. Mina dropped her eyes and left the main path to search for flowering tobacco. She stuck to the eastern side of the wood, carefully avoiding her tree. Soon she found a group of yellow blossoms and gathered them into her apron. She moved on, her soft boots silent, she herself little more than an apparition with a floating lantern. She found other blossoms behind moss-dusted stones and some near fallen logs blanketed in creeping vines. She tore them off at the base of their stems, keeping the point of her focus as sharp as she could. She stepped over a shrub, stumbled, caught herself against the trunk of a tree, walked on. When her apron held enough blooms for a dozen wreaths, she turned her back on the wood and headed home, trying not to think how the most beautiful thing in her world was shot through with so much sorrow.

Cole had never seen so many visitors in Holt. He worried that the swarming crowd would overturn his table and smash his lanterns. This was the last of the summer markets, and the atmosphere in Market Circle was feverish, tense, very different from what it had been in the spring. Now, winter loomed large in their minds. The hunters set out again and again, preparing for the coming storms. On market days, every craftsman in Holt was anxious to turn a profit. Cole was hoping to sell his prize lantern.

He scanned the crowd, his eyes moving inevitably toward Valour. She was talking with her friend at a table near the back, and she wore a crown of white flowers in her hair. He smiled, his heart expanding at the sight of her. Other craftsmen sold their wares nearby, and coins and food and wool and tools and belts and boots changed hands all around. He saw Evander spread a tunic across his table and showcase the embroidery on the neckline. His left arm was bandaged, his movements stiff. When the customer left without buying the tunic, Evander nodded and thanked him.

Evander's face was grave. Cole was trying to recall a time he'd seen it look otherwise when Evander's expression changed. His eyes brightened. The hard set of his mouth softened into a smile. His shoulders seemed to rise, as if a great weight had fallen away. Cole was curious to see what had brought on such a transformation. He followed Evander's eyes to the striking redhead with the crown of white flowers, and he sat down hard, suddenly sure that he would lose his daughter to the best man in the village, and sure that man would break her heart.

"Cole? What is it?" Ada asked. The frenzied pace of the day's buying and selling had kept her behind the table with her husband all morning.

"Our daughter's set 'er eyes on someone at last," he said.

"Aye," Ada said, glancing toward Evander. "A hunter." Ada was no fool. She'd already caught the looks passing between the two. "And that's not the worst of it. Was there ever a man so determined ta get himself killed." Ada put a hand on her husband's arm. "If we forbid it?" she asked.

"I find it hard to imagine refusing that man."

"Even fer the sake of our only daughter?"

"She loves 'im," Cole replied, remembering the conversation in his workshop. He gestured toward Valour. "Look at 'er. I've never seen 'er so bright. Would ya deny 'er this happiness?"

"Her happiness will be short-lived," Ada said. "Her grief will follow 'er all her days."

"Perhaps not. There's something about that man. He may live long and see good days and make Holt more prosperous still. He may surprise us."

Three customers came at once. They handled the charms and chains and admired the lanterns. One of the customers wore a belt with an edanna buckle. His tunic was heavily embroidered at the collar, and the hilt of his dagger was encrusted with colored stones. This was the man Cole had been waiting for. He made a move to bring out his prize lantern, then hesitated, taking a long look at Evander before coming to a decision. He left his masterpiece beneath the table, under a mound of cloths and wrappings, and spoke to the wealthy customer.

"I've edanna lanterns here with Fayrewood glass. Best workmanship in Holt, and nothing else like it in all Shiloh. What would ya like ta see?"

Cormac had grown accustomed to watching her from a spot near the back of the magistrate's cottage. There, he was inconspicuous, and he had an excellent vantage point. He stood in the dark under the eaves of the cottage while she stood in the midst of the crowd, illuminated by the flickering light of hundreds of torches and lanterns. At the moment, she was talking with Mina. His eyes ran over the crown of flowers, the flowing hair. Her face was radiant and full of color. *There's still a chance*, Cormac thought.

He cursed himself for hesitating. Valour had come to Holt in late winter. Now spring had passed, and summer was at an end, and still he hadn't spoken. Not really. Not as he wished to speak.

Evander will have her. Evander will have everything you desire. The familiar voice echoed the words that rang through all his waking hours. *There's still a chance*, he argued. He took a faltering breath and stepped away from the wall, moving steadily towards Mina's table at the back of Market Circle. He pushed through the crowds, keeping his eyes fixed on Valour. When he reached the table, Mina and Valour fell silent and waited.

Could I speak with you a moment? The words were there, waiting to be spoken. But when Valour looked at him, Cormac could not find his voice. He cleared his throat, glancing at Mina. Her expression was hard and fiery. He dropped his eyes to the table, where Valour's hand rested just behind a wreath of yellow flowers. He reached out and ran a finger lightly over the back of her hand. She snatched it away. Cormac cleared his throat again and looked up.

"What can I do fer ya, Cormac?"

It was Evander who asked, not Valour. He had appeared from nowhere, and Valour had stepped behind him and a little to the side.

Instead of responding to Evander or even meeting his gaze, Cormac watched the change in Valour's face as she looked up at Evander. Her eyes were adoring, and she shone. She was so bright, it almost hurt to look at her. She slipped her hand into Evander's, and Cormac felt as if the ground pitched and rolled beneath him.

Evander will have her. Evander will have everything.

He felt a sudden urge to drag Valour away from the crowd and lock her up somewhere safe, somewhere Evander could not touch her. But even as he fled Market Circle, he didn't give in to the inevitable. Cormac reminded himself that there might yet be a chance to win Valour. Evander had called another meeting. The man persisted with his ravings about the sun, and Cormac was beginning to wonder if he'd spent too many years holed up with Maeve and her visions. In a few hours, Evander might forfeit the respect of the men of Holt. He might lose all credibility, and with that, Valour's love. Cormac returned to his cottage and waited.

The men from Fleete were full of questions. They sat nearest Evander in Nolan's front room. Behind them were the hunters, and then the craftsmen, who slumped against the walls and sprawled over their chairs, exhausted. Evander told the newcomers of Maeve's dreams and how they seemed connected to many of the stories and legends that had been told for generations. From time to time, one of the men from Fleete nodded in agreement, remembering a tale he'd heard in childhood, but most of them were set against Evander. His words couldn't reach them.

"It's no surprise we've all heard the same stories, or near enough," one man said. "Doesn't make them anything more than stories, though."

At that, a general argument broke out, with some men mocking the others for giving credence to such foolish tales and others insisting that all the stories must have come from one source.

"What source?" someone asked, shouting above the din. His question was directed at Evander. The room quieted as the men waited for an answer.

"I don't know. In truth, I can't say that all the stories didn't begin in the mind of one mother rocking 'er child ta sleep." He sighed, leaning back against the stone wall. "But there is a chance that all o' them began with memory, that the tales are no storyteller's weavings, but the truth of our history."

"You'd seek *truth* in children's rhymes and the ravings of a mad woman?" a cold voice asked. Evander stood, and every face in the room snapped toward the tall man who stood beside the door. The men from Fleete assumed he was a local. The men of Holt assumed he'd come from Fleete. His hair was dark, his eyes startlingly blue.

"You'll speak no word against my mother." Evander said.

The stranger regarded Evander. The air in the room grew still, and cold. "Am I mistaken," the man replied, "or does your mother keep to her cottage, never showing her face, raving about visions she claims to have while she sleeps? Is she not the same woman who weaves her delusions into her embroidery and guards her flowers as though they were her children?"

Waves of fury and shame swept over Evander. There was nothing he could say in his mother's defense. This man spoke the truth. But how did he know?

The stranger cocked his head and lifted his finger, slowly, drawing every eye in the room to Evander's belt. "Is *that* the symbol of this woman's ravings? Have you branded yourself with the mark of a mad woman? Where do your loyalties lie, Evander, if not with the Clan of the White Tree?"

None of the men had been keen to speak against Maeve, but the question of loyalty to the clan set their blood boiling. There was a moment's pause while every man took a breath and opened his mouth, and then the room rang with speculations and empty accusations, with warnings against Evander's ambition and questions about the sign of the new clan. When Evander had had enough, he raised his hand and roared over the chaos, demanding silence.

"I'm not newly arrived in Holt," he began, eyes flickering toward the stranger by the door. "You've hunted with me," he said, looking into the faces of the hunters. "You've bartered and sold with me," he said, acknowledging the craftsmen. "We've fought the dragons together and bled together. You know me! I've no argument with my clan or its leaders, no argument with anyone, fer that matter. And I've no proof of any world outside this Shadow." He dropped his head, then lifted it again, and the look in his eyes was a look of unutterable weariness. In that moment, he looked much older than his years. "But I grow weary, weary o' the winters and the darkness, weary of hunting and being hunted, weary of watching my men die. I don't know whether I'm tired of fighting or whether I haven't fought hard enough. I only know that if there's any hope, any hope at all, of something more than this, I'd risk everything ta find it."

"Would ya risk *our* lives in such a quest? Our *families'* lives?" one man asked, the fear in his voice so thick that it spread like a contagion through the room.

"A fair question," the stranger said. "Would you risk the lives of these good men and their families because *you* haven't the strength to endure? These people are prosperous and comfortable. Would you have them give up their homes and their work and all they've ever known so that you might ease your weariness?"

Evander feared the effect of the man's words, feared his very presence, in fact. But a strange thing happened. Though a few men nodded agreement with the stranger, most did not. They were quiet, and many wrestled with the words "prosperous" and "comfortable." It was true that most of the craftsmen were considered wealthy by Shiloh's standards, but even the wealthiest among them understood something of heartache and loss. Some of them began to think that the comforts of colored lanterns and fine wool were rather a small thing, really. Cole would have given every scrap of edanna he'd ever touched to have Honour back. And Errol, as his time grew shorter, sometimes wondered what all his work had been for.

The poorest men in the room understood Evander's weariness only too well. And they could not, in a thousand years, accuse Evander of self-indulgence or indifference to the needs of his people.

No one noticed when the stranger left. No one noticed when Cormac followed him. After a time, Lorne broke the silence.

"They should hear the song, Evander, the one about the mountains."

He felt a fool, starting up a song before this grim assembly, but perhaps Lorne was right. Maybe the song was the only way to reach them. Evander began:

"Another day has died
The faded light now deeper fading
And still I watch the sky
Watch in sorrow, hoping, waiting

The endless mountains rise
Through seas of snow and cold winds wailing
And I would scale the heights
Ta find a warmth, a light unfailing"

Lorne joined in the song, then Chase. Lachlan pulled his pipe from his belt and played. Evander took heart.

"The Shadow covers all
This smoth'ring dark my nearest brother
What hope fer bright ones born
Who seek the bosom of another?

Another day has died
Another night descends, unyielding
No strength ta watch the skies
The breathless dark too heavy lies
In hope, I close my weary eyes
My fragile torch and lantern wielding."

Some of the men watched their feet when the song was over. Some watched Evander. Some wept.

"What of Ulff?" It was Reed who posed the question. Only one as young and impetuous as Reed could have been so bold. Of course, he wasn't supposed to be there at all, but that mattered little now. "If there's some realm outside Ulff's realm," he continued, "would 'e not be jealous of 'is captives?"

Evander was struck by the simple wisdom of it.

"Aye," he said. "It seems 'e would." Evander surveyed the assembly. "The risk is great, maybe too great. But I ask nothing of you now, only that ya think on it."

No one spoke, so Evander closed the meeting and dismissed them. The visitors from Fleete left quickly, along with many of the craftsmen. The others drifted out one by one, after offering Evander their support. Nolan excused himself and went to bed. Only Cole was left.

"Do ya wish ta die?" Cole asked.

Evander's brows rose. His mouth fell open. "No, truly. I've no wish ta die."

"Yer actions suggest otherwise," Cole said. "And yer words."

Evander waited.

Cole studied him. "I can't make up my mind whether you're a bit mad or whether the gods smile on ya. You take a very great risk in raising the hopes o' these people."

Evander felt intensely uncomfortable. He was sweating. He couldn't recall ever having such a reaction to any man.

"But ya have my respect, and my daughter's as well, it seems. Though I know it's not done as such, you've my permission ta marry Valour."

Evander was stunned, speechless. He'd only just finished arguing absurdities and impossibilities with a room full of hardened men. Now, he could find no words, none to explain himself, none to express his surprise, none to thank this man for offering his most priceless treasure. He took Cole's arm when it was offered, but that was all he could manage.

Twenty

Mina couldn't sit at home while the men talked of the sun and the future of their clan. She crept through the darkness outside the circle of light cast by the torches and fires and lanterns of Holt, and melted against the eastern wall of Nolan's cottage, near a window. The words were muffled, but she could distinguish tones of voice, and sometimes the source of a voice. She saw no one come or go. When the winds changed and the mountains echoed with thunder, as though a fearsome storm was blowing in, she did not know why. She could only listen, and tremble.

She heard Evander sing. Mina closed her eyes against the naked longing in his voice and gripped the rough stones of the cottage wall. How she ached for him! How she yearned for a country where no lovely thing was ever touched by Shadow!

There was no sense in what she did next. If her thoughts had been clear and ordered as they once were, Mina would never have done it. She waited until Evander's song was done and the men had dispersed. She waited until the house was silent, the candles and lanterns snuffed out. She waited several moments more. Then she cut through the shadowy pall of Market Circle, wound her way down toward the Cutting, and knocked on Valour's door.

Valour opened the door and stared. It was almost laughable the way her face changed, shifting from one expression to the next, one emotion to another. Mina saw surprise and disappointment, embarrassment and delight. *Why did I come here?* she wondered.

Valour spoke at last. "Come in!"

Cole and Ada were sitting at the table, their faces unreadable. Mina realized that she must have stepped into the middle of something, a heated conversation, or a disagreement. She looked to Valour, uncertain.

"Not a good time fer visitors, is it?"

Valour looked her in the eye and appeared to come to a decision. "Da's given consent... fer Evander and me... ta marry." She fiddled with her tree charm, watching Mina a moment before hurrying on. "It's not the way o' things, of course, and I haven't mentioned it, I know. It's only, well, I've only just realized... I..." Valour looked at her parents, at Mina. "Come," she said, taking Mina's hand and leading her out the back of the cottage to Cole's workshop.

Why did I come here? Mina wondered, frantic. *Why here? Of all the places to go!* She used the few hurried steps toward the workshop to regain control. It was only right, she told herself, only right that the best man in the village, the best man in Shiloh, should love the rarest beauty among them. It was right, and good, and she would rejoice with them. Somewhere in the depths of her, she held a dagger to her trembling heart and commanded it to rejoice with them.

It took all her strength of will to sit beside Valour and listen as she poured out every detail of her encounters with Evander, every nuance of her feelings toward him, every tender word he'd spoken to her. When Valour finally paused, Mina felt battered.

"I'm selfish and ridiculous, Mina. Fergive me. I've not given you a single breath in which ta speak! Have ya come from home? Did Chase say anything about the meeting? How I wish I could've gone ta hear Evander speak. He has such a way about 'im, doesn't 'e?"

"It went well enough," Mina answered, avoiding the details of how she'd gained such knowledge. "Some o' the men are beginning ta hear 'im, I think."

Valour shook her head in wonder. "The things 'e says! He's no end of ideas and thoughts and questions. He's no ordinary hunter." She leaned in and grasped Mina's knee. "He could well become Father o' the clan one day. Just think of it!"

Mina pulled away from Valour, confused. "He's no ambition ta be Father o' the clan, Valour. Haven't ya heard what he's been saying, about the sun?"

"Of course, I've heard 'im, Mina. His words are beautiful, powerful. Our people will love 'im fer 'is words, remember 'im by them."

Mina studied Valour, her eyes narrowed. How many hours had she spent in Valour's company? How many words, how many secret things had passed between them? But it was as if she spoke to a stranger, as if she'd never known Valour at all. "Evander doesn't speak ta gain the favor or the love of 'is people. That's not what 'e seeks. Evander seeks a better world, and he'll risk anything ta find it."

Valour shook her head. "Not anything, Mina. He wouldn't risk losing 'is wife. He loves me. And he's not mad enough ta try and cross the Pallid Peaks or set out inta the Black Mountains. Such a thing has never been done. Never!"

"How can we be certain?" Mina asked.

"We'd know, Mina! Some story or other would've drifted down to us —"

"What o' the stories we've already heard?"

"They're not the same . . ." Valour stopped, leaned back in her chair, sighed. "I don't understand. Are ya angry with me?" She did not ask if Mina was jealous, but Mina felt the thought, hanging between them.

"What if you're wrong, Valour?" she asked. "What if Evander does mean ta do this thing?"

Valour looked at the floor and shrugged. "Then he's mad."

Mina stood. "How can ya say that? How can ya love 'im and not believe in 'im?" She went to the outer door, avoiding Cole and Ada. She had no strength for farewells. "If Evander chose ta brave the Peaks this very night, I'd follow 'im." She watched Valour's eyes grow wide with shock and hurt.

"Then you're as mad as Evander," Valour said, and Mina disappeared into the shadows.

Knox couldn't remember a time when he'd been in such a foul mood, and two jugs of ale had done nothing to improve him. Last night he'd listened as Evander spoke of weariness, and he'd seen the effect of Evander's words on the men of Holt. He had the highest respect for Evander. He wanted to cheer him on like Chase and Lorne and Lachlan did. But he couldn't. He hurled pebbles into the pool with wicked speed and force, wishing the activity would ease and distract him, wishing he could find some release for his fury. But it was bound tightly round him, like a skin, and no amount of drink or violence could tear it free.

After a time, he stood to go, looping a finger through each of the empty jugs and heading up the hill. He'd taken only a few steps when a sound stopped him cold. It was a long, rising howl. Knox shivered, sweeping his torch back toward the east. He listened. The bog was full of sounds, of the deep, forlorn croaking of toads and the strange cries of unknown birds, of the slithering and squelching of slippery things in the sodden ground, of the shrieks and wails of other things for which the people of Shiloh had no names. But even the most frightful of these were familiar sounds to Knox. It was the keening howl of the wolf that gave him pause, that made him grip his torch too tightly, made his heart beat too quickly. He hated himself for being afraid.

Of course, he'd had plenty to drink. Perhaps his mind was as sodden as the bog. He turned back toward the village as a flash of gray appeared to his left. His torch followed the movement, casting light and shadow over a small figure running out of the bog.

"Wait!" he called. The gray-clad figure slowed not at all. He ran after it.

It must be a child, he thought as he ran. It was very small, but for all that, it was also very fast. Knox cursed the drink that had done nothing to ease his anger and nothing to speed his pursuit. On the edge of the village, in the shifting shadows cast by the torch outside the first cottage on the eastern edge of Holt, Knox caught her.

"Grey?!" he said, as he took her by the shoulders. She struggled against him at first, her eyes full of terror, until she recognized his face and gradually calmed.

"What in all this cursed dark were ya doing in the bog?!"

She took a shuddering breath and began to cry.

Knox knelt on one knee and seated her on his thigh, doing his best to comfort her with an occasional, "Now then," or "Ya musn't cry." When she'd calmed enough to speak, she rested her head against his chest and whispered.

"I like ta go exploring, sometimes. I grow tired o' the cottage, with Maeve always weeping and hovering and embroidering and humming strange, mad songs. Sometimes I can hardly bear it."

Knox nodded understanding, trying to imagine how long he would last in Grey's place. He threw in another "Now then," for good measure before Grey continued.

"I've been ta the Fayrewood, ta the furnace, and all through the village, but I wanted ta see the pool. I've heard about the black water that seeps in from Lake Morrison, and I wanted ta see it.

But I got lost, and …" Here, she choked back a sob. "… There was a wolf."

Knox looked down at her, lifting her chin so he could see into her great, red-rimmed eyes. "You heard it, too? A wolf?"

"I saw it."

"So near the village? Are ya sure, Grey?"

"Aye."

"And there was only one?"

"I think so."

Knox nodded and let go of her chin. It hadn't been the drink after all. There was one wolf, at least, hunting near Holt. It had happened before, in his father's time, packs attacking the village. But the hunters had organized, taken precautions, trained the women to use bows and arrows. The packs hadn't returned in a generation.

Knox rubbed the back of his neck, then ran his hand over his hair and forehead, down to his temples. He sighed. He had heard only one, and that was all Grey had seen. One wolf was not a significant threat. But if something was happening, if Holt had drawn the attention of the Shadow, and the forces of the dark were beginning to come against them, there was only one man who could possibly be responsible. Knox gritted his teeth and set Grey on her feet. He grabbed his torch and his empty jugs, his ears ringing with the cries of wolves and the voices of his dead brothers.

"I'll take ya home."

"Thank the gods!" Evander said, as Knox and Grey came in. Grey rushed to Evander and wrapped her arms around him. He buried his face in her wild hair, collecting himself, before setting her down in her chair by the fire.

"Grey, you've got ta stop this! I scoured the village and the

Fayrewood. It's thick dark now. Where have ya been?!" He looked toward Knox. "Where have *you* been? How did ya find 'er?"

Knox didn't answer, and Evander knew his friend well enough to see that he was fuming over something. The question was, what? Finally, Knox tossed the question to the child. "Tell 'im, Grey."

"I wanted ta see the bog," she said, her eyes very large and her voice very small, "and the black water from the lake." She paused, looking to Knox for permission to go on. He gave it. "And there was a wolf."

"So near?!" Evander asked Knox. "Did ya see it?"

"Heard it."

"Did *you*, Grey?" He squatted down in front of her and gripped the arms of her chair. "How did ya get away?! Wild, mad little slip of a child, ya risk too much!"

"Does she?" Knox asked. His tone snatched Evander's attention from Grey.

"Aye," Evander said, rising to face his seething friend.

"Where do ya suppose she learned such a thing?"

Evander shook his head. "You're full of ale, Knox. Go home."

"No! Not until I've spoken."

Evander waited while Knox chose a place to begin.

"I don't care if every other man in Shiloh falls under yer spell, Evander. It's madness, and ya must know it. It's one thing ta risk yer own mind, yer own heart, yer own life, but ta lead others ta their deaths, men who might've eked out a few more decent years with their families. It's *you* that risks too much."

"Not a man has been lost, Knox. Not a one of us has stepped inta the mountains."

"And yet we've still caught the eye o' the Shadow. Did ya hear what Grey said? A wolf in the bog . . ."

Evander dropped his head and sighed heavily. "I'll have ta see about it." He looked at Knox. "I don't like it, but so long as it's only one —"

"One is enough. It's just the beginning, Evander. Like ya said, no one has stepped inta the mountains yet. But more will come. I'm sure of it."

"I'll never understand ya, Knox. You'd risk yer life on a hunt, abandon all caution ta make a kill. You'd ride straight up ta the falls on a whim, just begging the dragons ta come out and play. But I've never seen a man so afraid."

Knox punched him, and Evander stumbled back, dazed. He'd hardly gotten his feet before Knox came at him again, his fist flying. In the last second, Evander caught his arm and twisted, bringing his own fist up under Knox's chin and propelling him backward into the table. Evander heard the jolting crack of Knox's skull against the sturdy wood.

Knox groaned and lifted himself painfully, taking extra care to see that his feet were beneath him and steady. One hand touched the back of his head and Knox winced and swore.

"I'm sorry, Knox," Evander said. "You're in no state ta talk tonight. I shouldn't have let it go so far."

Knox flashed him a look of loathing and love and humiliation and grief, and left. For the moment, at least, he was emptied of his fury.

Twenty-One

It was early autumn. The winds were fitful, coming sometimes from the west and sometimes the north. On some mornings, the hillside was dusted with frost. The leaves of the Fayrewood were a mingled green and gold. Mina caught their distant luster as she stood in Market Circle with the villagers. At the head of the group, facing the crowd, Nolan stood. In front of him, their hands clasped and their faces luminous, were Evander and Valour.

The ceremony was unusual. Marriages were not much celebrated in Shiloh. But all of Holt knew that Cole wouldn't allow his daughter's union to be marked by so little as a branch of belladonna nailed to a doorpost. Cole had spread a small banquet for the villagers, and he'd paid Lachlan and a few other musicians to play while the people danced.

Mina shifted her weight and abandoned all attempts to listen to Nolan's speech. By the look of the fidgety crowd, he'd lost everyone when he launched into some obscure account of Grosvenor's marriage. Mina decided to make use of the time. She'd spent the days since her argument with Valour practicing, retreating from the noise around her and the chaos of her heart into the quiet of her mind. She'd known this day would come, so she'd set about regaining control.

She's lovelier even than the Fayrewood today. It was the first thought that presented itself as Mina watched Valour. Her red hair was arranged so beautifully. There were tiny, thin braids tucked into larger braids and flowers woven throughout. Her shift was embroidered with threads of every imaginable color. Though the sign of their clan was a white tree, it was almost never represented as such. It was quite the reverse on Valour's shift, with bright leaves and flowers, birds and branches, roots and vines spreading over snow-white fabric. Mina sighed, touching the tiny embroidered tree on the neckline of her own shift. It was brown. Her shift was gray. It was a finer weave than the one she usually wore, but still, it was nothing to Valour's.

That's as it should be, she thought. She was plain, with brown hair and eyes, and her shift suited her. Valour was remarkable, and her beauty deserved the compliment of the richly colored shift.

I love her still. Mina resisted this thought at first. She hadn't spoken to Valour since the argument, and she couldn't shake the feeling that she'd been somehow betrayed. She'd thought she'd known Valour, and she hadn't. And yet, she couldn't help loving her. Mina loved Valour for her love of the Fayrewood, for the hours they'd spent with their legs dangling over the side of her branch, listening. She loved her for her beauty, her candor, her easy chatter, for the innocent light that had shone in her eyes when she showed Mina her panes of colored glass.

But I fear for Evander. The argument had left Mina with a sense of dread, as though she'd swallowed a stone and it still rolled around in her belly. If she didn't know Valour, Evander surely didn't. What would he say when he discovered that he and his lovely wife sought two very different things?

All through Nolan's address, Mina had avoided looking at Evander directly. Even on the edge of her vision, he was so strong, so radiant. Finally, she looked. She drank in the sight of him. Inside, she was hollow, aching. The winds tore through her without mercy. Her eyes were hot and scratchy with unshed tears.

I love him still. I'll love him always. It couldn't be helped. She would love Evander as she loved the leaves of the Fayrewood, as she loved the thundering grace of the Fell horses as they rode into the hills. Mina could love those things fully without the smallest hope of possessing them. It would be enough. It had to be.

There was silence when Nolan finished speaking. He lifted a lantern from the ground near his feet and lit it, raising it over the heads of the couple. Gasps of wonder and little cries of delight rose from the crowd. This was Cole's prize lantern. It swung gently on its hinge, sending out shafts of green and gold and amethyst light. It was so bright, so alive. The lantern almost breathed. Mina kept her eyes fixed on it, on Cole's masterpiece fitted with Valour's glass, so that she would not see the kiss that was happening beneath it.

The rush of the wind changed to a focused, pulsing beat. A roar broke over the assembly, and Nolan cried out as a great, black talon scraped along his forearm and slid into the ring at the top of the lantern. The dragon rose, billowing blue flame, then turned and wheeled back toward the Pallid Peaks.

Another dragon descended. The torch fixed to Nolan's roof caught fire, and the crowd dissolved, men running to retrieve their weapons, women herding children to safety. But the dragon seemed intent on leaving no place of refuge for the villagers. It wheeled over Holt, plummeting in among the panicked people, careening into the corners of cottages and sending roof tiles crashing to the ground.

The cries and screams, the reek of the beast, the heat and smoke from spreading dragon fire hardly came into Mina's mind. She stood very still, watching as the Fayrewood lantern moved slowly toward the Peaks, clutched in the talons of the dragon. She watched as it shrank to a tiny point of light. She watched as it was swallowed by mountains and Shadow.

Mina realized that she was alone. Market Circle was abandoned. She stood near the wall of a cottage, beside a pile of firewood. In the rush, she must have been overlooked, forgotten. She walked over to the Cutting and wound her way through the workshops. No one saw her or spoke to her, and she failed to draw the dragon's attention. At home, she opened one of the trunks against the wall and pulled out her winter coat, her father's dagger, and an extra pair of wool socks. From shelves and baskets, she took a water skin and some cheese, some potatoes and a few berry cakes, some string and a leather cord. She strapped on her belt and tucked the smaller items into the pouches. The rest she shoved into a wool sack. Then she took her brother's quiver, full of new arrows for the next hunt, and his bow, and slung both over her shoulder. She wondered vaguely why Chase had not come back for them. She thought of Reed, for a moment, and her father and mother. But their faces were indistinct. What she saw clearly was Evander and Valour, the man she loved and the friend she loved, with the Fayrewood lantern suspended above them.

So much lost. The dragons had come again. They'd stolen the loveliest lantern (Mina saw Valour's grin as she held up the golden pane) from the loveliest woman in Shiloh. They'd stolen a moment of perfect joy from a man who'd known too little of joy. What else would they steal before the night was over? Someone's helpless baby? Someone's son? Someone's wife?

Mina decided that the dragons had taken enough. And she was going to take something back.

It was simpler than she expected. One of the horses must have broken free from the stable. She found it running, agitated, on the western edge of the village. She whistled for the horse and took its bridle, shushing it and stroking its neck. It was a blue roan mare, saddled and ready to ride. Mina couldn't recall the identity of the horse's owner. She could only assume that he had intended to ride her and that she'd bolted in terror of the dragon.

Something nudged at the corners of her mind. *Light*, she thought. She stepped into one of the nearest workshops and took a few vats of tallow, a flint-and-iron, two torches, and an old lantern with smashed panes. She pulled herself onto the mare and set out. From behind her, far away, came the cries of the villagers and the shrieks of the dragon. Ahead lay darkness, and the distant roar of the falls, and the howling of the wind in the mountains.

It was the worst attack Holt had seen in many years. The dragon escaped, unhurt, and four villagers were lost. Nolan's daughter, Aster, was consumed in a blast of fire from the dragon's mouth. Nolan ran to defend her, but his dagger was no match for the dragon's claws. He fell beside his daughter, and Cormac wept over their bodies.

Jameson shielded his wife from the fury of the dragon, throwing himself between Tilly and the beast. He died in Tilly's arms. A little boy called Allan was sitting in his cot, trembling and terrified, when the dragon's tail smashed into the wall of his cottage. His small body was crushed by falling stones. A dozen cottages were at least partially destroyed, and the people fought fires late into the night.

All thoughts of celebration were forgotten. When the darkness thinned towards morning and the winds banished the smoke of the dragon's wrath, the men of Holt gathered. Their magistrate was dead, their village devastated. They were standing in Nolan's front room, waiting for direction, when Cole asked Evander what needed to be done.

"You'd put yerself under Evander's command, after *this* night?" Cormac said. His grief had given him a voice at last. His face was smeared with dirt and stained with tears. He had a wild, unbalanced look about him. No one answered.

"This wasn't like any attack I've ever seen," Cormac continued in a quavering voice. "That dragon came with a purpose."

"They always come with a purpose," Lachlan said.

Evander saw Knox's taut expression. He knew exactly what his friend was thinking, and he was grateful that Knox refrained from speaking his thoughts aloud. Better that Cormac did it.

"It was a warning, I tell you." He looked pointedly at Evander.

There was a pause. Every man in the room took Cormac's meaning. They'd all felt the focused cruelty of the dragon's attack. It had toyed with them, tormented them.

"How could it be a warning?" Lorne asked. "What do the dragons know of our doings?"

"Who can say what the creatures of Shadow know?" Cormac said. "Or what the Lord of Shadows bids them do?"

"But why?" Lachlan asked. "We've embarked on no journey, made no proclamation. What could we have done to invoke such a vicious attack?"

It was Evander who answered. "We've marked ourselves with the sign of a new clan. We've spoken openly of venturing out ta find the sun." He dropped his gaze to the floor. He felt the terrible weight of his words, the terrible price his people might pay for his choice. "If he's jealous of 'is captives, as Reed believes," Evander said, "there's no knowing what Ulff might do ta hinder us." He looked into Knox's eyes, acknowledging his friend's fears and his warnings. But instead of swelling at Evander's admission, Knox seemed to deflate. He looked tired, defeated.

"There's something else," Chase said. Evander hesitated to look at him. He knew what grief he would see in Chase's face, and he had little hope that Chase could forgive him if he was at all responsible for the loss of his father. He needn't have worried, yet. Chase was staring at the floor between his boots. "Mina's missing."

"Yer sister?" Evander asked.

Chase nodded.

"Have all the cottages been searched?"

Chase nodded again.

"Has anyone else gone missing?"

"Haven't yet found my blue roan," Lorne said.

"Some things had been taken from the cottage," Chase added. "My bow and quiver, namely, but also a coat —"

"Could she have set out fer Fleete?" Evander asked. "Perhaps she thought it wasn't safe . . ."

His knuckles grazed the scar under his chin. He tried to draw his focus back to the immediate needs of the villagers. "Chase," he said, "we'll look into it. In the meantime, there's work ta be done." He set most of the men to the task of repairing the damaged cottages, for winter was fast approaching. Others were assigned to build pyres for the dead.

But Evander was unsure of how to address the matter of the missing girl.

"You've searched the Fayrewood?" Evander asked Chase, when the others had set about their appointed tasks.

"Aye," he replied. "And Reed as well."

"Valour should go. She's been there with Mina many times, I believe. She may prove some help in the search." Chase nodded.

"In the meantime, I'll send Lachlan ta Fleete. It's likely she's there, Chase. Any number o' things could've sent 'er in that direction."

He gave Evander a penetrating look. "Ya don't know Mina."

Evander put a hand on Chase's shoulder. "Lachlan will ride fast. We'll soon have word."

"Not both o' them in the same night, surely," Chase said. "Not Da and Mina both, surely."

Evander ached for him. In a few hours, Chase would watch his father's body burn, and there would be no time for him to rest and grieve. There was too much to be done. Evander closed his eyes, utterly lost for words of comfort. He pulled Chase into an embrace and let the boy cry on his shoulder for as long as his pride would allow.

Before long, Chase pulled away, wiping his eyes.

"I'll send Valour ta the Fayrewood within the hour," Evander said.

They walked out together without noticing Cormac, who sat in a chair near the front of the room in mute astonishment and rage. *He'd* lost his father and his sister in the same night. *Both* in the same night. What's more, he was the new magistrate, and no one had seen fit to mention it. Men who stood in firm opposition to Evander's ideas about the sun had rallied behind him in the moment of crisis. Cormac might just as well have kept his mouth shut, for all his words had accomplished. His words mattered not at all. He could have fallen beside Nolan and Aster, and it would have made no difference, for, magistrate or no, it was Evander who led the people of Holt.

Twenty-Two

The blue roan stayed with Mina as she waited out the night under cover of the falls. Inside the rush of water, there was a kind of stillness, and Mina was dozing when the dragon that had wreaked havoc in Holt wheeled over the falls and returned to its mountain lair.

She woke in a panic, the mad, incomprehensible, reckless, senseless thing she was doing finally settling over her. But the trials of recent days had strengthened Mina, and she was coming back to herself. She retreated from the paralyzing dread into the quiet of her mind. She breathed. She closed her eyes and breathed again. Her first thought? *I can't climb with all this gear.*

She spread her coat over the damp ground and emptied the wool sack, repacking it with the food, the socks, the cord, and the tallow. She tied the string at the top of the sack and laid it beside the smashed lantern and the quiver. She closed the coat around them and rolled it up, looping it through the handle of the bow. Then she tied the bundle with string and strapped it to her back. The flint-and-iron and the dagger stayed close at hand in the pouches on her belt. She filled her water skin and tied it to her belt. The blue roan waited all this time. Mina hoped the lovely mare would reach Holt unharmed. She spoke gentle words of thanks and farewell before slapping her rump and sending her off.

The mountains rose, gray and unyielding, until their peaks were lost in Shadow. But behind the falls, a crumbling ledge wound up and out of sight. Mina made for the ledge.

It was a steep, scrambling climb, but it was not so very different from climbing trees in the Fayrewood. She just had to be sure of her balance and her footing (her boots were ideal for the task), and she had to be sure of the integrity of whatever she used to pull herself up. Slippery rocks were no better than thin, brittle branches. But if she was careful, if she was patient, if she trusted that another path to the top would always present itself, she could scale the southernmost wall of the Pallid Peaks. Mina took heart.

Near the end of her ascent, there was a bit of an overhang, and Mina had to work around it. She found handholds and footholds to the left of the ledge, and these she took one by one, never allowing her thoughts to rest on the force of the winds that tugged at the bundle on her back and whipped her hair into knots. She was red-faced and puffing when at last she hoisted herself over the ledge. To her left, the water plunged over the cliff, crashing into the pool below and cutting its way toward Holt. She peered over the falls, catching her breath at the sight of the sheer drop and the birds that circled over the rising mist. *It wouldn't do to drown now*, she thought, *not after such a climb.* She backed away from the falls and took a steadying breath before turning and crying out in astonishment.

To the north, an enormous lake filled the valley between mountain slopes. The lake was silver-grey, its edges foamy white, and green-tinged fir trees surrounded it. Mina had half expected the interior of the mountains to be charred and barren. It was, after all, the home of the dragons. But whatever lurked in other corners of the Pallid Peaks, this place, at least, was beautiful. Clouds of fog and mist rolled over the water, but the Shadow did not settle down among the mountains. Mina smiled to herself as she imagined the Shadow, like fabric, catching and snagging on the sharp points of the Peaks. *Perhaps one day the whole thing will tear away,* she thought.

Evander's song came to mind. She'd heard Chase sing it while he sat in the cottage fashioning arrows. She couldn't recall the words, but she thought one of the verses spoke of the mountains. It seemed the right song to journey by. She set out for the lake humming.

Valour was miserable. Her white shift was smeared with mud and soot. Her hair stank of smoke and sweat, the frayed ends of her braids falling into her face as she picked her way through the wood.

Everything had gone wrong. The dragon had taken her lantern, or Evander's lantern. It was Evander's now, and she was his wife, though all thought of their union had been forgotten in the aftermath of the attack.

She'd hardly seen him since their kiss. She hated that so many tasks, so many people vied for Evander's attention. She hated herself for resenting the people of Holt in their genuine need. Four were dead, and the lanes of the village were filled with rubble and the charred fragments of now-unrecognizable possessions. And Mina was gone.

"Mina!" Valour called her name as she scoured the wood, knowing the search was vain. Mina would not hide in the Fayrewood while her people suffered. If she were injured, she would know what to do. Mina always knew what to do. If Chase and Reed failed to find her here, then Mina was not in the wood. Valour doubted that Lachlan would find her in Fleete, either. It was not like Mina to run. Valour had seen her hide, blend in, disappear. But she'd never seen her run.

Valour climbed into Mina's tree, laid back against Mina's branch, and allowed the endless motion of the leaves to calm her.

She knew Mina thought her false for marrying Evander when she did not share his vision. It had never occurred to Valour that Evander might act on his grand words. In private moments, alone with her thoughts, she imagined him leading Holt, or perhaps leading the clan. But if Evander had no such ambitions, if he truly believed in a world beyond the Shadow and a great light called the sun, Valour was cruel to hide her doubts. Mina had known it. Mina had stood with Evander. Her words still rang in Valour's ears. "I'd follow 'im," she'd said. And Valour had called her mad.

The worst of it was that Mina's words cast a strange light over her disappearance. Valour went through every detail again and again. She always ended up at the same conclusion before dismissing it as impossible, unthinkable. If Mina would follow Evander in his quest for the sun, then Mina was willing to brave the mountains. And if Mina had packed food and weapons, a water skin and coat, and taken a horse out of Holt, she had not fled the village in terror. Mina had set out on a quest of her own.

Valour's tears flowed into her matted hair until she was weary beyond crying. When she left the Fayrewood, she went first to Mina's cottage. She told Tilly and Reed and Chase of her fruitless search and watched her words steal the anxious hope from their faces. Then she went home and took a clean shift from her trunk and headed for the Cutting.

Evander was relieved when he reached the cottage. Cole and Ada were on their way out the door, taking food to Cormac and his mother. They assured him that they'd be gone for most of the evening and told him Valour was bathing in the stream. He thanked them, stepped inside, and waited for his wife.

Nothing had gone as planned. He felt that he had failed Valour, though he couldn't pinpoint how. He hoped that the extraordinary lantern, and not his words, had summoned the dragons. But either way, the day of his marriage would always be remembered with grief instead of joy. And he'd hardly seen his wife since their kiss. She'd been waiting for him after this morning's meeting, and it had taken all his strength to send her away again to search the wood for Mina. If only he and Valour could have a cottage of their own. But Evander could not leave Maeve and Grey to fend for themselves. Grey had reluctantly agreed to move into the back room with Maeve, and Evander and Valour were to have the front room. A curtain had been hung in the adjoining doorway. Evander sighed and jabbed at the fire with an iron poker. He wanted to give her so much more.

Now, at last, and beyond his wildest hope, he would have a few hours alone with his wife. He sat down at the table, then rose and paced again. The wait was maddening.

She came through the door, and her hair was wet. It fell over her shoulders in strands of deep, crimson red. Her cheeks were flushed, and she fumbled with the latch as she closed the door behind her. Her soiled coming-of-age shift hung over her arm. The one she wore now was grey, and unadorned.

"It makes no difference," Evander said aloud.

Valour pulled back toward the door. "What?"

Evander closed his eyes, shook his head in frustration. He didn't want to spoil this. "I meant . . . it makes no difference what ya wear." He searched for the words. "You're so lovely."

Valour's expression changed. The color in her face deepened. She took a tentative step forward and hung her filthy shift over the back of a chair.

"Nothing's gone as it should, Valour, my love. Fergive me."

"It was none of yer doing. The dragons came, and that's all." She lowered her eyes, took a breath, and rushed ahead. "I'm sorry I couldn't do more. I wish I could be some use ta these people, but it seems all I can do is envy them."

"Envy?" he asked.

When she raised her eyes to him, she looked uncertain, almost shy. "You've seen nothing but them, since the dragons came."

One of the logs on the hearth fire split and settled down into the embers with a sigh. Evander covered the space between them in two long strides. He had surprised himself, during the Dance of the Lantern Light, when he wiped the tears from Valour's face. The depth of his longing had frightened him. It was infinitely more so now. Valour's beauty awakened his every desire. He wanted her so desperately.

He offered a hasty prayer, to whichever of the gods might be listening, that he would not hurt her. And then, he let himself go.

Twenty-Three

They found the blue roan the next morning. It was standing outside the stable, drinking from the stream, as though nothing in particular had happened. Lorne breathed his relief and patted her neck and led her to her stall.

When Lachlan returned from Fleete, he met with Evander and Valour in Mina's cottage.

"They saw nothing of 'er? Nothing at all?" Evander asked.

Lachlan shrugged. He had already answered the question, though it was clear to everyone why Evander pressed him. Tilly and the boys were desperate for word of her. The appearance of the horse had not encouraged them.

"Perhaps the horse means nothing. She could be here still . . ." He stopped before laying out the gruesome possibilities. She could have gone too near the Turn. She could have encountered the wolf that was prowling near the pool. She could be pinned beneath one of the piles of rubble scattered around the village. Evander rubbed his eyes.

"You're forgetting the food that was missing, the weapons, the coat," Chase said. "Mina knew what she was doing and where she was going."

"I think she went after the lantern," Valour said, her voice small in the crowded room.

Tilly groaned and shut her eyes, allowing her head to fall back onto her chair. Chase nodded to Valour. "Aye. It's what I've been thinking."

Evander turned to his wife. "Ya think she went inta the Peaks, fer a *lantern*?"

"Fer *my* lantern," Valour said. "And yours." An odd look came over Valour's face, as if some new thought had come to her, as if she suddenly understood something.

"What is it?" Evander asked.

She shook her head and gave Chase a pained look and said nothing.

"It's like 'er," Chase said.

"How so?" Evander asked.

"She's tough," Reed replied.

"Stubborn," Valour added, "determined, strong, skilled. She knows every plant in the Fayrewood and its use."

"I taught 'er ta ride and shoot myself," Chase said.

"If Mina went alone inta the Pallid Peaks," Evander broke in, "what good will riding and shooting do 'er? She's lost to us."

The room went very still until Reed said, "You didn't see 'er charge the dragon."

Chase stood and spoke to Evander. "I'm going after her."

Tilly's eyes flew open.

"Ya can't, Chase," Evander said.

"Who are *you* ta say such a thing? Of course I'm going after her!"

Evander shook his head. "We'll not last half the winter on what we've caught this summer, Chase. All our families will starve if we don't set out again soon. We need you here."

Chase slumped back onto his seat. "You'd risk anything in

search o' the sun, but nothing in search of Mina."

The words stung. Evander's voice, when he answered, betrayed his sorrow and regret. "There are no small risks now, Chase. I'm sorry." He couldn't look at Tilly and Reed as he took Valour's hand and stepped outside. Lachlan followed.

"Any other news from Fleete?" Evander asked, when the door was shut.

Lachlan hesitated.

"Tell me."

"The magistrate asked that I bring a message ta the people of Holt."

"Well?"

"He says anyone who'd wish to avoid Evander's fate is welcome in Fleete."

Evander sighed. "Anything else?"

"They say you're as mad as yer mother."

It was not what Evander wanted to hear before bringing his new wife home to his cottage for the first time.

He settled Valour in the front room. He'd cleared out a trunk for her things, and he encouraged her to use the table and shelves as she liked. She seemed relieved when he didn't invite her into the back room to visit Maeve.

He pushed the curtain aside and looked around for Grey. There was no sign of her, but that came as no surprise. Evander had given up trying to keep her in or near the cottage.

Maeve was in her chair, rocking and stitching. When Evander reached her, she looked up sharply, startled. Her eyes gradually focused on Evander, and she set her embroidery aside and pulled him down in front of her. He knelt in front of her chair, holding both her hands.

"They're coming, Evander. Ya mustn't go too far. They're close now."

Evander read the panic in her eyes, and he held her hands more tightly. "The dragons, Ma? Do ya mean the dragons are coming?" he asked.

"Aye, the dragons," she said. "And others as well." Her voice fell to a whisper. "They have eyes here, in the village. They know, and they're coming."

Evander remembered the wolf that Knox and Grey had seen. "Have ya seen the wolves in yer dreams, Ma? Is it wolf packs that are coming?"

Maeve dissolved into tears. She stroked the backs of Evander's hands with her thumbs. "Oh, my son, my son. Don't go. Please, don't go!"

Evander pulled her into his arms and held her while she cried. He stroked her hair, and, after a time, sang softly over her. It calmed her, and she fell asleep, and Evander placed her in her cot and covered her with blankets. He walked to the windowsill, thinking to sit in the chair by the window and clear his mind of his mother's words before he went back to his wife. But something stopped him cold, and he never reached the chair. The flowerpot rested in its usual place, but the velvet-black flowers were dry and shriveled. They slumped over the edges of the pot on limp brown stems. The windowsill was spotted with drops of red. The bleeding flowers were dead.

Evander was shaken. His mother had hovered over those flowers for as long as he could remember, and this sudden change in her compulsive behavior jarred him. Was Maeve beyond hope? Was she lost forever in the world of her dreams? Or did her warnings bear some weight?

Surely not. What could threaten him so terribly, if not dragons or wolves? Who had eyes in the village? Perhaps his mother was speaking of Ulff. Evander shivered, and the fire guttered. *Enough of this*, he said to himself. He left his sleeping mother and the dead flowers and went to the front room, seeking comfort in Valour's arms.

Seeker

Mina didn't know whether the Pallid Peaks swarmed with ten thousand dragons or only ten. She didn't know if all of them occupied one massive lair, or if every cave housed a dragon of its own. She didn't know which dragon had taken the lantern, didn't want to think how the panes of colored glass might already lie smashed on some rocky crag deep in the mountains. What she did know was that the lake stretched far to the north, filling the valleys. There were moments when the mist and fog rolled away and she caught glimpses of it, its silver-grey waters disappearing only at the farthest limits of her vision.

She decided to follow the shoreline. Where new mountains burst up around the valley, there would be canyons and passes, and any of these she could take if she chose. But the lake would be her guide. If she could find the water, she could find her way home.

She had traveled a day and a night, skirting the edge of the lake, listening to the soft lapping of the water on her left as she climbed over ledges and scattered stones and picked her away among the trunks of the fir trees. The trees were covered in a shy fur of greenish moss, and the sound of the needles moving in the wind was so unusual to Mina that she often stopped to listen, trying to pick up their language. Until now, the Fayrewood trees were the only trees she'd thought much of. It was their lush motion, their rich colors that filled her mind. The fir trees were utterly unlike them, yet when she touched their trunks in passing or used their branches to pull herself over unstable piles of rock, she felt a sort of fondness for them. In this lonely country, they seemed like friends.

Passing the night was difficult. Mina had her flint-and-iron in her pouch, and she could easily have built a cheerful fire beneath the trees and made camp on a bed of fir needles. But she was afraid the light would draw the dragons.

She'd argued with herself at first, until she stepped out from the shelter of the trees and stood on the shore of the lake, looking up. Far off, flashes of blue fire appeared in the black sky. Mina held her breath, watching. When she was sure that none of the fires was coming any closer, she released it in a rush, and thanked the gods that she hadn't risked a fire of her own. She returned to her little camp under the trees, wrapping herself in her coat and leaning against a springy, moss-covered trunk. It wasn't as comfortable as her tree in the Fayrewood, but it would serve. She nibbled a little of her food and emptied her water skin and slept.

It was her back that woke her. It was cramped and stiff. Sometime during the night, the soft, mossy trunk had transformed into a lumpy iron rod. She groaned and pushed herself to a stand. Her hands and feet were stinging with cold. It took a bit of rubbing and stomping before they felt like they belonged to her. She cursed herself for forgetting her gloves. In Holt, it was early autumn, but in the Peaks it was nearly winter, and the cold might well prove a more formidable opponent than the dragons. She went out to the water, broke through the sheet of ice that crusted the shoreline, and refilled her water skin. Then she set off, northward again, along the eastern edge of the lake.

After a few hours of quiet travel, a dragon's roar pierced the sky overhead. Mina crouched behind a boulder as currents of foul air surged through the trees. She waited, her heart hammering against her chest. When another, more distant, roar told Mina that the dragon had passed her by, she leaned around the edge of the massive stone and looked toward the lake. The dragon was circling, the light of its eyes reflected on the surface of the water. It slowed, dove, and rose. Something dark and slimy wriggled in its talons, sending out sprays of glinting water droplets. Mina closed her eyes and slowed her breathing. She pushed all thought of the lake creature's fate from her mind.

When the dragon was gone, and the only sounds were the lapping of the water and the rushing of the wind, Mina continued her northward journey.

Twenty-Four

Every leaf in the Fayrewood was golden, but the people of Holt hardly noticed. The craftsmen were rebuilding walls and repairing roofs, and preparing for the last market days before the snows came. And the hunters were leaving.

Jameson's death had left his band short by one man. Such a thing was not uncommon, of course. Evander's band had been two men short for some time. But Reed had begged to be allowed to go in his father's place, and the hunters would have none of it. They knew the boy would be a danger to himself and every man in the group.

So when Jameson's men left Holt, very early, Reed was leaning against the door of his cottage, pitching bits of turf into the lane and looking forlorn. When Evander's men mounted their horses, nearly an hour later, Reed stood in the same spot, his expression unchanged.

Evander rode up beside the boy. "Reed," he said. "I've a task fer ya, while we're gone. Are ya willing?"

Reed scowled at him. "If I'm too young and troublesome ta help on the hunt, what use could ya have fer me here?"

"I'll not play games with ya, Reed. Are ya willing or no?"

Reed considered. He gave a short nod. "Aye, I'm willing."

"No one's changed the torches. They were extinguished after the attack, but not replaced. The task should've been assigned already, but with everything, well, it slipped my mind. You'll need ta soak the cloths in tallow —"

"I know how ta make a torch," Reed interrupted.

Evander's brows rose. "Alright then. I leave it ta you. I'll expect ta see fresh torches when we return."

Reed nodded, and Evander rode out with his men.

Never in his life had Evander endured such a frustrating, disheartening hunt. It was not so much that the game wasn't there. His men could hear the thunder of hooves as herds moved in the distance. They could see the tracks, the droppings. But whenever they closed in on their prey, the wolves barred the way. Over and over, when the hunters advanced, the wolves cut them off. What little they caught served only to feed them. There was nothing left for their families, nothing to set aside for the winter.

After a third day of fruitless pursuit, the men camped on the southern edge of the foothills. They sat around the fire in an uneasy quiet, each with his own thoughts. Knox rubbed salve into a long gash on his arm and wrapped it with strips of cloth. Lachlan tried to play, but found he didn't have the heart for it. He put his pipe back into his belt after only a few notes.

Evander's thoughts hovered around Holt, and the women he'd left behind. Ever since Knox had seen the wolf near the pool, he had worried about leaving the village. The craftsmen had some skill with a bow and arrow, and most of the women, but it wouldn't be enough. If the packs moved in quickly, in great numbers, his people would be massacred. Evander was sure of it. He wished he knew where Grey was roaming that night, or if, by some miracle, she was actually tucked into her cot. He worried about Maeve's state of mind, for the image of the dead flowers still plagued him. And he thought of Valour. He'd asked Errol to keep a particular watch on her, and the old man had been thoroughly insulted that Evander would even consider the alternative. It was a foolish thing to do, of course, and unnecessary. Her parents would make sure she was well cared for. But Evander hadn't been able to help himself. He didn't like to be away from her.

He watched Chase, whose blank face was fixed on the campfire. It grieved Evander to think what Chase must be feeling. To lose his father was grief enough. To lose his sister in the same night . . .

For all his talk of bright worlds beyond the mountains, Evander had not the faintest hope that Mina would return. He'd envisioned his quest to find the sun as a series of bloody hunts. He and his men would face one enemy after another, whole hosts of enemies, perhaps. And if they survived, a new sun-lit country would be their reward. He didn't believe for an instant that one girl could journey into the Pallid Peaks and face the dragons and live to tell of it. He wished, for Chase's sake, that Mina had died in the attack. As it was, the cruel possibility of his sister's returning would torment him to the end of his days.

"Lorne," Evander said, seeking a distraction from his dismal thoughts, "I think we could use a tale tonight. What say you?"

Lorne nodded and thought for a moment. "My daughters like best ta hear about Linden and Callista and the birth o' the Fayrewood. My grandmother told me the tale when first she brought me ta the wood. Her mother had done the same, and so it had been fer generations. I still remember my first sight o' the trees in spring, the pink blossoms falling ta the ground like snow." Lorne smiled as he remembered. "Do ya know I only took my youngest this year? She's eight. First thing she did was ask me why I'd waited so long ta take 'er." He waved a hand, as if brushing this thought aside. Then he leaned back against his pack and gazed into the darkness above the campfire and began.

"My grandmother told me that Callista, the goddess of beauty, and Linden, the maker o' the trees, met together long ago. Callista wept, for winter snows had blanketed the world, and there were no flowers. Linden wept, too, for the winter winds had torn the leaves from the trees, and they looked barren and dead, and he grieved fer them. Linden and Callista longed ta put an end to winter, but even the gods were not given such power. So they sat and thought and planned. At last, Linden brightened.

"'Let us make a wood,' he said, 'that would grow in the coldest part o' Shiloh, right under the shadow o' the Pallid Peaks.'

"'The snows would still cover it in winter, and the winds tear away its leaves,' Callista replied.

"'True,' Linden said. 'But icicles would hang from the largest branches and clusters of ice crystals from the smallest, and the snow would carpet the ground.'

"Callista's eyes brightened as she began ta see what Linden saw. 'If this wood is lovely in winter, it must be something more wonderful in spring. When the weather warms, let the falling snowflakes become the falling petals of pink blossoms.'

"'In summer, let the wood spill over with life and beauty. The green o' the leaves will put ta shame the leaves of any other wood. The ground will be covered with flowers, and the trunks o' the trees with flowering vines,' Linden declared.

"Callista smiled. 'In autumn, the wood will blaze like embers, like lantern light, like the sun. Let the leaves be pure, unblemished gold.'

"Then the immortals chose the spot. It was a bitter corner o' the world, with the Peaks ta the north and the Black Mountains ta the east. It was a place most desperate fer beauty. So they stood, in one mind, in the center o' the valley. And the Fayrewood sprouted up around them. Seedlings grew ta saplings. Branches spread. Trunks thickened. Leaves unfurled and mosses crept and vines climbed and flowers opened, all in a moment's time. Then Linden and Callista smiled on their work, and the light o' their faces fell on the wood and lingered. And still the Fayrewood stands, lovely in all seasons, and even the winter cannot rob it of its beauty."

"You've added the line about the sun, Lorne," Evander said.

Lorne laughed. "Aye. Seemed fitting."

Chase spoke from the other side of the fire, surprising everyone. "What do ya suppose Hallam sees, and Alistair, now they're gone?" He spoke without bitterness. "Do they see the immortals? Or the sun?"

Knox rose and left the camp. Evander called out to him, knowing what a risk he took in stepping away from the fire, but Knox ignored him. And no one else had any answer for Chase. His question remained, suspended in the air around them, until they were too weary to wrestle with it anymore, and sleep took them.

Mina had crossed over the roots of three towering mountains. Where one ended and another began, the winds came barreling through the mountain passes. They rattled the needles of the fir trees and tossed Mina's hair as she picked her way along the shoreline. She had caught a rabbit and some sort of large bird she didn't recognize. Twice she'd risked fires. Her hunger had driven her to that. But Mina had built the fires under the thickest stands of trees, and, as soon as the fires caught, she'd all but smothered them, leaving just a low bed of crackling branches on which to cook her meat. The resulting meals were ashy and half-raw, but they sustained her. She'd even saved a few scraps for the journey ahead.

More precious than the food she'd caught, though, was the knowledge she'd gained. The people of Holt knew very little about the dragons. They didn't know what the dragons ate. They didn't know if the dragons worked together or kept to themselves. They didn't know if the dragons mated and produced offspring or if they were spawned by Ulff himself, or if the dragons lived for many hundreds of years, and those they saw had dwelt in the Peaks since the world began.

But Mina had learned much on her journey. She'd seen the dragons hunt and fish, and she knew they had a taste for the black serpentine creatures that lived in the lake. She knew that the dragons usually kept to themselves. She'd watched them hunt alone, fly alone, and she was almost certain she'd seen one enter a cave on a cliff overlooking the western side of the lake. It entered the cave alone, and though she kept her eyes trained for hours on the spot where it disappeared, she never saw any other creature come or go.

Mina had also discovered that dragons did not live forever. Along the edge of the water, on her third night in the Peaks, she'd stumbled upon a skeleton that could only have belonged to a dragon. It was a small comfort. Of course, it was still possible that the dragons lived through ages of men, still possible that some of Sirius's offspring inhabited the Peaks. She wondered, fleetingly, if the spawn of the infamous dragon would recognize a daughter of Grosvenor, if they would hunt her with special vengeance. But she banished that thought. It didn't serve her.

Her newfound knowledge was invaluable. If the dragons hunted for food, and if they lived alone, she might be able to enter a dragon's lair while it was away and find nothing within to threaten her. There was just the small detail of finding, among all this vast mountainous wilderness, the single lair in which the lantern was secreted. If the lantern remained in one piece, that is.

This is madness, she said to herself, and remembered the last words Valour had spoken to her. In this place, the words were a boon. Any comparison with Evander seemed to Mina a great compliment, and, now she thought of it, there was something unspeakably freeing about surrendering to madness. Besides, the mountain passes were calling. She stepped out from under the cover of the trees and cast a longing look at the silver-gray lake before filling her water skin and turning east.

The land rose as it moved toward the mountains, and the air grew colder. Mina was glad of her extra socks. She concentrated on the feel of the wool against her tired feet. It was the only thing to do in such a place, at such a time: focus on the nearest, clearest things. At any moment, the enemy could come, and things could go shatteringly awry. She could die. But Mina was masterful at focusing her mind on the immediate. One step, one breath, one thought. The sound of lapping water disappeared. The trees thinned. She liked the trees, liked the cool dark and the sound of the needles overhead, the spring of the needles under her boots. A bird sang in a high branch. She did not recognize its call.

Then the trees came to an abrupt end, and gray slopes rose to left and right. She hooked her thumbs through the straps on her shoulders and disappeared between the mountains.

While Evander was away, Valour spent as little time as possible in her new home. She could not quite bring herself to think of it as her cottage, or even hers and Evander's. It was so definitively Maeve's cottage. Even with the curtain drawn, Valour was unnerved by the power of the quiet presence in the back room. When she was not working with Errol or talking with her mother, she visited Moss or helped Emmeline with Fayre and True or walked in the Fayrewood. In the evenings, she went reluctantly home to prepare a meal for Maeve. She ate alone, cleaned up alone, and sat alone beside the fire. She climbed into her cot alone and lay awake wishing for Evander's return.

Grey might have been a comfort during those solitary evenings, for she listened to Valour and asked her many questions. But she vanished so often and stayed away so long. Valour never asked Grey where she went. She knew that Evander and Grey had settled the issue between them, and she trusted Evander's judgment. She knew also that the child was very wild. Keeping her locked in the cabin would do her no good.

Valour sat in front of the fire, fiddling with her charm. She wasn't sure if she wanted to curl up on her cot and cry herself out or run through the village screaming. As much as she disliked her new living arrangements, her parents' cottage no longer felt like home. She couldn't think where else to go. And she missed Mina, and tried not to think of her, and failed. Knowing that Mina had loved Evander only added to her suffering. When she thought how much Mina had given and how much she had taken from her, she could hardly breathe. She hadn't been to see Tilly or Reed, because she couldn't quite bring herself to visit Mina's cottage without her there. And Errol was at odds with her. She couldn't keep her mind on her work. She'd ruined half a dozen batches in as many days. And Evander was gone, and she longed for him.

A thought struck her with such force that she broke her charm from its edanna chain.

Nothing is going to change.

Mina, very likely, was lost to her. She thought of her last angry words to her friend and blinked away the tears that rose unbidden. And, much as she tried to avoid the fact, this cottage was her home. Maeve and Grey might well go on for many years doing exactly as they did now. And Evander would always be off hunting. She would always be wondering if he would walk over the hill with his men or if, one day, Rogue would crest the hill with Evander's body strapped to his back.

The cot, she decided. She would go to the cot and cry. But when she tried to stand, she found she could not. She covered her face with her hands, and wept.

"Valour."

She looked up and saw him, standing on the threshold, and her relief was so great, she hardly noticed the slump of his shoulders or the dull cast to his eyes. Evander was home, and, more than anything, Valour wanted him to take her into his arms and tell her that everything would be alright. She wanted him to tell her that all of this would change, that he would soon be Father of the Clan of the White Tree, and she could tinker with her glass, and their days would be quiet, and he would never leave again.

But when she saw his face, Valour stopped. His eyes had always been something like an old fire, with little sparks of light that illuminated the otherwise unremarkable brown. On this night, there were no sparks. There was no light at all. Valour sat in his chair and watched him as he leaned against the doorway. He didn't come in.

"I'm going ta the Fayrewood. Wanted ta let ya know I was home, and well."

He was not well. They had only just begun to know each other, but Valour could see that much. "Let me go with ya," she said.

"Not tonight, my love. Please. I just need . . ." He sighed and hung his head, as if an explanation required more strength than he could muster.

"Go," Valour said. "I'll wait fer ya." It was not what she wanted. She wanted him to hold her. She wanted his courage, his hope, to seep into her bones.

"Don't wait," he said, and looked at her. "Please. I . . . we may leave again tomorrow."

"So soon?" she said. "Was the hunt so bad?" Of course it was. It must have been for Evander to look as he did, act as he did.

"Sleep, love. I'll tend the fire when I get back." He stepped out into the night and shut the door behind him.

She listened, for a moment, to the ringing silence of the cottage. She left the chair and curled up on her cot and cried herself to sleep.

Twenty-Five

Evander spent most of the night on the familiar stone in the heart of the Fayrewood. Lorne's story had reminded him how much he missed the wood, how hungry he was for the peace he'd always found there. But when he arrived, he found no solace in the fluttering gold leaves that caught the light of his lantern and set it dancing. The beauty of the Fayrewood failed to move him, for his vision was clouded by fears and cares.

Riding home from the hunt, with Rogue's nose pointed toward his lovely young wife, he'd known something was wrong. His stomach had twisted in knots at the thought of returning to her. But why should that be? Evander could make no sense of it. Had they been married ten days? He tried to count them in his head and then abandoned the effort. Hallam had said it was good to have a wife to come home to, and it was. And he loved Valour, truly. Her presence and her beauty were a balm to him. Taking her into his arms again should have been a delight, a relief. So why this sense of dread? He explained the feeling away, blaming the unsuccessful hunt, his fatigue, Maeve's failing mind, the recent attack. But none of those things touched the heart of the matter. As Evander crossed the Cutting, a dreadful truth settled over him.

Valour could not satisfy all his longing. She was not enough.

He was afraid she would know his thoughts, that she would read them in his eyes. He couldn't stay with her in the cottage. Better he should clear his mind here in the wood. The rustling of the leaves and the rushing of the wind were beginning to have an effect. He leaned against the tree behind him and sighed.

He wondered what it would be like to be settled, to be content. Whatever it was he sought seemed always to pull away from him and vanish, like failing lantern light in the devouring dark. He wondered if he ought to embark on his quest to find the sun this very night. But he was afraid of the Turn, afraid of the wolves and dragons, afraid of what catastrophe awaited him, his family, his people, if he took such a risk. Yet he feared staying here in Holt. His restlessness only grew with the passing of time.

He thought, unaccountably, of the girl who'd ridden into the mountains alone.

"Mina," he said aloud.

It struck him how very alike the two of them were, he and Mina. He hadn't noticed before. He felt a sudden, piercing sorrow for the loss of one so brave, so mad. And he wondered if, when the time came, he could find the courage to do what she had done.

Mina was lost in the mountains. Whenever the word "lost" rose to her mind, she pushed it down vehemently. But it was true. She'd entered the pass behind the third mountain north of the falls, and several hours into her trek, she had reason to think she'd chosen well. A dragon wheeled into the narrow gorge and landed on a crag of rock high above. She heard the wings slow and stop, heard the scratching of great talons against stone, and saw pebbles fall to the ground. The dragon had returned to its cave.

For a moment, Mina's heart raced. This could be *the* dragon, and the lantern could be just overhead. She inspected the wall of rock to her right, but she couldn't find even the smallest foothold. She went further, beyond the place where the pebbles had fallen, searching for some path up the side of the mountain. There was none. So Mina was forced to go onward, deeper and deeper into the mountains.

The gorge she had entered, that single lane between peaks that could so easily lead her back to the lake, suddenly split into two paths. Mina had to choose, and she took the path to the left, the one that led north. This path climbed and turned many corners and intersected with other paths before heading steeply downhill. By nightfall, Mina had descended into a wooded valley. The lake was far behind her. When the dark grew so thick that she could hardly make out the trees that blocked her path she wrapped herself in her coat and lay down on the fir needles and slept.

In the morning Mina ate a little cold rabbit, her last scrap of potato, and a few crumbs of a dried berry cake. The water in her water skin was bitterly cold. It made her throat ache to drink it. She decided she had better wrap it inside her coat if she was to keep it from freezing.

She spent the next two days crossing the wooded valley. At night, dragons circled high above. Why they came together, she could not tell, but she watched as their fires wove in and out, over and around and through one another in some splendid and terrible design. When they broke from their dance, they spread out singly, moving toward every corner of the mountains, and disappearing into caves and gorges.

Mina had almost reached the northern end of the valley. She was straining ahead to see what lay beyond the trees when she stepped on an unstable bit of ground. Her foot twisted beneath her, and she fell forward, crying out. She knew before she hit the ground that her ankle was sprained. She'd done it as a child, before she'd learned how to climb a tree. She lay on the ground a moment, focusing. Then she pushed herself up on her hands and knees. She fought the urge to cry out again, hissing, instead, as she sucked air through her teeth. Scooting backward and leaning against a tree, she remembered what Moss had done for her when she was small. The apothecary had wrapped her ankle, tightly, and she'd given her tobacco leaves to chew for the pain.

Mina was certain there was wild tobacco growing somewhere in this wood. She'd seen it once or twice near the lake, and it must be here as well. But first, she took her dagger and cut a strip of cloth from the bottom of her shift. Wincing, she removed her boot and peeled away both socks. She gently probed the ankle, searching for the least painful spot, then held the end of the cloth with her thumb and wrapped the bandage as tightly as she could bear. She tied a small knot, pulled her socks and boot on, and rested against the tree a little longer. She pushed herself up, testing her weight on the ankle. Again, she hissed at the pain, at the clumsiness of her movements. She needed the tobacco.

Mina turned south, prepared to limp back into the wood in search of the plant. But it was no use. The valley had grown too dark. Mina could not distinguish the trunks of the trees from the heavy night that cloaked them. She slipped off her pack and set it on the ground. She leaned over and untied the cords, laid the bow aside, unrolled her coat, and removed the broken lantern. She hurriedly wrapped and tied the coat, returning it to her back.

Tobacco. It was the next thought, the needful one. But for a moment, it slipped from her grasp. Mina was exhausted. She could feel her ankle swelling, feel the painful pulsing of blood against the tight wrappings. Hunger gnawed at her. Her empty belly protested more with every day that passed. She sagged against a tree. Though she rarely gave herself permission, she let her mind drift, let it wander back to the place of its greatest delight.

Evander. She remembered his face, remembered his hands so capable and beautiful. She remembered the deep resonance of his voice as he sang to the men gathered in Nolan's front room. Her heart gave a little whimper. More than anything, she wanted Evander to have all that he desired. The thought gave her courage.

She pulled the flint-and-iron from her pouch and crouched over the broken lantern. She struck the pieces together. A spark caught, and the oiled wick flared with light. Mina held her breath, waiting for the wrath of the dragons to descend. Nothing. But for the circle of light cast by the lantern, the wood was black and still. She looped a finger through the hook at the top of the lantern and moved with as much speed and stealth as her swollen ankle would allow.

She'd just caught sight of a wilting tobacco plant when the dragon came. There was no roar, no fire, only the sudden, stunning pain of the dragon's claws clamping down on her shoulders and arms, and the hot reek of the beast, and the pulsing of its wing beats, and the clanking of scale on scale.

She was lifted above the trees. The rush of air from the dragon's wings snuffed out the lantern light. Then there was only darkness and wind and pain. Then new, shattering pain, and her face scraping against jagged stones. Then nothing.

Cormac and the blue-eyed stranger sat across the table from one another in Fleete's only inn. The stranger tossed a handful of coins on the table and invited Cormac to order what he liked. Cormac ordered cherry ale, the finest drink in Shiloh. He wanted the stranger to see him as a man of wealth and influence, as someone to be reckoned with. He sensed already that he wouldn't succeed.

"Didn't get yer name, after the meeting," Cormac began.

"Hadrian," the stranger said.

"You're from Fleete, then?"

"No."

"Ah, well." Cormac shifted in his chair. This man unnerved him. At first he thought it was the eyes. They were astonishingly blue, and cold. But Valour had blue eyes, and Maeve. He'd seen blue eyes before. No, it was something else. Cormac couldn't get any idea of the man's age, and he very much wanted to. Hadrian's hair was dark, his skin smooth. But he was certainly not young.

"You've yet to give your reason for asking me here," Hadrian said, his gaze falling full on Cormac.

"Fergive me," Cormac said. "As I told ya after the meeting in Holt, I don't stand with Evander. His notions about this 'sun' were madness ta begin with." Cormac's confidence grew as his loathing for Evander surfaced. "He toys with my people, and rather than reject 'im fer the traitor and fool that 'e is, they rally behind 'im. His madness *spreads* through the village. Something must be done."

Hadrian stared at him. He let the silence stretch before he asked, "Do you know how dangerous he is?"

Cormac opened his mouth to reply, but Hadrian spoke first. "You can't imagine how dangerous."

For one blissful breath, Cormac felt relieved, vindicated. At last, someone stood with him against Evander! Someone else saw Evander for the grasping, traitorous madman that he was. Then Hadrian's face broke into a smile. Cormac gripped his mug. He was afraid.

"Something can be done," Hadrian said. "You can offer Evander a warning."

"Me?"

"Why not? You're a clever man, Cormac, to have thought clearly and spoken sense while others fell under Evander's spell." Hadrian looked at him with something like amusement. "Tell him it's his quest or his people. He can take his pick."

Cormac gaped. "His quest or 'is people? So, if Evander sets out ta find this 'sun' of his, the people of Holt will die?"

Hadrian leaned back in his chair and glanced at the wall, as though he was tiring of the conversation. Cormac wished he'd never come. He'd been the one to initiate this meeting, but he realized now that he'd never been in control, of any of it. He felt like a pawn, like a child.

"All of 'is people? What of those who don't follow?" Cormac asked.

"They'd be wise to leave Holt," Hadrian answered.

"And if Evander stays put? If nothing changes?"

Hadrian's brows lifted slightly. "He keeps his people."

He realized all of a sudden that Hadrian had left him entirely out of the reckoning. He himself was inadvertently calling the people of Holt *Evander's* people. Once again, he was alone in his father's front room, magistrate in nothing but name, overlooked by the men who should have followed him. "They're my people!"

"Are they?" Hadrian asked. His eyes narrowed, their cold light growing colder still. "Are you part of the Sun Clan, Cormac?"

Cormac paled. "That's madness," he whispered.

Hadrian's gaze lingered on him, appraising him, until sweat beaded at Cormac's temples.

"Good," Hadrian said. He stood and dropped a leather pouch onto the table. It jingled when it landed. He took a quick look around the room. "Fleete seems a decent enough place for men accustomed to the cold and the winds." His black cloak brushed softly against the floor as he walked out of the inn. The night swallowed him up. The door swung shut. Cormac was left alone with more edanna than he'd ever seen and enough cherry ale to dull the acute sense of disquiet that had settled over him during his brief meeting with the blue-eyed stranger.

He stayed in Fleete that night and slept overlong the next morning. The jarring gait of his horse's hooves as he traveled home over the hills made him wish he'd foregone some of the ale. But at length, he did reach Holt. He rode straight to the stable on the southern end of the village, ready to confront Evander with Hadrian's warning. But the stable was empty. Evander and his men had gone.

Twenty-Six

Three clay pots fell and shattered, scattering powdered ores across the floor of the cave. Valour cursed.

"Where's yer head today, my girl?" Errol asked, pushing her aside and gathering the fragments of pottery. "Gone off with Evander again, has it?" He scooped up a handful of the now useless powder and sifted the mixture through his fingers. "Ya might ask 'im ta leave it with ya, next time 'e sets out, eh?" He tried to wink at Valour and failed. The loss of the ores was too irritating. Valour wasn't looking at him anyway. She sat on a stool near the door, her braids unraveling, her face bleak.

"He doesn't love me, Errol."

"Who?"

"My husband," Valour answered.

Errol rose from his cleaning and tossed the broken pots into a scrap barrel in the corner. "Evander? I don't believe it fer a minute. What's got ya talking this way?"

Valour hesitated, embarrassed. Of course, Errol knew nothing of women or marriage. Perhaps he wouldn't think her foolish. "He didn't want ta see me when 'e came home last. He wanted ta go ta the Fayrewood instead. We've not been married a month, and already he tires of me."

"Did ya smash all 'is pots? Bust the windows out of 'is cottage?" Errol asked, eyes twinkling with mischief.

"Errol," Valour warned.

"It'll vex any man, even the best of us. That's all I'm saying," Errol said, and smiled.

"Ma warned me, and Da as well," Valour continued, ignoring Errol's teasing. "I knew it would be hard when 'e was gone, knew I'd miss 'im and fear fer 'im. But I never imagined that during the few, precious hours we had together, he could want something other than me." She looked at Errol. "What's the good o' my beauty if it can't even secure my husband's love?"

Errol walked to Valour's side and took a strand of her hair in his gnarled, maimed hand. "Oh, Valour. Is that why the gods blessed ya with beauty? Ta win a man's love and keep it?" He squatted down in front of her and took both her hands in his. She snatched them away, angry at his words.

"And what is the use o' colored glass and finely-wrought lanterns, Errol? I love 'em as much as anyone, but we craft them ta sell, ta feed us and clothe us, ta secure our comfort. Why else would we make such things?"

Errol stood and took a step back. "I'd not thought ya as ruthlessly practical as that, my girl. I've made a good living, sure, but I'd come ta the furnace and watch the slow flow o' the molten glass and find pleasure in my work if no one ever came ta Market or paid me a single coin."

"Fine words, Errol, but you've all ya need, and yer life is nearly done. What would it matter if ya sat in yer cottage surrounded by Fayrewood lanterns until ya breathed yer last?"

Errol's eyebrows rose, and she wished the words unsaid, but her pain was flowing now, and the words came with it. "If my hair and eyes, if this body guarantees me nothing, why wasn't I born plain? Is it just the cruelty o' the gods? Do they mock me? Why marry at all if it only brings more heartache? Why bear children if only ta watch them die? Why make lovely things when the dragons carry them away?" She made no sound as she cried. She sat tall and defiant while the tears ran down her cheeks.

Errol came and leaned over her. He rested his hand on her shoulder. "My girl," he said, "you've forgotten the Fayrewood."

She waited.

"What's the good o' the Fayrewood?" he continued. "It offers no shelter, no food, nothing but a few herbs that are easily found elsewhere in the foothills. If it serves no purpose, why not cut it down? We could use the wood in the furnace."

The color drained from Valour's face. The thought of the Fayrewood trees being felled to feed the fires of the furnace! It was unendurable. She thought of Mina, of Mina's tree. She felt sick.

"I've seen the colored wood. Don't go as much now. My legs aren't what they once were. But I know the beauty o' that place, and it isn't wasted. And perhaps my word on the matter is worth little, seeing as I've never married, never had children. But I've noticed a thing or two in my years, Valour. Much of what people do makes not a lick o' sense. In this cursed darkness, where men are falling ta the wolves and women are dying in childbirth and boys and girls are starving, it's madness ta marry. It's madness ta bear children, madness ta make lanterns and gather flowers, madness ta sing and dance. It's madness ta hope, really, when we've seen nothing ta hope for. But people do it anyway, against all reason. I've seen it time and again. People can't stop hoping, and beautiful things feed their hope." He brushed Valour's cheek with his thumb. "Yer beauty gives me hope, my girl."

"Do ya think there's any truth in Evander's words, Errol? Do ya think there really is a sun?"

"I couldn't say," Errol replied. "But to imagine a light beyond this darkness, well, that is hope indeed."

They were silent for a moment. "Why not go home and rest?" Errol said. "You've done quite enough today."

Valour caught the gleam in his eyes this time. He winked at her, and she managed a weak smile. "I'll clean up," Errol said, shuffling her toward the door. "Out with ya."

The first thing Mina was aware of was her face. The right side was raw, and it was pressed against a rough stone floor. Even the slight movement required to look at her surroundings awoke her to the bright, intense pain of the torn skin on her face. Something under her cheek was faintly sticky. *Blood*, she thought.

For the time being, she gave up on her surroundings and concentrated on her body. She thought she was whole. Arms and legs, fingers and toes, seemed all to be where they'd been before. She could sense them, distantly, beyond the layers of pain and exhaustion. That was good. Her right ankle made its presence more forcefully known. The ankle throbbed, her blood pulsing against the tight wrapping. Well, at least the knot had held. The ankle would mend in time.

She would not have moved if she hadn't been so thirsty. She wondered how long she'd been asleep, or unconscious. Her mouth felt as though it were stuffed with wool. It occurred to her that her water skin might not have survived the flight. She didn't want to die of thirst in the darkness. She was trying to lift her arms, to push herself up, when she remembered the dragon's talons. He'd caught her by the shoulders, with her right arm bound against her and her left dangling loose. Her right shoulder was sore and tender, but the left exploded with pain when she tried to move it. She could feel the place inside her left shoulder blade where the talon had penetrated.

She flopped back against the floor, forgetting the raw skin on her face. When it scraped against the stones and fresh blood seeped from the wounds, Mina gave a strangled sob. She took a moment to catch her breath, allowing the waves of pain to subside. She closed her eyes and focused on her knees. She released a slow breath and pulled her knees forward, toward her chest. Every bone, every muscle protested, and her ankle screamed. She stopped again, this time focusing on her right hand. She spread her fingers on the floor and used that hand to push herself up. She rolled onto her left hip. Then, with the breath hissing through her teeth, steadied herself and sat up.

Her water skin was still tied to her belt. She fumbled with the cord, loosened it, and lifted it to her lips. She took a few grateful gulps and returned it to its place.

Now that she was upright and her thirst was not so distracting, Mina considered her surroundings. She wanted very much for her instincts to be wrong, but she knew she was in a dragon's lair. She remembered the flight and the wind and the dark. She closed her eyes and listened. Apart from her own breathing, the only sounds she could discern were the dripping of water from ceiling to floor and the wind. She opened her eyes. The view differed little from what she saw when her eyes were closed, except that, to her right, perhaps ten paces distant, the darkness was thinner. There was a sort of hole that was more gray than black. To her left, the darkness thickened as it plunged into the mountain.

She picked up a handful of broken stones and tossed one toward the mouth of the cave. It flew out into the wind and disappeared. The second she threw ahead of her, and it made a sharp crack against the opposite wall. *Not so very wide,* she thought. The next she hurled to her left, toward the bowels of the cave. It splashed into a puddle some ways back without ever finding a wall. She made an awkward half turn to throw a stone behind her, and jumped when it bounced off the cave wall and struck her in the small of the back. Mina was overjoyed at this discovery. She inched haltingly backward, until she leaned against the wall. It was a relief to have solid stone at her back instead of a dark unknown. Comforted, Mina rested her head against the stone and fell asleep.

Evander and his men did not return for market day. The village was full of visitors, though, and the air was alive with questions and tales, with assumptions and accusations. People began to notice the sign of the Sun Clan. Here and there, craftsmen were using the sign to mark their work. Many of the hunters now wore the sign on their belts. Tilly had even embroidered the sign on Reed's tunic, and the boy had more than a few strangers question him about it.

Sales were good. This late in the year, the craftsmen lowered their prices. They'd have plenty of time to work over the long winter, and they could easily replenish their wares. In autumn, their chief goal was to line their pockets with coins, and line their shelves with supplies.

Maeve's embroidery sold well. Valour manned the table this time, and her mother came and sat with her when she could. Valour was glad of the company, for the bustle of market day brought thoughts of Mina fresh to her mind. And Evander was gone, and Valour was burdened with loneliness and a sense of foreboding.

At the end of the day, she packed up the remaining pieces and returned to the cottage. She'd made up her mind to accept Evander's home as her own, made up her mind to accept Maeve as her mother. She wanted to be brave, like Mina and Evander, and this was a beginning.

When she opened the door of the cottage, she dropped her basket to the floor and smiled.

"Grey?"

The little girl sat in her chair by the fire, working away at a scrap of embroidery. She dropped the needle and cloth on the edge of the hearth when she saw Valour, and jumped up to greet her.

"I didn't expect ta see ya," Valour said, wrapping Grey in a hug. "I worry about ya, Grey." She held the girl until she started to squirm. "You're not eating enough, surely."

"I always take something with me," she said.

Valour scooped some vegetables from a basket by the wall. She took two knives from the shelf, gave one to Grey, and started on supper.

"You do the peppers," she said, and Grey did as she was told.

They worked in silence for a while, chopping, loading vegetables into the kettle, filling it with water, adding herbs and a few precious hunks of salted meat.

"I don't like it when Evander leaves," Grey said.

"Nor do I," Valour said. She built up the fire under the kettle and sat down across the table from Grey.

"The cottage is strange when he's gone," Grey continued. "It's too still."

"Grey," Valour said, and the girl's bright eyes looked at her expectantly. "I've not asked about yer ma and da. I didn't want..." She stumbled over the words and stopped.

Grey shook her head, once, and looked down at the table. She ran her finger along a twisting bit of grain in the wood. When she spoke, it was in a whisper. "I don't like ta remember."

"I'm sorry." Valour took Grey's small hand in hers. "You've a home here, ya know."

"There's a wolf near the village."

Valour swallowed. She crossed to the other side of the table and put her arm around Grey's thin shoulders. "Ya don't have ta be afraid. Just stay close ta the cottage. We'll watch out fer ya."

Grey looked at Valour. "What if Evander goes away ta find the sun?"

"He won't leave us, Grey." The girl's eyes searched her face. She was not convinced. "I promise," Valour said. "Now, the kettle's nearly boiling. If you'll watch the pot and stir it a bit, I'll check on Maeve."

Grey hopped up and went to the kettle while Valour stepped through the curtain into the back room.

Maeve was lying on her cot, the blankets twisted beneath her. She stared at the dead flowers on the windowsill and sang a little of her song. "Loose yer hold, stain the ground. All is lost that once was found." Valour pulled a chair up to the cot and sat down. Maeve had been singing the same words, off and on, since Evander left last, and nothing Valour said or did moved her.

Valour had offered to wash her hair. She'd brought soap and oil, and a bucket of fresh water, but Maeve refused to sit up. Valour was grateful that the woman still ate a little and drank a little, that she still went outside to relieve herself. But she was frightened of what Evander would find when next he returned.

She reached for Maeve's hand, but Maeve tucked it under her shift and picked up the tune of her song. Valour looked at the blank blue eyes, the filthy golden hair, and she was overwhelmed with pity for Maeve. She'd lost her husband so soon. She'd raised her son alone. What had it been like for her when the dreams began? Valour wondered what Maeve had felt the first time someone accused her of madness. She wondered about the dead flowers in the window and the years of sitting, day after endless day, in the same dark room with the same haunting visions.

"Maeve," she said, her voice gentle and pleading. "Won't ya come and have some supper with us? Grey's home, and we've got a stew going."

Maeve sat up, suddenly alert, and slipped her legs over the edge of the cot. Valour gasped in delight and relief. Perhaps Maeve was coming out of this difficult spell. Perhaps she was improving. The woman made a quick move toward her chair by the fire, and Valour smiled, thinking she would join them for supper and embroider in the front room afterwards. But as Maeve pushed aside the curtain and entered the other room, firelight flashed on the long embroidery needle she carried in her hand. She brought no cloth. Valour bolted after her. By the time she reached the table, Maeve had come up behind Grey and lifted the needle to the girl's neck.

"Maeve, No! Stop it!" Valour screamed. Grey spun around and raised an arm to shield herself. Valour wrenched the needle from Maeve's hand and threw it into the fire, and the older woman collapsed in a weeping, quivering heap on the floor. Grey retreated to the far corner of the cottage while a rattled Valour hauled Maeve back to bed. She took a blanket from the floor and spread it over her with trembling hands. She touched Maeve's forehead lightly, searching her eyes for . . . something. There was nothing to see. Her blue eyes were blank and unfocused. Valour sighed and left the room.

"She's getting worse," Grey said, without emotion, as she ladled soup into two bowls.

"Aye," Valour replied. She slumped into her seat at the table, feeling as if she'd aged a hundred years in a few weeks. She'd never known such weariness. "Are you alright, Grey?"

The girl nodded. They sat across from one another and ate their supper in stunned silence. When the dishes were cleared and Valour asked Grey if she was ready for bed, Grey shook her head. "I'd like ta walk a bit."

"No, Grey, please. It's late. I'll walk with ya tomorrow."

But Grey was already stepping out into the night. "I'll just go down ta the stable," she said, and was gone.

Cormac didn't wait for Evander's return. As the men cleared away the tables at the end of market day, he spread the word. The men of Holt were to meet in *his* cottage after supper. It was underhanded, for Evander's best supporters were hunting beside him. But Cormac didn't care.

When everyone was assembled in the front room, Cormac repeated Hadrian's warning. He was careful to change the phrasing. He wouldn't stand before the men of his village and call them 'Evander's people.' But he took pleasure in relaying the awful message. Without Hadrian present (or Evander, for that matter), Cormac was all confidence and righteous indignation.

There was a moment of disbelieving silence after he finished. Some of the hunters were disgusted with Cormac, and they left at once. "I'll not sit here and listen ta this," said one, on his way out. "Not from you, Cormac, and certainly not without Evander here ta speak fer 'imself." He slammed the door behind him, and Cormac scanned the faces of the remaining men. Cole spoke next.

"I agree," he said. "It's right Evander should be here, and 'is men."

"If you're so offended, Cole," one of the craftsmen snarled, "why have ya stayed?"

Cole gave the man a hard look. "I've stayed because I'd be a fool ta dismiss such a warning."

Cormac broke in. "It was my wish that Evander should be here ta hear this. But I've no say in what he and 'is men do. I only speak in the interests o' the men of Holt, of their women and children."

Another craftsman spoke up. "But this could be just an idle threat, could it not? Why should we believe the words of a stranger? What power could 'e have over an entire village and all its people?"

"Aye," another said. "What reason do ya have ta fear this threat, Cormac?" He looked around the room, spurred on by a few approving looks and nodding heads. "How are we ta know it's not some tale you concocted ta silence Evander?"

Cormac bristled. "I've not come ta speak ill of Evander. I've called ya here ta protect you and yer families from harm! Do ya not see how dangerous he is? If Evander persists with 'is wild ideas, his absurd plans, everything we've come ta know and love could fall ta ruin."

He stopped, looking into the eyes of the men of Holt. How long he had waited to stand before them, to speak and be heard, to lead! His blood rushed and sang with the joy of it. He was magistrate now, and he would defend his people from the madman and preserve the village of Holt. When he spoke again, his voice filled the room.

"I've no more wish than any of you ta be driven out o' my home. And if we're ta stay here, between the Cutting and the Fayrewood, if we're ta see our village grow and prosper, if we're ta see our children grow and prosper, we ought ta think twice about Evander's proposals. If we've any wish ta live out our days in peace, we may have ta silence Evander completely."

He'd gone one step too far, and Cormac knew it. Several men stood and left, some cursing, some shaking their heads, some giving Cormac a warning of his own with their fierce looks. But a handful of men remained. They were comfortable, prosperous men, mostly. They had much to lose, and, therefore, much to fear. They talked well into the night, considering what might be done about Evander.

And when they took their torches and lanterns and made their way back to their cottages, they heard the howling of wolves in the hills.

Twenty-Seven

Mina woke to the clanking of metallic scales and the grating of talons against stone. She didn't dare move. It wasn't terribly difficult. She was so weary, so sore. Her body felt as if it were made of tallow, as if her edges had grown soft and melted into the wall and floor.

Gray light filtered into the cave and fell on the dragon. The beast was eating. Mina shut her eyes against the gruesome spectacle. She wished she could stop her ears as well. The dragon's jaws splintered the animal's bones. Innards splattered and squelched on the floor. And beneath it all was a low thrumming, a sound that came from within the dragon. Mina did not know if it was a sound of breathing or of pleasure. It could have been the sound of the monster's inner fire or the rush of black blood in its veins.

When the meal was finished, the dragon lumbered towards the back of the cave. Mina stopped breathing. She waited, melted against the wall, while the ragged edge of the dragon's wing brushed across her ankles. When it reached a point in the cave where no light could penetrate, the beast settled onto the floor.

Mina felt the stirring of the air as it drew in its wings. She stole a few quiet gulps of air while she waited. When the hiss and rumble of the dragon's breathing took on a steady rhythm, Mina guessed that the dragon slept.

She breathed more easily then, filling her lungs again and again, until her head was clear. With shaking hands, she untied her water skin and drank. The water was relieving, but it made her fiercely aware of her empty belly.

My pack. If it weren't for the pain that racked her body and the cold and the hunger and the dread knowledge of her likely fate, she might have laughed aloud when she realized that her pack was still strapped to her shoulder. The wound from the dragon's claw had kept her from noticing anything else on her left side. But there it was, hanging heroically from one cord. She leaned forward, sliding the pack off her shoulder with her right arm and setting it in her lap. She untied the cord and unrolled the coat. The torches were there, useless though they seemed. There were a few slimy scraps of meat. Her stomach growled so loudly when she saw them that she caught her breath and jerked her head toward the dragon. The rhythm of its snores didn't change. She devoured the meat, licking her fingers when she finished. There was a carefully hoarded bit of berry cake that she stuffed into her mouth without the least remorse. She'd been saving it for a time of desperate need, knowing it would keep better than fresh meat. If this was not such a time, she shuddered to think what was.

That meager meal exhausted Mina. It took no effort at all to direct her mind away from the scabs developing on her face or the throbbing in her shoulder and ankle or the frigid damp of the cave. She was far too drained to think. She left the coat and its contents in her lap and fell at once into a deep sleep.

Seeker

In the days that followed, Mina's greatest torment was the question of why the dragon allowed her to live. The dragon came and went, ate and slept. It landed with a clangor a few paces from her feet, and Mina quailed. It tramped past her and settled down to sleep, and Mina's heart hammered out a desperate rhythm. It roared, and sweat beaded on Mina's skin. The terror of the dragons was woven through all the years of her life, and it could not be undone. Mina's fear only grew as the days stretched.

She watched the mouth of the cave, noting the change in the light and marking the passing of time. During the night, she couldn't tell the wall of the cave from the mouth of the cave, so complete was the darkness outside. By midday, the air was gray and hazy, and she could just make out the opposite wall. But she came to dread the daylight, for that was when the dragon slept, when the smoke that came curling from its nostrils and the charred, sour stink of the beast almost smothered her. That was when Mina longed to sneak to the mouth of the cave and lean out and breathe the cold, clean air of the winds that cut through the valley. But she didn't dare risk it. She tore another strip of cloth from her shift instead, and tied it around her face and pressed herself against the wall and sometimes fell into a fitful, uneasy sleep.

Each day, late in the afternoon, the dragon woke and lumbered to the door of the cave. It spread its wings and forced them downward. Mina watched its armored tail, its long talons, as they rose and disappeared. Not long after, the dragon returned with something to eat, and Mina endured the sounds of another meal. When bones cracked and splintered in the dragon's jaws, Mina did not think how her own body could soon be broken or how no one would stand beside her funeral pyre and sing, for no one would know that she had died or how or when. She did not think of those things. She refused to think of them.

She thought of her family, though, and her village and her people. She closed her eyes, and she could see them all. There was Reed, snatching berries from the bowl, and Da, making ambitious plans. There was Ma, stirring the kettle on the fire, and Chase, telling her about his last hunt. She saw Moss, sitting in her rocking chair and rubbing her knees. She could almost smell the apothecary's shop, with the roots and herbs dried and powdered and simmering in pots. In her mind, she walked the lanes between the cottages of Holt. She visited the sheepfold and the stable and mumbled greetings to the sheep and the horses. She wandered into Emmeline's cottage to see how she fared and to kiss the bright faces of Fayre and True. For a time, that was as far as she could go. To remember any more, in the barren dark of the dragon's lair, seemed cruel, intolerable.

When it had eaten, the dragon left again. Mina never knew where it went or what it did during the long night hours, but she soon learned that it never returned until morning. One night, when her water skin was empty and Mina could think of nothing but her thirst, she took an enormous risk. She used the flint-and-iron to light one of her torches. She was breathless with terror, and she allowed the torch to burn for only a few minutes. But it was enough time to reveal shallow pools of water on the floor of the cave further back. Mina thanked the gods, hobbled to a spot where water dripped from the ceiling and collected in a hollow in the rocks, and filled her water skin. She rushed back to her usual place, fearing the dragon's imminent return. But as she'd seen, the dragon did not come until morning.

Mina grew bolder. When she began to recover some of her strength, and her ankle was sound and the torn skin on her face had scabbed over and the wound in her shoulder pained her a little less, the night hours became precious. Sometimes Mina slept, too weak and hungry to do anything else. But sometimes she picked through the remains of the dragon's meal, in search of something palatable. And sometimes she made tentative explorations of the cave.

And each morning, when the dragon returned with a roar that

shook the walls, Mina prepared herself for death. She knew it was coming. She saw it in the dead cold of the dragon's blue eyes.

But each morning, when the echoes of the dragon's fury had finally stilled, the beast turned away from her. It tramped to the back of the cave, black wings billowing behind, and settled down to sleep.

Evander was growing wild with desperation. He and his men were five days into this hunt, and still they'd caught no more than a few rabbits. When they happened upon a band of hunters from Fleete, Evander was shocked to see their horses burdened with their kills. When Lorne questioned them, they assured him that their most recent hunt had been no different from any other. They were optimistic about their store of supplies for the long winter months, and they were returning to Fleete in high spirits. As they set off, they laughed. The phrase 'mad as Evander' drifted back.

Evander was not immune to taunts. The word 'mad' brought back too many troubling memories from his boyhood, of furtive glances from the villagers and rumors about Maeve's visions and her health. As a boy, he had challenged anyone who spoke ill of Maeve, or questioned her sanity in the slightest. He'd never imagined how much those accusations could sting when they were aimed at him.

His men tried to bolster him when they noticed him sitting in his saddle, staring at nothing.

"Don't listen ta them, Evander," Chase said.

"Fools," Lachlan called out.

Lorne slapped Evander heartily across the back, and Knox moved Frost alongside Rogue as they rode west, through the foothills. "Buck up, my friend," Knox said. "It's not over. We could take down a herd this very day."

Evander looked into Knox's eyes and knew that his friend didn't believe a word he'd spoken. "Knox," he said, his voice low and bare. "I've spent my life playing and hunting with you, accepting every challenge ya offered. I've saved yer life more than once, and you've done the same fer me." He paused, studying the reins in his hands. "Do you stand with the men from Fleete? Do *you* think me mad?"

They rode in silence until Knox could formulate an answer. "I think ya want too much, Evander. If you aim ta father a new clan, I think you'd be better off going home and starting one with that beauty o' yours. I don't understand why ya can't be satisfied with that. Many men would give their lives fer half so much joy." Knox was silent for some time. When he spoke again, his voice trembled. "If I'm ta die, and I surely am, I'd rather die here, with these men, doing what I must. I'd rather die laughing, riding Frost ta the falls with the wind on my face. I can't understand why any man would walk inta the arms o' the Shadow, knowing what must come."

"It's not death I seek, Knox, whatever you think."

"What then? What is it you seek?"

"Life!" Evander replied. "And there's none ta be had here."

Knox stared at Evander, at a loss. "I'll never understand you."

"So it seems," Evander said, and moved Rogue to the head of the group.

Valour sat at her parents' table, eating supper. Her hair was pulled back into a single, hasty braid. She was wondering if any flowers still bloomed in the Fayrewood. She thought Maeve might be persuaded to eat a bit if there were flowers in her room. And she was wondering when Grey would return, when Evander would return.

"I fear fer Evander." Valour thought the words as her father spoke them aloud. She blinked, and looked up from her bowl.

"What?"

"I wanted ta tell ya before ya heard it from anyone else," Cole said. "There's been a warning. Cormac met with a man in Fleete who says Evander must choose between 'is people and 'is quest."

"A man in Fleete? Why should a stranger care what Evander does?"

"That's what troubles me. If Cormac threatened Evander, I'd think nothing of it. But I've an idea who might have made this threat. There was a man who came ta one o' the meetings, a man I've never seen. He's not from Fleete, that's fer sure." Cole looked over Valour's shoulder, remembering. His face was troubled. "When 'e spoke, I was afraid. More than that, I felt . . . hopeless, as if there was no such thing as light, as if there'd never been."

Valour sat very still, letting the words sink in. "What power could such a man hold over us?"

Cole shook his head. "I don't know. But Evander's talk o' the sun can no longer be seen as mere words. We're all at risk now, and you not least, my daughter."

Valour leaned back in her seat and made a statement that sounded more like a question. "But none of it matters. All o' this is idle worry, and speculation. Evander won't go. He'd never risk so much. He'd never leave me here."

Her mother glanced at her father, waiting for him to speak. Cole's voice was soothing, his words careful. "Surely not. But we'd hoped that, when Evander returns, ya might speak with 'im."

Valour laughed, and the sound was bitter, desperate. She could never find the words to tell her parents what she felt. She was ashamed to acknowledge her violent changes of mood over the past weeks, ashamed to confess her fears about her husband and her future, ashamed to admit that she may already have failed as a wife. Besides, she was sure . . . she'd promised Grey . . . that Evander was not a man to leave his family on a whim and venture off into the Shadow, seeking death. She was sure, wasn't she? She looked at her parents then and realized, with horror, that they were not sure, not at all. They were counting on her to keep Evander contained, for his sake and hers, for their sakes and the sake of all the villagers.

"He could have many good years here, Valour. You know it as well as we do. He could lead the clan."

Valour stared at her father. She rose from the table, leaving her meal half-finished, and left the cottage without a word. She clung to the hope that this was all a foolish waste of energy, that Evander would not have married her if he didn't intend to stay with her. But her whirling thoughts could not crowd out the fear that Evander was indeed mad enough to rebel against the Shadow Lord and seek another home. If such was her husband's ambition, his ultimate hope, what victory could she possibly find in robbing him of it? How could she secure her happiness by stealing Evander's away?

Twenty-Eight

They were surrounded. The wolves were everywhere, coming by twos and threes, growling and snapping as they ran. Their eyes lit the darkened plain, and Shadow trailed behind them. It was Evander who'd taken the risk, moving his men south of Lake Morrison and close to the Black Mountains in a frantic search for game. Now, Knox bled heavily from a gash in his arm, Chase from a wound to his leg. The hunters circled Lorne and lit their arrows, sending them two at a time into the fray, but the Wheel, minus two of its spokes, was not nearly so effective as it had been. And their arrows wouldn't last. The flaming shafts flew into the advancing wolves, and, here and there, enemies dissolved in fume and smoke and blew away. But it was not enough.

They might have made a run for it, turning north, and driving their horses until they reached the foothills, if it had not been for the lake. The wolves lined the banks, black fur against black water, with mist creeping between.

Evander touched his arrows to Lorne's torch, and the older man gave him a meaning look and a brief nod. Rogue halted, sensing Evander's indecision, waiting for the muscles in Evander's legs to guide him forward or back. Tears sprang to Evander's eyes, for he saw Lorne's meaning. Lorne was ready to die, ready to fall with his men. And he was at peace.

"No," Evander breathed. He looked at each of his men in turn. Lachlan was nudging his horse out from Lorne's torch, launching his arrows into a group of five fast-approaching wolves. Chase's face was grim and set, and he loosed his bowstring with a fearsome grace that was terrible and beautiful. Knox shouted and cursed the wolves that closed in on him, firing individual arrows in quick succession. Lorne smiled a little, reading Evander's face and understanding.

"No!" Evander cried. "Not now! Not yet!" Somewhere deep within him, far beneath the weighty realm of his suffering and doubt, his dissatisfaction and fear, Evander knew the world was not as it should be. Too many things had been lost to the darkness. Innocent things, lovely things, bright things. He would not be the next to fall. He was more than fodder for the wolves. He threw his bow over his shoulder and jerked Rogue's reins. The stallion reared. As the horse's hooves pawed the air, Evander's skin flared. His men stared, and their horses pulled away from the dazzling light.

When Rogue's hooves hit the ground, Evander shouted a battle cry, drew his dagger, and charged north. His men faltered, their vision filled with the blazing fury of him. They watched in awe as the wolves gave way, those ahead of him slowing their charge, changing course, veering off. The wolves on either side turned and fled. Their growling and snapping had ceased, and they were subdued. Lorne and Chase joined in the cry and bolted after Evander, scattering shafts of light as they went. Lachlan smiled and joined them. Knox came last, his face unreadable.

The wolves faded into the Shadow, and the company rode north, slowing their horses only when they had come within the foothills and found a reasonably defensible campsite. They were returning to Holt with no meat. They had wounds to dress. Their store of arrows had dwindled: less than a dozen among them. Yet, apart from Knox, they were a cheerful group around the fire that night. They were going home, all five of them. And their faces still shone with the joy of their escape and the conviction that good things were coming to them.

Knox could not understand it. He should have been relieved, grateful. But he sat against his pack scowling. He felt cheated. When Evander smiled, Knox could think of nothing but the delirious bliss of pounding his face in.

His death had come to meet him, and Knox had been ready. It was an honorable way to leave the Shadow Realm, risking everything to provide for his family, falling as he defended his friends against a host of Shadow Wolves. Such a death would have honored his fallen brothers.

But Evander had robbed him. Now he would return to his mother and younger brothers empty-handed. There was no honor in starvation.

Lachlan's voice interrupted his seething. "We've not planned a route, Evander. If we set out tonight, ta find the sun, would we journey north or east?"

"My mother's dreams have never been so clear, not enough ta give any direction. None o' the songs or stories either, so far as I can tell." Evander looked to Lorne for confirmation. The old man shook his head.

"I've thought on it a good deal, of late," Evander continued. "There's no easy path. Either we brave the Peaks and the winter and the dragons and starvation, or we risk the Black Mountains. I wish we knew something more of them. They could be far more deadly than the Peaks. Or far less."

"Well, so long as you've got a plan ..." Lachlan teased, and Evander grinned.

"I'm half inclined ta begin at the Turn," Evander said.

Brows rose all around the camp. Knox clenched his fists. There were some deaths less honorable even than starvation.

"I know it sounds mad," Evander continued. There were snorts of laughter from Lorne and Lachlan. "But, as far as we can tell, the Turn leads straight inta the Black Mountains. I fear it above all other paths, and so I wonder if it isn't the right one."

Knox could sit silent no longer. "No more o' this, Evander! How many times have you accused me of recklessness? Yet you'd throw away yer life, their lives, fer a fool's hope. It *is* madness!"

His words were more powerful than a blow to the face. He could see it in Evander's eyes, and he was satisfied. He stood and grabbed his pack. He thrust a torch into the campfire, and, when it was lit, mounted his horse.

"Knox!" Evander called. Knox didn't turn, didn't slow. He took Frost's reins and urged her out into the night.

The bobbing light of Knox's torch was swallowed by darkness. None of the hunters were surprised. They were accustomed to Knox's outbursts. But his angry words and his swift departure had dampened their hopes and stolen the luster from their glorious escape. The rest of the evening, they spoke practically of routes and supplies. Not one among them was willing to bring his wife or his children or his mother on such a perilous quest. Not yet. They all agreed that a band of men should go first, to cut a path to a new world, if such a place could be found. Then, they would return for their families. It was a reasonable plan. The hunters already risked their lives almost daily, and their wives and children knew that every farewell could be their last.

No final arrangements were made that night. No one committed to a date of departure. But things were taking shape, and Evander fell asleep with the verse of a song running round in his head.

"The endless mountains rise
Through seas of snow and cold winds wailing
And I would scale the heights
Ta find a warmth, a light unfailing."

Mina had no good reason for avoiding the back of the cave.

When walking had become easier, she'd explored the mouth of the cave. She'd been bold enough to attempt it in the afternoon, as soon as the dragon had gone out in search of a meal, for she'd wanted as much light as possible. She'd stepped out onto the lip of rock from which the dragon took flight and peeked over the edge. The mountain fell away, sheer rock plunging far, far down to a valley she could not see. She felt dizzy. She crawled back inside the cave and took several slow breaths, trying to steady herself. This was nothing like shimmying down from a Fayrewood tree, nothing like her scramble over the path beside the falls. There was no escape from the dragon's lair by that route.

This knowledge should have made her even more determined to search the back of the cave. Still, night after night, she made excuses, putting it off, busying herself with meaningless small tasks or merely staring out into the obscure world beyond the mouth of the cave.

But one evening, after the dragon had finished a meal and gone out again, and Mina had choked down a slimy scrap of raw meat, she determined to do it. She unrolled her little pack and removed one of the torches. She never let them burn for long. Even so, she'd had to tear more strips of cloth from her ever-shortening shift, wipe them in the drippings from dragon's meals, and wrap them around the ends of the torches to replenish her light.

With a little sigh of satisfaction, she took the flint-and-iron from her pouch and lit the torch. The warm light bolstered her courage. She took the torch in her right hand and let the fingers of her left hand graze the wall as she pushed into the palpable darkness of the cave.

The winds were picking up now, as autumn drew on. She could hear them whining and gusting outside. Water collected on the ceiling and dripped steadily into little pools on the floor. The stench grew worse as she made her way deeper in. Her progress was slow. She explored the floor with the toes of her boots before taking a step, and she was never sure quite where to shine her torch. She remembered falling into the Cutting once, when she was little. Until Chase pulled her out, she had been suspended in a strange world, a world where up and down had lost their meaning. The darkness of the cave was rather like that. There was black beneath her feet, black on either hand. The roof of the cave shrank away from her, veiling itself in black. Mina swam in a river of darkness, hardly able to distinguish up from down, left from right. They seemed all to be the same. She kept a fierce grip on her torch.

She began to fear that she would lose herself in this darkness. She had almost determined to turn around when something glinted in the torchlight. It was low to the floor, on the opposite side of the cave. With just a heartbeat's hesitation, Mina let her left hand fall away from the steadying presence of the wall and stepped toward the flash of light. As she approached, many shining things captured the light of her torch and sent it bouncing over the walls and the floor of the cave, over the surface of the water in the little pools. Mina reached the mound, crouched down, and gasped.

She stretched her left hand toward the nearest treasure and lifted it by the iron loop at the top. It was a lantern. In the shock of her capture and the suffering and terror that followed, Mina had almost forgotten that she had lit a broken lantern just before she was taken. It came back to her with brilliant clarity as she surveyed the pile of lanterns before her. This was the dragon's hoard, its collection of bright things. Stolen things.

She stood. With an unsteady hand, she raised her torch until it shone on the top of the mound. And there it was. Even before the panes of colored glass and the exquisite edanna filigree tossed the torchlight around the cave, Mina knew it would be there. After so many days in the dark, alone, in pain, Valour's lantern might as well have been the sun, so glad was she to see it.

Mina took the lantern from its perch. She scooped a bit of carefully hoarded tallow from the tiny vat in her pouch and spread it in the hollow around the lantern's wick. Then she lit the lantern and extinguished the torch. The light flickering through the green and amethyst panes of glass awakened her memories of the Fayrewood. She ran her fingers over the clear pane and turned the gold pane to the front.

The leaves will all be golden now, she thought. Mina fell against the wall and slid to the floor. For the first time since she'd come to the dragon's lair, she wept, great sobs racking her body as she cradled the lantern in her hands. All the longing and sorrow she'd buried beneath the pressing demands of survival came bubbling up. She walked through the Fayrewood as pink leaves fell like snow. She led Valour through the arching trees and saw the wood anew through her eyes. She lay on her branch, with her leg swinging down, and watched the swaying branches above. She saw Evander as he walked in the wood, as he took someone else into his arms, as he kissed his new wife beneath the loveliest of all Fayrewood lanterns. And her heart shattered all over again, and she clutched the lantern more tightly still.

When her tears were spent, and Mina was empty and quiet, she dried her face on her sleeve and looked at the lantern once more. It was a lovely thing. It was made by people she loved, and it belonged to them. Mina would return it. Soon.

Fearing that the dragon might notice the absence of its greatest treasure, she replaced it on the top of the mound. She lit her torch and extinguished the lantern before making her way back to her seat near the mouth of the cave. She sat down and drank a little water, beginning at last to plan her escape.

Twenty-Nine

Reed was the first person to greet Evander when he rode into Holt. The boy walked up with an air of importance and just a hint of a swagger. He looked quite pleased with himself.

"You've replaced the torches, I take it," Evander said.

"Aye, every one," Reed replied.

"Good man," Evander said. "Yer da would be proud." He didn't think before he spoke. They were the right words, and Evander knew it. But it pained him to see the shadow pass over Reed's face. The boy said nothing else. He retreated back into his cottage, not even greeting his brother when he rode up beside Evander.

"Let me tend the horses," Chase said, snatching the reins from Evander's hands. "You find Knox."

Evander nodded, hating that this should be his first task on coming home. He needed to talk to Valour, especially after the way they'd parted last. But Chase was right. If Knox was drunk, there was no knowing what manner of trouble he would find.

Evander went straight to the pool. He couldn't count the times he and Knox had sat together and watched the black water seep in from Lake Morrison. He knew it was the likeliest place to find his friend, but Knox was not there. He jammed his torch into the soft soil near the pool and stepped into the Fayrewood. He filled his lungs with the clean, crisp air of the colored wood, and walked northward along the central path. Above him was a canopy of pure gold. He stopped to listen, and closed his eyes, the weight of his errand falling away. The tossing leaves and swaying branches had a hushed, calming rhythm, like a mother's heartbeat, like her soft singing.

He opened his eyes. Knox leaned against a tree, watching him.

"I forgot how..." Knox stopped, considering. "'Beautiful' doesn't seem the right word, does it? Not enough."

This was not the Knox Evander expected to meet. He waited. "Thought I'd be drunk, didn't ya? That was my intent. Brought a jug down ta the pool, but I tossed it in." Knox rubbed the back of his neck, tousled his hair, and dropped his hand. He looked Evander in the eye. "You're impossible, ya know. I can't win. If I join ya on this fool's quest, I'll face all the things I fear most. But if I stay behind, I'll despise myself ta the end o' my days. All I wanted was ta die in my own way. It's not so much ta ask." Knox shook his head. "I was furious with ya. And then I came in here, and I ..."

Evander nodded. He understood.

"I can't think how many years it's been," Knox continued. "And hardly anyone ever comes ta the wood. I thought it was because o' the Turn. That's what I told myself, anyway. Is that what we all tell ourselves?"

Evander gave him a sad smile.

"But it isn't that. The Turn's got nothing ta do with it. It's the beauty we can't bear. It's too much. It ... hurts." Knox swallowed hard.

"Knox," Evander began.

"I'm a coward," Knox interrupted. "Naught but a coward. I don't want ta die like my brothers. I don't want ta die at all."

"Knox," Evander tried again.

"I don't want ta lose you either, Evander. I can't let ya go alone." Knox rubbed his forehead, then looked up, his eyes rising to the fluttering golden arch above them. "Do ya suppose the sun is as lovely as this?"

Evander's smile spread over his face. "Come with me, Knox, and we'll find out."

Knox returned a lopsided grin. "I guess you've forgiven me, then, fer knocking ya down?"

Evander laughed, a brief, sharp burst of air. "It's easily forgiven, my friend. Ya did nothing o' the kind."

Knox slapped Evander across the back with his usual jovial brutality, and the two made their way out of the wood. Evander's steps were light as he went to find Valour.

The state of things in the cottage was not at all what Evander expected to find when he returned home, luminous and full of hope. Grey was wounded. There was a bright red welt on her arm that looked something like a burn. He joined Valour, who was hovering over Grey, applying salve to the girl's arm as gently as she could.

"How did this happen, Grey?" Evander asked, searching Grey's wide, blinking eyes.

She paused, looking down at Valour as she wrapped strips of cloth around the arm. "I got too close ta the fire."

"Which fire?" Evander asked, turning to Valour. "How long has she been gone?"

"Two days. She's only just returned."

Evander walked to the window to collect himself. He loved this child, but Grey complicated everything. If he and his men set out before the year was done, as he hoped, how could he leave Valour with this wisp of a girl who roamed the foothills, disappearing for days at a time and then turning up injured?

He went to kiss the top of Grey's head. "I don't suppose it does any good, telling ya ta stay close." He squatted down in front of her, looking into her eyes. "There's a chance, Grey, that things'll grow more dangerous in the coming days." He touched her wild dark hair, wrapping the strand of grey around his finger before letting it spring back into place. "Will ya make me a promise? Will ya stay closer, ta Valour and me, and Ma? It's all I'll ask fer now."

Grey's eyes brightened. She nodded.

"Valour," he said. "I'm . . . I wanted . . . there's so much I want ta say." Her eyes, as he spoke, were full of something he couldn't define. "I'll go in and see Ma, and then, can we talk alone?" He squeezed her hand and passed through the curtain to the back room.

He was not prepared for what he found. His mother was huddled under a soiled blanket. Her hair was matted and dull. The mattress stank. Maeve's chant had worn itself down to three words. "All is lost." She sang the words, or whispered them, falling silent for a time before picking up the chant again. Evander ran to her and touched her shoulder. His first reaction was mingled pity and horror. But those were quickly overwhelmed by a torrent of wrath.

"Valour!" he called. She pushed the curtain aside, her head shaking as she came near. "What's happened? She's wet herself. She's filthy!"

"She wouldn't move. I tried," Valour began. "Yer leaving —"

"What does my leaving have ta do with it?"

"It wasn't 'til after —"

"I've gone many times over the years, fer many, many days. She was alone then, and perfectly well. Why should she be any worse now? When you and Grey are here?"

"Why?" Valour asked, her eyes flaming. "Why *now*? Perhaps because everything's falling apart!"

"What do ya mean?" Evander asked.

Seeker

"It's not just Grey and Maeve. It's the whole village! Cormac's come from Fleete with a warning, Evander. They don't want ya talking about the sun anymore."

"What?! Who? Who sends a warning?"

"I don't know 'is name, only that 'e says ya must choose between yer quest and yer people." She came closer, and Evander took a small step back.

"Someone's sent a warning that I must choose between my quest and my people?! I don't understand. Who has the power ta threaten the people of Holt? Is it the Father o' the clan? Does 'e think I provoke the villagers ta rebellion?"

"It doesn't matter, Evander," Valour said, approaching him again, with a hand extended. "You can end it. The people of Holt will follow where you lead. Gather the men and tell 'em it's time ta think of other things, to improve the village's defenses against the dragons, or expand the furnaces, or anything. They'll have something ta work toward, and the threat will mean nothing, and we'll be safe."

She touched Evander's arm, and he stared down at her hand as though it were some repellant, unfamiliar thing.

"In the Fayrewood, and here in this cottage, we talked o' the sun, of a better world. You spoke of yer sister, of wanting something ya never had."

"Aye, I did. And I feel that still. But there's much that I *do* have, here. Yer words are beautiful, Evander. Yer stories and songs. But they're not enough, surely, ta blind ya to all that you already have?"

Evander looked around the cottage as though he were making a hasty inventory of what he already had. He looked down at his wife, his radiant, exquisite young wife, and felt suddenly desolate. Abandoned. Betrayed.

Valour's eyes pleaded with him. Her grip on his arm tightened. She stepped in close, grasping both his arms. "We need you,

Evander. Yer ma and Grey." She blinked back tears. "I need my husband here. Evander, I need you."

He had to get away, away from the warmth of Valour's touch, away from Grey and her bandaged arm, away from his fading mother. He saw the hurt and shock in Valour's eyes when he pushed her aside. But, no. He had to leave. He'd come home to tell his wife of his escape from the wolves, of the plans his men were making, of Knox's change of heart. He'd come home to tell his mother that he was closer than ever to finding the elusive light of her dreams, to tell Grey that he would find her a world where no wolves would threaten her. He'd walked through the door with all these words on his lips, and what he'd found were a mother and a child who seemed beyond hope or aid and a wife he did not know. He stormed out of the cottage feeling savage. And lost.

Cormac rode into Fleete and asked after Hadrian. The owner of the inn told him that Hadrian was expecting him. That unsettled Cormac, for he had sent no word ahead. He went, as he was directed, to the rocky summit of the hill. It was a strange little village, Fleete. The shops and stables and cottages were strewn haphazardly around the stony crag that broke from the top of the hill and braved the winds from the mountains.

Cormac found his way to the top and stood shivering in the wind. The sky was thick, swirling overhead like soup stirred in a kettle. He held his lantern high, searching, stumbling along in its pale light as freezing rain began to fall. It pricked his skin like tiny arrows. He wished he was home, in the warmth of his large cottage, stretched before the fire.

Just ahead of him, a blot of darkness appeared. Cormac moved his light toward the shape. He cried out, nearly dropping the lantern and shattering the glass on the stones, when two gleaming blue eyes appeared in the dark form, and white teeth flashed.

Hadrian was smiling.

During the whole of their exchange, Cormac never got a clear view of his companion. The lantern light sought other things to illuminate. It shied away from Hadrian, bending around his black cloak. They spoke only a few words to one another. Cormac told Hadrian the names of the men who'd agreed to help him silence Evander. He told Hadrian what they intended to do and when.

"Market day," Hadrian said, dismissing Cormac's plan. "Everything will be settled."

"But what if Evander isn't in the village?"

"He will be."

Mina found the tunnel after three nights of searching, when her last torch was all but useless. She'd spent her days formulating plans for escape, considering every possible scenario. When she slept, her rest was uneasy, and she woke with a sense of extreme urgency. She had to get home.

She'd determined that the only way out of the cave was on the back of the dragon. She would take the lantern while the dragon hunted and tuck it in her coat. She would wait while the dragon ate its meal. Then, when it made ready to fly toward its nightly destination, she would leap onto its back. She'd thought about plunging her father's dagger between its scales and holding onto that, but it was risky. She could injure the dragon and send both of them plummeting to the floor of the valley. More likely, she would just enrage the beast, and it would turn its head in flight and burn the flesh from her bones. Either way, on the verge of escape, Mina's death loomed, imminent and violent as ever.

Then she found the tunnel. She'd ventured farther back each night, astounded at how deep the cave cut into the side of the mountain. On the fourth night, her torchlight shone on a crack in the wall. It was wider than her shoulders, and it rose high above her head. Mina reminded herself that the crack might be nothing at all, might lead nowhere, might be impassible just a few paces beyond this wall. But the dragon had only been gone an hour or two. There was time to explore.

Mina hurried back to her place at the front of the cave. She gathered everything into her pack and slung it over her shoulder. She passed through the freezing darkness, through the reek of the dragon, through the noise of water dripping from the roof of the cave and plopping into shallow pools. She went to the dragon's hoard and took the lantern. By this time, her torch was going out, the flames sputtering around the bottom of the cloth. She stuck it gingerly into the lantern, touching one little tongue of flame to the wick. It caught, and the cave shone with the colors of the Fayrewood. Mina dropped the dying torch. It fell into a puddle of water and hissed and smoked and rolled over to the bottom of the dragon's hoard, disturbing the mound of lanterns. Something showed its face then, something bright that had lain hidden for who knows how long. Mina bent to pick it up. It was a panel of beaten edanna, well made, that must have broken from the framework of a lantern. In its face a large circle was cut, and inside the large circle was a much smaller one. The two circles were linked by a strange assortment of short and long, straight and curved lines. Mina's heart skipped a beat. This was the same device that Maeve embroidered into her finest work. This was the sign Evander had chosen to represent the Sun Clan. And here it was, secreted in the depths of a cave, lying forgotten at the bottom of a heap for years uncounted. This symbol had doubtless inhabited the cave long before Maeve began to dream. And that could only mean ...

Mina laughed aloud, and the sound echoed through the cave. That could only mean that Maeve was not the first to see the sun. Others had seen it. And the images that appeared and reappeared in the old stories and songs were more likely the memories of their ancestors than mere fabrications. If she read the symbol rightly, then there was a time before the Shadow fell, and there was a sunlit world beyond its reach.

Mina put the edanna panel in one of the pouches on her belt and made her way to the crack. She stepped out of the blackness of the cave and into another darkness. She took a few steps, the sound of dripping water growing more and more faint. The fingers of her left hand found the water skin tied to her belt. It was full. The line between her brows softened, and she pushed on, gathering courage from the lantern light. Her soft boots made no noise on the floor of the tunnel, but the sound of her breathing was very loud in this stillness. She stopped once and held her breath. No roaring, no distant wind, no swaying branches, no water. Nothing. She held it a little longer, until the pounding of her pulse distracted her from the silence. She exhaled, and the air came out in a puff of white. She walked on.

After an hour or so, the roof of the cave dipped down. Mina stooped and continued, holding the lantern in front of her. There was time enough. If the tunnel came to an abrupt end, she could still return to the dragon's lair. That prison, terrible though it was, held the promise of water and the occasional scrap of raw meat. Mina smiled to herself, marveling at how she could reason and rationalize, how she could lie to herself. She had no intention of turning around. She couldn't. With the lantern light going before her, she felt as if she were journeying toward the sun. She wished Valour could see how extraordinary it was, how much beauty it recalled in even so dark a place as this.

When the roof dipped again, Mina crawled. With her teeth, she held the ring at the top of the lantern. She persisted, on hands and knees, until the tallow ran out, and the lantern went dark.

Mina stopped. She sat against the wall of the tunnel, fighting her rising panic, her tangled fears. She took them captive, one by one.

I'll die here. It was the first thought she found, perhaps because it was larger than the rest, and it seemed to pulse. She took a deep breath, drank from her water skin, and wrestled with that. In truth, she could've died before ever she reached the falls. Since she left Holt, death could have taken her a hundred times over. How often had it passed her by in the dragon's lair? Yet here she was, with the lantern in her hands. Valour's lantern. Evander's lantern. Already, she'd done impossible things. Perhaps she could do more.

Evander. I must see Evander again. That was the second thought. Its edges were jagged, and it hurt her when she picked it up. It wouldn't be easy to see him, now he was Valour's husband. But if he was happy, if he was content, if Mina could see him smile, see the light in his eyes . . .

She doesn't believe him. This was the third thought, and the "she" was Valour. Mina didn't know what to do with this one. She didn't know if the edanna panel would restore Valour's faith in Evander. She didn't know if Valour had any desire to seek a better world, if she was even dissatisfied with her life beneath the Shadow. Mina set the thought back down among the others.

I'm hungry. This thought was most easily dealt with. Mina reminded herself of all the long winters she'd survived. More than twenty. She'd gone hungry on many days, had lain awake hungry on many nights. She had water, and if she could get down into the valley, there was hope of finding food. She would live.

It's not as dark as it was. This thought surprised her, and she wondered if the tunnel was coming to an end and light was leaking in through some outlet up ahead. She looked to left and right, checking her theory. But beyond her, in both directions, the darkness was complete. It was the area nearest her, around her body, where the dark was thinnest. She lifted a hand and looked at it. It shone with just the faintest tinge of silver light. She wiggled her fingers. In the perfect silence, she heard them. They moved with a kind of humming energy that was not unlike the trees. She'd always imagined, when she touched the bark of the Fayrewood trees, that she could feel the sap running through them. What flowed through her veins, she wondered, that could fill the empty silence and illuminate the dark?

*The dragons come for bright thing*s. This thought was more surprising than the last, for Mina had never imagined herself as something worth stealing. She knew that the dragon had taken her from the valley because it coveted her lantern. Now she understood why it had kept her. *It might have been me, and not the lantern, that the dragon most prized.*

This thought gave Mina new strength. In light of it, the dark of the tunnel seemed a small thing. She tucked the lantern inside her coat and crept forward on hands and knees.

Thirty

Maeve's dreams changed again. When she slept, she saw the sun hanging high in the sky. It was golden and full of promise. For one perfect moment, she felt its warmth on her face. Then the Shadow came. It crept into the edges of her vision, eating up the blue sky, swallowing the light. The darkness crowded in, until the ball of fire shrank to a pinpoint of light, and disappeared. She woke and whispered, "All is lost."

After coming home and finding it no home at all, Evander spent the day in the stable. He took special care with the horses, and, when he was inclined, shared his sorrows with Rogue. He should have gone to one of his men. They believed in him, and they could have rekindled his hope. But Evander had long made a habit of isolating himself from those he needed most desperately. People like Errol, like Lachlan, like Chase, like Mina, they moved on the borders of his world, absolutely vital and totally unseen. The ones who tormented him, who opposed him, who deceived him, those he clung to.

It was a cruel turn of fortune that Valour should prove faithless only moments after Knox had come around. Evander told Rogue how cruel it was, and how often he wished he could be satisfied with his life in Holt. The black stallion nickered and munched his supper, and Evander fell asleep in the warmth of the hay.

The next day he went to his men, asking if they'd be ready to set out on the following morning. The hunters were eager to go. Their time was short, and they were desperate for a successful hunt. Only Lachlan protested.

"We'll miss market day," he said. "And it's likely this will be the last." Lachlan earned a few coins for his playing on market day, and the money would go further toward feeding him through the winter than another unsuccessful hunt.

"We've got ta try," Evander replied. "And we need you."

Lachlan agreed, and it was settled.

The men thundered out of Holt next morning. They'd just ridden out of the foothills when they pulled up. The air was full of the baying of wolves. There were many hundreds. They moved like dark water flooding the plain, their flashing eyes a sea of candle flames.

"By the gods," Lorne breathed.

"Back!" Evander cried.

The hunters raced toward Holt.

The darkness was thinning, softening, and it was not merely Mina's radiance that worked the change. The tunnel was coming to an end. She could hear the wind, just ahead. Her palms and her knees were bruised, her neck aching; her nose and cheeks burned with cold. But Mina beamed, and any man who saw her then, wounds and all, would have wondered how he could've ever overlooked a woman as fair and bold as she.

Sharp, searing light appeared. It spilled into the tunnel, frightening Mina, then disappeared as quickly as it came. Mina feared dragon fire, but the color wasn't right. This was something new.

When she reached the end of the tunnel, she peeked into the open, clinging to the hope that she was not suspended high above the ground and as trapped as she'd been in the dragon's lair. Her hope was rewarded. The tunnel opened not on a cliff, but on a rocky slope dotted with snow-blanketed fir trees. Ice hung from the branches of other trees in long, crystalline fingers. Further down, the slope spread out into a wide, forested valley.

A little shudder of relief passed through Mina as she crawled out of the dark tunnel and into the gray light of a Shiloh day.

Wait.

Mina realized with a jolt that this was not like any Shiloh day she had ever seen. The green of each fir needle, the brown and gray bark of each trunk and branch stood out in sharp contrast to the white of the snow. There was too much light. She could see clear across the valley below. She looked up, toward the ever-present hovering dark she knew so well.

The Shadow was different here. In Holt, it had weighted her every waking step. In the Peaks, it had watched her and cloaked her enemies. Here, on what Mina guessed was the northern border of Shiloh, the Shadow was distant, thin, like threadbare fabric. It could tear apart at any moment.

When the fabric of the clouds did pull away, and the light broke through, Mina shielded her eyes and cried out. She fell to the ground, squinting against the sharp, sudden radiance. As her eyes adjusted, she slowly came to see how the icicles glinted, how the snow sparkled.

Her tears spilled over. She couldn't contain them. She could hardly breathe. The clouds shifted, cutting off the light, but Mina had no doubt what she'd seen. The sun.

"What's wrong?" Valour asked, when Evander came running through the door. He'd only just left.

"The wolves," he said, his eyes searching the room. "They're coming."

"What —"

"Where's Grey?" he demanded. "Don't tell me she's gone out!"

Valour held up empty hands. "What could I do?"

Evander leveled her with a cold stare. "Stay here with Ma. Not one foot outside this door, do ya understand?!"

"Evander —"

"No, Valour," he said, silencing her. His words sank in when the door slammed shut.

The wolves were coming.

Coming where? Coming when? How many? And what of my parents? And Errol? What of Emmeline and the babies? What am I to do with Maeve?

Valour went to the back room. Since her argument with Evander, Maeve had not eaten. She'd taken no water in more than a day. Nothing Valour said or did moved her. She was silent and still, and her eyes were closed.

And the wolves were coming.

When? How many? And what was she to do?

Valour wondered, and despised herself for wondering, if this was Evander's doing. Could it be possible that Evander had already chosen his quest over his people? If he had, what was to become of them?

Mina was faced with an impossible choice. Before her was the wooded valley, with high, breezy clouds and the sun riding over all. What waited in the far north, she could not tell, but it sang of life and promise. Behind her were the Peaks and the dragons, the falls and the foothills, a little village shrouded in Shadow, and everything she had ever loved. She unfastened her coat and held the lantern in her hands, thinking how frail and small was the beauty of the Fayrewood lanterns. They were nothing to the glory of the colored wood. And none of Maeve's dreams, and none of Evander's words, and no tale or song she'd ever heard could have prepared her for the splendor of the sun. One glimpse of its bright rays had broken her heart and healed her wounds.

The north called to her. It spoke her name. *Mina*, it said. *Come out of the dark*. But her people cowered in Shadow. Her mother was there, waiting for her. Chase was there, and Emmeline. Valour was there, and Evander.

It was hard to turn her back on the valley and clamber over the tumbled slopes toward the southern side of the mountain. It was hard to walk back into the Shadow after her eyes had seen the sun. Her face streamed with tears as she came around the mountain and her view of the northern valley was blocked. But Mina had made her choice. She'd forfeited her freedom so that she might bring hope to the people of Holt.

Thirty-One

Evander and his men hurried through the village, alerting the people of danger, and summoning the men to a meeting in the magistrate's cottage. They rushed to the furnace, shouting for Errol. They corralled the craftsmen in the workshops along the Cutting. They called through doorways, banged on windows, and the men of Holt came running. When they were assembled, Cormac was first to speak.

"We were warned of this!" he said, pointing a finger at Evander.

"Warned of what?" Cole said. "What's happened?"

"Wolves, coming in great numbers," Evander said.

"How many?" someone asked.

Evander shook his head. His men looked at the floor. The others understood. Too many to count.

Evander looked at Errol. "It's happened before, hasn't it?"

The old man shifted his weight. "Aye. We put tallow 'round the village and lit it. But we've used all the extra tallow on the torches."

Evander and Chase noticed Reed at the same moment. He was trying to hide behind a large man near the back, but he'd revealed himself by looking Evander in the face when Errol mentioned the torches.

"Reed!" Chase called. "This is no place fer children."

"Let 'im stay," Evander said.

There was quiet again. Then a voice muttered, "We'll fall ta the wolves trying ta defend ourselves from the dragons."

"It's just as Hadrian said!" Cormac shouted. "The village will fall, and it's your doing!"

"Bonfires, then," Evander said, ignoring Cormac. "It'll give us some advantage, if we can move quickly enough."

"How long?" someone asked.

When Evander hesitated, the men paled. Even Cormac was silent. Finally, Evander pointed to five of the craftsmen.

"Gather what fuel ya can, now. Get fires started along the southern edge o' the hill. Go!" They jumped to life and hurried out the door.

Chase spoke next. "The women, Evander. The children. What of them?"

When Evander faltered, Chase tried again. "We've not much of a plan ta defend the village. Can we not get them out before . . . ?"

But how? Evander knew he could never get Maeve out of Holt before the village was overrun. And what about Moss? She could scarcely walk. What about Emmeline and the babies?

"North," Knox said. "They'll see no wolves if they go north o' the foothills. They can travel along the plain and then down inta Fleete. They'll be safe there fer a time." He nodded assurance. It was the best way, the only way.

Evander agreed. "We can't force 'em, though. Lachlan, would ya go with Chase? Spread the word. Any who wish ta flee should meet in Market Circle." He looked around the assembly. "Who will lead them?"

Cormac volunteered. Evander hadn't noticed the bundle of supplies waiting by the door until Cormac grabbed it on his way out. Apparently the new magistrate had already made ready to retreat.

"I'll need yer arrows, men," Evander said, turning to Knox and Lorne.

"There'll be no more hunting today, I suppose," Lorne said.

Knox smiled and slapped Lorne across the back. "Don't trouble yerself, Lorne. It's likely there'll be no one left ta feed this winter anyhow."

They hastened through the village, commandeering arrows wherever they could be found. The air rang with the howling of the wolves. When they reached the edge of the village, daylight was failing. Just out of sight, the dark line of the horizon moved, as black shapes swarmed over the hills.

"I won't go," Valour insisted.

"The others are prepared. They're waiting. Please, my daughter, see the sense in this!"

"No," Valour said again. "I won't leave Maeve and Grey. I won't leave Evander. Da, I can't. I'm sorry." She took his hands in hers. "Tell Ma I'll see 'er soon. Either we'll come ta Fleete, or she'll come home."

"Please, Valour," Cole whispered. She felt the tremor in his hands as he spoke. "Please."

She leaned in and kissed his forehead, blinking back tears. "I've already chosen, Da." She saw that he understood. He pulled her into a fierce embrace, then turned and left without a farewell.

Valour took a cloth from the table and dipped it in a jug of water. She wrung it out and folded it, carrying it back to Maeve's cot. She leaned over the wasted body, wiping Maeve's forehead with the damp cloth.

"Maeve," she said. Then, more tenderly, "Ma."

No response.

Valour could hear shouting outside the cottage. And now, through the thick stone walls, the windows, the heavy wooden door, she could hear the cries of the wolves. She took Maeve's hand and tried to sing. But the tune faded away, and she forgot the words, and it was hard to think while the wolves were closing in. *There must be hundreds*, she thought. *Oh, Grey. Grey!* Valour pressed her face to Maeve's hand and wept. How she wished she could be like Mina, holding the reins of her mind so tightly, never allowing her thoughts and fears to overwhelm her. But sorrow and terror swept in with unstoppable force. Valour let them come.

When at last she lifted her face and let go of Maeve's hand, it dropped like a stone. Maeve, the first Dreamer, was dead.

Mina found a little stream that was not yet fully frozen. The snow was piled along its banks, and slabs of ice hindered the flow of water, but it moved. She filled her water skin and followed the stream, hoping it would lead her to the lake. Hoping there was only one lake.

On her second day outside the tunnel, Mina killed a rabbit. She'd seen it hop out of a little hollow in the snow, and before she'd even thought to wish for her lost bow, she'd thrown her father's dagger. It stuck fast near the rabbit's tail, and Mina closed her eyes to the twitching of the pitiful creature as she crushed its skull with a stone. Her fingers were clumsy with cold by the time the carcass was skinned and gutted. Mina was too ravenous to care.

That night she sheltered under a ledge of rock lined with dripping icicles. She made a small fire out of pine needles and another strip of her shift. Waiting for the rabbit to cook required almost more patience and restraint than she could muster. She checked it repeatedly, singing her fingertips on the outer portions only to find that the inner portions were bloody and raw. She occupied herself by catching the fat that dripped from the roasting meat.

Finally, her supper was ready. Mina tore off a hunk of meat and dropped it into the snow to cool it before taking a bite. No meal had ever tasted so sweet. Mina licked her fingers and licked the bones and fell asleep, leaving the fire to burn as long as it would.

Next morning, she set out with new vigor. Thoughts of her aching shoulder and her countless cuts and bruises fell away. She began to imagine her homecoming. She wouldn't want the whole village to see her. That would be awful. But when Chase saw her, and her parents ... Her heart gave a leap at the thought of seeing them again. And what would Valour say when she saw the lantern, whole and shining? Perhaps then she would believe in the impossible.

And Evander. She sighed, laying aside the question of how she could ever find the strength to look into Evander's face and speak the words, *I saw it. I saw the sun.*

Of course, none of that mattered now. Not yet. The river was widening, and she could see trees ahead. She picked up her pace, following the river down and down, into a broad, still forest of snow-dusted evergreens. The snow on the ground was powdery and dry. It hushed her footfalls as she ran, following the path of the water through the wood.

As the light faded, Mina stopped to drink and rest. She leaned against a mossy trunk, inhaling the rich scent of the fir needles. A sound rose to her ears. She held her breath to be sure. She exhaled in a rush and ran toward the murmur of water lapping against ice and stone. It seemed only a few steps before she exploded out of the wood and stood on the edge of a wide lake. Thick plates of ice stretched from the rocks at her feet, reaching toward the ice that gathered on the far shore. *The far shore.* Mina's eyes grew wide. She could see the opposite shore of the lake! She lifted her hand. Shafts of silver light leaked out of the sleeve of her coat. She marveled at the sight of her fingers, brighter than lanterns, illuminating the mountain lake. She'd found her way back. Laughter bubbled up inside her.

She never heard the rush of air or the vast, slow beat of dragon wings. The bursts of blue fire were eclipsed by her own radiance. She knew nothing, nothing but her glory, until the dragon's claws closed on her. Her right shoulder was held fast by two talons in front and one in back. On her left side, talons sank deep into the flesh below her ribs.

As she rose over the lake, the silver light died away, replaced by the erratic explosions of many blue fires.

Thirty-Two

There were only a few dozen men, spread thin. Evander ran between the bonfires, setting the craftsmen to maintaining the fires and scrounging kindling from every possible source. The hunters were positioned between the fires, arrows poised to pick off any wolves that broke from the horde.

No one slept. The next day was market day. Or it would have been. No one thought of that. No one thought how they were burning up all the firewood they needed to survive the winter. They could think of nothing but the onslaught. The wolves snapped and snarled, and there were never enough arrows. No matter how carefully the hunters conserved them, there were never enough.

When morning neared, and the light began, almost imperceptibly, to change, Evander sent Reed to the Cutting with buckets. He brought them back full, and the men drank, no more than one or two at a time, and returned to their stations solemn and sweating.

Evander paced between bonfires encouraging his men, taking shots when he could, wondering why he didn't mount Rogue and ride out into the midst of the wolves, blazing like he'd done only days before. The answer was simple. He feared that his men would follow, feared they would all be lost. The wolves were too many. What could they possibly do against so many?

As the day wore on, a group of wolves surged forward, leaping upon the men of Holt in a vicious assault. Two men fell before the wolves were dispatched with flaming arrows. Three others were wounded, and these Evander sent to Moss. Meanwhile, a little knot of wolves used the distraction to advantage, making its way to a weak point in the line and sneaking into the village. They roamed between the cottages, sniffing the air and calling to one another. When a little boy heard them and opened his cottage door to see what was happening, they swarmed.

The sound of the child's screams never reached Evander. When Valour came running, against his specific instructions, she held a torch in a trembling hand. He could see in her eyes that something was dreadfully wrong. He motioned for Knox to follow and ran after Valour. Evander saw the wolves, three standing over the boy's body, and two breaking away. He told Valour to hide. He and Knox nocked two arrows apiece, lit them, and let them go. Five wolves dissolved in vapor and smoke.

At the same moment, Cormac was leading a band of women and children down into the hills north of Fleete. They'd crossed the plain without incident, and they could still hear the roar of the falls behind them when Tilly's voice rose in a wailing lament. The others turned, following her gaze to the blue fires that came spilling over the falls.

The blood drained from Cormac's face. Here was the hideous fulfillment of Hadrian's warning. Cries erupted all over the group as women and children realized what Cormac already knew. The dragons were heading for Holt.

Seeker

"There are too many! We need another plan!" Lachlan was shouting. Sweat dripped into a long gash on his forehead.

Evander stared at the body on the ground. It was a tangle of torn cloth and torn flesh. But it had been a child, only moments before. "Get the others out," he said. "All o' them. Lachlan, you know who's still in the village. Send Cole and Errol ta meet them at Market Circle. Go now!"

Lachlan ran.

"Valour!" Evander called. A mass of flame-red hair appeared around a doorway, and Valour came. "Can Ma ride?" Evander asked, taking her arm.

Her head gave a tiny shake, her eyes filling with tears. She bit her lip.

Evander read the truth in her face, and he shrank within himself. The frenzied cries of the villagers, the roaring of the bonfires, the howling of the wolves, everything quieted. Evander heard it all as from a great distance. His people ran by, scooping children into their arms, snatching blankets and water skins and weapons. He didn't see them. He didn't feel the soft wool of Valour's shift or the ache of his muscles. Somewhere, far off, horses thundered past.

His mother was gone. The woman who'd unleashed the radiance of the sun on his mind, on his world, was dead. Never again would she dream of a light so great and bright that it burned up the Shadow. The Dreamer was lost, and her dreams with her. Only Evander was left, with his memories of her sad songs and her embroidery and her absolute conviction. Evander looked at the branded symbol on his belt, at the wolves that covered the hills.

"Evander!"

He understood, gradually, that Valour was screaming at him, shaking him. He turned, raised his eyes. The sky was full of dragons.

He gripped Valour's arms.

"Evander!" Valour cried, and he saw her, weeping, trembling.

She was so beautiful. He blinked, turned, pulling her with him. He had to get her out.

Black wings beat the air. The torches on top of the cottages blazed with blue fire. Evander dragged Valour toward Market Circle, shielding her when a wall collapsed and stones tumbled across their path. As they neared the northern end of the village, a dragon swooped down. Something dark fell to the ground and made a small gasping sound.

Evander rushed to the body and found it slumped forward. He pulled the pack from its back before turning it over and laying it gently on the ground. Valour fell to her knees and sobbed.

Mina. She was deathly pale. She made a weak motion toward her pack. Her shift was short and ragged. Channels of dried and drying blood streaked her left leg. Evander found the wound in her side.

"Can ya stay with 'er, Valour?" he asked, shouting above the din. She looked back terrified, nodded. Evander ran toward the bonfires, searching for Chase. He didn't have to explain. When Chase saw his expression, he left the dwindling line of men who fought back the wolves and followed Evander.

"Mina!" he cried, when he saw her. Chase dropped to the ground, pulled her into his lap, and rocked her in his arms. Valour was kneeling nearby, holding something in her hands.

"By the gods!" Evander said, recognizing the lantern. "She found it?"

"It was in 'er pack," Valour said.

Evander looked at Mina, wondering at her. She'd gone into the mountains and found what she sought. It was impossible. It was madness. And she'd done it. Tears rose in Evander, a torrent of tears that begged to be shed. He crouched beside Mina, looking into her eyes. She was watching him intently. Her lips fluttered.

"Mina?" Chase asked. He searched her face, then lowered his ear to her mouth and waited. He looked up at Evander, shaking his head. "She saw it. She says she saw it."

Evander took one of Mina's hands and held her fingers lightly. "What did ya see, Mina?"

Her face lit. She smiled at him. "The sun," she whispered.

She made another weak motion toward her belt. Then her eyes, fixed on Evander, lost their focus and closed.

"Mina!" Chase cried.

Evander placed Mina's small hand on her chest and allowed her words to ring in his head for a long moment. The sun. The sun. The sun. It was there, and Mina had seen it.

A horse screamed as it fled from the dragons. Evander was jarred from his reverie. He stood, pulling Valour away from Mina and hauling her to Market Circle. Women and children huddled on the edge of the circle, against the walls of cottages. Cole guarded them, loosing flaming arrows whenever the dragons descended. Errol was there. He was helping Moss into a saddle. Emmeline was there, with Fayre strapped to her back and True in her arms.

Evander called to Moss. "Is this everyone?" She nodded, and Evander looked to Cole and Errol. "Go on, then! There's no time!" The villagers streamed down the hill.

Evander pulled Valour to him and kissed her, remembering all she had awakened in him. "I'll come fer you, my love," he said.

She shook her head and wept and fought him, "No! You'll be lost like everything else. Come with me, Evander! Please!"

He leaned in, his face against hers, his mouth to her ear. "Not everything is lost, Valour. Find yer courage. Remember Mina. There's hope yet."

She stilled, and pressed the lantern into his hands.

"I'm sorry," she whispered, and seemed unable to find any other words. She looked at the lantern once more before turning and running to catch up with the others. Evander lingered, watching, until Valour took True from Emmeline's arms, and Cole embraced her, and Errol put a protective hand on her shoulder. Then he spun back to face the desolation of Holt.

Thirty-Three

The fire was wrong. The dragons swept over the village, circled, shrieked, chased fleeing ewes and horses. But Evander couldn't see that they were trying to burn Holt. It was all but impossible, for the cottages were built of stone, their roofs of slate, and the dragons were too large to get in among the cottages and destroy them from the ground.

Yet the village was burning. Windows shattered, and blue fire billowed out from *inside*. He studied a nearby cottage. The torches at the corners of the roof were bright, but the flames were moving, dripping, sliding down the cottage wall, onto doors and window frames, finding their way in. There was plenty to devour inside the cottages. Blankets and cots, tables and chairs, woven rugs, and whatever fuel had not been taken to feed the bonfires.

Reed. He must have replaced the torches before the tallow was dry. It had run down into so many little wooden nooks, transforming the cottages into massive torches, just waiting to be lit. It was a simple mistake, a child's doing. And Holt would burn for it.

Holt may well have burned anyway, Evander thought. He was

caught somewhere between wild hope and utter despair. He ran through the village, pulled Chase away from Mina's body, called to a handful of men who were not busy dismantling the bonfires and spreading flaming logs in a long, solid line across the southern edge of the hill.

They made for Chase's cottage. The torch on the roof had not yet caught fire. Evander and the others rushed inside. They found Reed in a corner, crying, but whether he grieved for his sister or whether he had realized his mistake, Evander couldn't tell.

There were a dozen men in the room. All were sweating, bleeding, their faces drawn, their eyes over-bright.

Evander said what all of them were thinking. "We can't stay."

There was a moment of quiet, as the men panted and looked at one another with questions in their eyes. The village would burn. Holt would be overrun by wolves, leveled by dragons. By now, that was certain.

"Seems like as good a day as any ta start our quest," Lorne said.

Evander looked at him. "I wondered if we mightn't go on. I think I will regardless."

"I'll go," Chase said. His eyes were red, his face stony. He stood beside Reed with his arm around him. He gave Evander a helpless look. "He should've gone with the others."

Evander nodded as tiles scraped overhead. The walls shook, rattling the windows in their frames. Shouts and cries rose from the men outside.

"Who else is with me?" Evander asked, looking at Lachlan.

"Ya know I'm going," Lachlan said.

"Are we the Sun Clan or aren't we?" Knox said. "Besides, it's not as if we had any meat fer the winter. If I'm ta starve, I might as well do it with you."

"Evander!" Lorne pointed to a window. Blue fire was eating into the frame. The glass pane cracked and fell.

"We've no time!" Evander said. "Are there any others?"

"Aye," one of the hunters answered. "There are men who'd go with ya, Evander. But where? How?"

Evander remembered the lantern he'd hurriedly hooked onto his belt. "The Fayrewood," he said. "The wolves won't go there. It's our best chance."

Evander saw the fear in their eyes. With the wolves cutting off escape to the south, the dragons to north and west, there would be only one way out of the Fayrewood. They would have to go through the Turn and journey into the Black Mountains.

The walls shuddered again. Roof tiles scraped and slid, exposing a corner of the cottage to the open air.

"Take what ya can: weapons, food, blankets. And spread the word. Any man who would journey with the Sun Clan must get ta the Fayrewood with all speed. I'll see what horses I can gather."

The men poured out of the room. Only Reed was left, and Evander could hardly bear to look at him. His face was desolate.

"It's my fault," he said.

"Think no more of it, Reed. You've only spurred us on toward our quest. Now get yer things. And hurry!"

By the time he reached the stable, blue flames were licking up the hay and gliding across the wooden beams in the ceiling. The horses had broken from their stalls and run wild over the village, fleeing the wolves on one hand and the dragons on the other. Evander grabbed what bridles he could reach and ducked out of the building. He passed his cottage, where fires were eating up the door. They would soon find the cot he had shared with his wife, the basket with his mother's embroidery, and countless other testaments to a people and a time that were vanishing before his eyes.

The flames would find his mother. It was fitting, he supposed, that the cottage should serve as her burial mound. Evander touched one of the stones that jutted from the wall, closing his eyes against the rising grief, and remembered Grey.

Where was Grey? She wouldn't have stayed in the cottage. Maybe she'd seen one of the groups making for Fleete. Maybe she'd gone with them. Maybe she hadn't. Maybe she was lost. Evander roared in impotent rage and hurried on.

He found Rogue and Frost circling the hillside between the village and the Fayrewood. They calmed a little, on seeing him and hearing his voice, and he just managed to put a bridle over each of their heads. He led them down toward the guttering wall of fire that was their only protection against the wolves. Reed was there, and Chase. Knox arrived with perhaps twenty others. Lorne came, coaxing three horses. Ropes were tied around their necks, and the blue roan was among them. Lachlan ran up, waving his pipe in the air. "Dropped it," he explained.

"Do we wait fer anyone else?" Evander shouted.

One of the hunters spoke up. "Some o' the men hope ta make it ta Fleete. This is it."

Evander nodded, and led men and horses into the Fayrewood.

The floor of the Fayrewood was littered with brown-gold leaves, and gusts of wind from the mountains and the dragons' wings sent more of them fluttering to the ground. It was strange to walk in the lovely wood, when the familiar sound of the wind in the trees was joined by the baying of the wolves as they tore through the village. Evander gripped Chase's shoulder and let go, acknowledging their shared grief. While they made their escape, the bodies of women they loved were burning.

But Chase was distracted with Reed. In spite of Chase's pleading, the boy kept wandering off and falling to the back of the group.

He seemed unsure of his place, and eager to hide his shame from the older men. Chase's agitation grew as they neared the Turn.

Knox came up beside Evander. "It's as ya said all along, my friend. We'll take the Turn and see what befalls us."

"Aye," Evander replied, looking into the darkness beyond the Turn. The trees quivered. His eyes could never bring them into focus. There were unnerving cries from unknown creatures. Mist covered the ground. Evander felt the sweat trickling down his back. "Now we come to it, I think I'd prefer the Peaks."

There was a disturbance in the group. Someone at the back called out, "The trees!" Evander turned with the others to see blue fire race across the branches of the Fayrewood trees, leaping from leaf to leaf. It was too much. Evander shut his eyes and dropped his head. How complete was the destruction of his home! The village and the Fayrewood would burn, and only the colored lanterns would linger, like memories, like ghosts of forgotten beauty.

Now, truly, the Turn was their only hope of escape. Evander lifted the lantern from his belt and lit it.

He stepped beyond the Turn, and his men followed, falling silent as they came in among the dark trees. They kept their arrows ready, their hands on the hilts of their daggers. They'd missed the beauty of the Fayrewood because of their fear of the Turn, and they all thought now how wise they had been to stay away, to warn their children away. They were thinking, too, of the wives and mothers, the sons and daughters, who crept under the shadow of the dragons, under the shadow of the mountains, seeking refuge in Fleete. They hoped their dear ones would never know the savage terror that closed in on them now.

Chase's frantic voice broke the tight silence. "Evander, where's Reed?"

He was not with the others. Chase ran back towards the Fayrewood.

There was no sign of him. Then Evander noticed a small figure coming toward them, through the trees. "Reed!" he called. "Is that you?"

The figure kept its steady pace, and Evander took one step off the path, into the trees with the shivering bark, and stretched his lantern forward. He squinted. "Grey?"

The girl stepped up to him and wrapped her arms around his neck. He clung to her a moment, then held her at arm's length. "How did ya get here? Ya shouldn't be here! I'd hoped you'd gone on with the others, toward Fleete."

Grey put a tiny hand on Evander's cheek. "Don't go, Evander. Ya mustn't go off on this mad quest and leave me here with the wolves."

"We can't stay. There's nothing left, Grey," he said, "This quest is our last hope."

"Oh, Evander," Grey replied. "So foolish, so deceived."

As she spoke, her skin darkened. Her large eyes bored into Evander's, flashing with green and gold fire. Her nose grew impossibly long; her teeth lengthened, the ends narrowing to sharp points. Her wild black hair shortened and spread over her body, the gray streak stretching into a long line of gray fur that ran the length of her hide. She snarled. Hands and feet sprouted claws, and the hand that rested on Evander's cheek was yanked back, leaving bloody gashes.

Evander and the wolf pulled away from one another. The quivering trees of the dark wood shrank, shifting, taking wolf forms. They fell on the Sun Clan.

Further back, where the Fayrewood burned, a dark man with blue eyes stood watching. The Lord of Shadows had sent him long ago, when Maeve had first begun to dream. For years, from a distance, he'd seen how those dreams shaped Evander, how the boy grew into a man driven by longing and purpose, a dangerous man. He'd sent Grey to haunt the cottage and the stable, to pursue the hunters in the guise of a wolf, to mingle with the Fayrewood trees so that she might see and hear everything.

Ulff would be pleased.

Hadrian smiled while the Sun Clan was slaughtered.

Knox fell, shot with a stray arrow. Evander tried to reach him, but a wolf took hold of his leg. He flung the lantern at its head, and its black fur caught fire. The beast vanished, and the lantern fell to the ground. Evander looked up to see Chase fall beside Knox. In the next breath, Chase's body was covered in a writhing mass of fur.

As the wrath of the Shadow fell, Evander remembered Mina, remembered her shining face when she spoke of the sun, remembered the impossible quest she'd embarked upon and completed. In the end, it was the courage of a woman he'd never loved, a woman he'd never noticed, that saved Evander. Suddenly, the army of shifters, and the dark wood, even the bodies of his fallen clansmen faded from his vision. He saw the sun in his mind's eye, as his mother had described it to him. It hung in a sky of clear blue, brighter and warmer than anything he'd ever seen or known. And all Shadows fled before it.

A fire was kindled in Evander. It leapt from his skin and seared the hides of the yelping wolves. "The sun!" he cried, and the darkness trembled at the sound of his voice. Lorne and Lachlan took up the cry. They, too, shone with brilliant light, illuminating the wood.

All three escaped the shifters, journeying on foot along the western edge of the Black Mountains. They entered the Pallid Peaks at the start of winter. But the winds and the snows and the dragons were no match for them, for they began to guess their strength, and they knew that their Enemy feared them. In dark places, in hunger, in distress, they remembered Maeve's visions and Mina's triumph and took heart. One morning, while Lachlan played a new tune on his pipe, they came upon a wide, forested valley far to the north. High, thin clouds pulled away, and the sun broke through.

Epilogue

No morning glories grew in Fleete. Valour always grieved for them in late spring and summer when the walls of the village cottages were bare. There were no bleeding flowers either, no Fayrewood, no Dance of the Lantern Light. There were no ores, no colored glass, no Cutting Stream. Fleete was prosperous enough, in its own way, but when Valour thought of all that was lost in Holt . . . well. It was enough loss for a lifetime of grief. She supposed she should be grateful that there were no bleeding flowers, for they would only have reminded her of Maeve. The Fayrewood trees would only have reminded her of Mina. Colored glass and the Dance of the Lantern Light would only have reminded her of Evander, who had not returned.

Her life was altogether different, and sometimes she thought that the beauty of Holt, and all that she'd known there, had been only a passing vision, something akin to Maeve's dreams. But that thought wouldn't stick, not when she looked into the face of her son and saw Evander.

She kept herself busy. There was plenty of work to do. Either she was caring for little Hallam or helping Emmeline with Fayre and True, or she was cooking and cleaning with her mother, or working with Errol at the furnace.

One morning, Valour sat on a stool while Errol added fuel to the fires. "Do ya ever think we should've gone with 'im?" she asked.

He turned to her, bushy eyebrows raised. "With Evander?"

"Aye."

"It was my duty ta get you and the others out," he said. "I don't wish it undone."

"But do ya wonder if things could've been different?" she asked, gloved hands crossed over her leather apron.

"Aye," Errol said, sighing deeply. "I know it could've, but as much as I worry over it, I can't think how." He removed his gloves and sat down beside her. "I do wonder if any o' them found their sun."

"Mina saw it," Valour said. "I've wondered time and again if she was just wild with pain, but 'er face . . ." Valour shrugged. "She got the lantern. There's no knowing what she saw."

She stood up and went to the furnace, hoping some activity would ease the ache. "I'm tired of sitting safe and comfortable while those I love venture great things. Honour did it first, ya know. She struggled, and died, and my birth was easy. Mina went inta the Pallid Peaks ta reclaim my lantern — Evander's lantern. She brought it all the way back ta Holt." Valour struggled with the words, choking on them, but determined to go on. "I stood there like a fool and a coward, with the lantern in my hands, and watched 'er die." She wrapped her gloved hands around the iron rod that held the molten glass in a bowl on its end. "My husband sent me ta safety while our village was overrun. He set off in search of a better world, fer me, and fer our children. And I did nothing."

"Ya saved 'is son, Valour. Ya did as 'e asked."

"But I want ta do more! I want ta honor them. What good were their sacrifices if I sit idly by, wasting my days in fear and regret?"

"Be sure o' yer hands before ya pour that glass, my girl," Errol warned. Valour knew better than to ignore him. She took a calming breath and pulled the bowl of thick orange liquid from the furnace. She walked carefully to the iron molds where the panes would cool and tipped the bowl to fill the first. Molten glass flowed out.

"I want ta do something," Valour said. "I want ta find my courage."

Errol stood and shuffled up to her, hoping to offer comfort, but something caught his eye. "What in all Shiloh . . . ?"

Valour watched, too, amazed. The molten glass, instead of spreading out into its mold, was taking shape. As the bowl emptied, and Valour lowered the iron rod, the gold-orange glass brightened to shining silver and formed itself into a long cylinder. Markings appeared, etched into the side. On either end of the cylinder were circles of clear glass. Errol used tongs to pick it up. He brought it near the furnace, where the light was brightest, and read, "Until the day breaks, and the Shadows flee away."

Valour caught her breath. "What is it?"

"I've never seen the like." He touched a calloused finger to the cylinder, and, finding it cool, raised it to his eye. Valour waited, impatient.

"Can't make out anything but the furnace," he said, passing it to Valour, "but this is the work o' the gods. It seems they smile on you, my girl."

She turned the silver glass in her hands. "Why should they smile on me?"

Errol's eyes twinkled. "Well, as I recall, when that gift arrived you were making plans."

Valour's lips parted in a little gasp. "Could we go, Errol? Do ya suppose we could go after Evander and find the sun?"

"Ya know," he said, "in all my years at the furnace, I've never once let the dragon fire burn as long as it would. I've always put it out ta keep the others from suspecting. But, truth is, there's no telling how long it might last." He rubbed his old hands together, and Valour slipped the glass into her apron pocket before throwing her arms around him. She pulled away abruptly.

"You'll go with me, won't ya?"

"Aye, and I think there are others who might wish ta do the same."

It was decided that Ada would stay in Fleete, with Hallam. Valour wept over his cot every night before they set out, stroking his dark hair and telling him how she was going to find his father, the Light of the Sun Clan, and singing to him until he fell asleep. Emmeline insisted on going, and bringing Fayre and True with her. "It's what Hallam would've wanted," she said, and Valour didn't argue. Cole came as well, and Moss, on horseback. There were others who joined the company: women seeking husbands and sons, and a few men who could no longer endure the passing of years and the accumulation of regrets.

They left Fleete on a summer morning and journeyed south. They planned to purchase supplies in the village of Dunn, and, from there, travel over the Black Mountains in search of the sun. But someone in Dunn suggested another plan. Valour embraced the girl with wild black hair and captivating green-gold eyes, weeping for joy that she had escaped the destruction of Holt.

Grey suggested a path through the Whispering Wood that would lead them to a gap in the Black Mountains. Valour and the others rejoiced, but they were no match for the wolves of the Whispering Wood. Valour fell, and Moss and Cole and Errol and Emmeline. Some few escaped, bloodied and wild with fright. They took their lanterns, burning with blue flame, over the Black Mountains. And the silver glass fell into the undergrowth, lost and forgotten, lying in wait.

Seeker

Their voices echo still, in the winds that whip down from the mountains, in the rush of the stream that winds its way around the forgotten village and plunges into the pool where lazy currents of black water drift below ice-crusted banks. But all else is silent. Charred stones and decaying boards, like discarded bones, peek through a blanket of snow. The lanes that wind between the shells of collapsed cottages are empty apart from the snow that collects in ever-rising drifts. The furnace in the hillside, once bright with fires and the varied colors of cooling glass panes, is cold and black.

To the east is a strange, broken forest. The blackened stumps of ancient trees squat on the ground, shouldering their heavy snow burdens. Hundreds of years of fallen leaves and flowers rot beneath the snow, in layer upon layer of death. No man who sees this desolation could envision the gentle rain of pink petals in the heart of the Fayrewood in spring, or the clear green of the fan-shaped leaves in summer, or their transformation to vivid gold in autumn. All of that is lost.

When the snows thaw, little clusters of bleeding flowers will spring up again on the hillside. Nectar will gather on the tip of each folded, velvet petal and fall to the ground, sinking like blood into the soil. The flowers could tell the tale. They remember the colored wood and the bright lanterns, the loveliness that blossomed, for a time, beneath the Shadow. The remnant that retreated to the village of Fleete could tell it, too, though their version could hardly be trusted. The others are gone, lost. Women of great beauty and courage and children who hardly knew how much they had to fear vanished in the tangled gloom of the Whispering Wood. Fierce warriors, men of skill and daring and cunning, faded into the darkness of the Black Mountains, never to return.

This is the story of the Sun Clan, the *Lost* Clan, and all that was lost with them.

Pronunciation

Evander – ee-VAN-der

Mina – MEE-nuh

Valour – VAL-er

Maeve – MAYV

Fayrewood - FAIR-wood

About the Author

Helena Sorensen believes in the transformative power of words and stories, and in the power of the voices that speak them. Before she became a mom, she studied music, taught English, and dabbled in poetry and songwriting. These days, when she's not playing "royal ball" or "royal feast" with her daughter or doing science experiments with her son, she's hiking with friends at Radnor Lake or talking books with her husband. Of course, she might be at her kitchen table writing fantasy novels. She is the author of *The Shiloh Series,* including *Shiloh, Seeker,* and *Songbird.*

You can read more of Helena's work at www.storywarren.com and www.helenasorensen.com.

Sign up for Helena's newsletter (http://bit.ly/SorensenNews) to stay up-to-date on future releases!

Don't Miss

Available Now: the rest of
The Shiloh Series
Get more details at Amazon.com
or at HelenaSorensen.com